Also available

Blart: The Boy Who Didn't Want
to Save the World

Blart: The Boy Who Was Wanted
Dead Or Alive – Or Both

BLART

The Boy Who Set Sail on a Questionable Quest

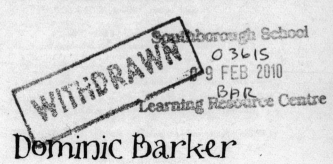

Dominic Barker

BLOOMSBURY

Acknowledgements

I would like to thank Michael Barker, Kate Clarke,
Suna Cristall, Jude Drake, Ele Fountain, Caroline Hill-Trevor,
Ian Lamb, Nancy Miles, Paul Nash, Helen Szirtes,
Colette Whitehouse and David Wyatt.

First published in Great Britain in 2008 by Bloomsbury Publishing Plc
36 Soho Square, London, W1D 3QY

A CIP catalogue record of this book is available from the British Library

ISBN 978 0 7475 9357 7

All papers used by Bloomsbury Publishing are natural, recyclable products
made from wood grown in well-managed forests. The manufacturing processes
conform to the environmental regulations of the country of origin.

Typeset by Dorchester Typesetting Group Ltd
Printed in Great Britain by Clays Ltd, St Ives Plc

1 3 5 7 9 10 8 6 4 2

www.bloomsbury.com/blart

To Dick and Jez

Chapter 1

There were pigs for as far as the eye could see. Piglets playing in muck. Sows standing in muck. Boars lying in muck. All in all there was a lot of muck.

And there was Blart.

Asleep and dreaming in his bed in the palace of the King and Queen of Illyria, Prince Blart, husband of Princess Lois and an Official Saver of the World (twice), gave a little snore of pleasure.

Perhaps he would not have done so had he known that at that very moment two black-clad agents of Anatoly the Handsome, Prince of Styxia, eldest son of Gregor the Grizzled and one-time suitor of Princess Lois, were sneaking towards his bedchamber, armed with daggers. Their orders – to make sure Blart never awoke from his dream.

Back in that dream it began to rain. But not any ordinary kind of rain. It rained apples. Juicy green apples fell from the sky, landing harmlessly in the muck surrounding the fat, contented swine.

Meanwhile, the two agents of Anatoly the Handsome slipped stealthily into the room.

But Blart was too soundly asleep to be disturbed. He watched the pigs munch happily on the bounty from the sky as, adding to the gaiety of the scene, the sun suddenly burst brightly from behind a cloud.

If only Blart had known that what seemed to be the sun shining was in fact a light creeping across the pillow as the two agents raised a lantern over his bed to check whether the slumbering body belonged to the youth they had been detailed to kill.

But Blart was one of the few people who slept on his front with his face squashed deep into the pillow and, despite their proximity, the agents of Anatoly the Handsome were unable to tell whether the sleeping boy was their quarry.

'Oh,' whispered the first agent, who was called Uri, when the lantern revealed the anonymous back of a head.

'Is that him?' hissed the second agent, whose name was Mika.

'Don't know,' replied Uri.

'This is his chamber, isn't it?' said Mika. 'It must be him.'

'The palace is big and there are many corridors. We could have taken a wrong turn.'

'Shall we kill him anyway?' suggested Mika, raising his dagger.

Uri shook his head. Mika was younger than Uri and

lacked his extensive experience when it came to killing people. Uri knew that in cases like this you only got one chance.

'We must be absolutely sure. If we kill the wrong boy then Anatoly's wrath will be terrible. He will tell his father.'

Both men shivered at the thought of what happened to people who displeased Gregor the Grizzled.

'What should we do, then?' muttered Mika.

'We must wait,' answered Uri in hushed tones. 'We have time. It is still dark. People turn over in their sleep all the time. When one is on a mission to kill, one must be patient.'

Uri and Mika waited, but Blart, still happily in the land of pigs and muck, didn't move at all, much to the annoyance of the two killers who stood over him.

'This is not working,' said Uri after they had watched for some time. 'We must amend our plan. He is too sound a sleeper. You pull him back and, if it is the right boy, then I will strike.'

Silently, Mika slunk round to the other side of the bed, leant over Blart and gently, ever so gently, began to turn him away from the pillow. Little by little, he moved Blart until he was lying on his side.

'Stop!' ordered Uri.

He raised the lantern to reveal Blart's face and compared it with the description he had been given by Anatoly the Handsome.

'*Head too big.* Yes. *Eyes too close together.* Yes. *Squashed nose.*

Yes. *General look of stupidity and idleness.* Yes. It is Blart,' confirmed Uri.

'Now can we kill him?' asked Mika.

Uri nodded and unsheathed his dagger.

Blissfully unaware of his impending death, in his dream Blart watched as a large boar trotted towards him.

In the real world, Uri raised his dagger.

'Can't I do it?' asked Mika. 'You always seem to have all the fun.'

The boar approached ever closer to Blart.

Uri shook his head, took careful aim at Blart's heart and prepared to use his ultra-sharp blade.

Nothing in the real world could save Blart now.

Uri's dagger plunged downwards.

But fortunately for Blart, he was not in the real world. Suddenly the boar reared up.

Blart had been handling pigs all his life and he knew that a boar could be a very dangerous beast indeed. He threw himself back from the deadly trotters.

Which meant in the real world, just as Uri attacked, Blart's limp, defenceless body suddenly came to life and flung itself across the bed, taking Mika, who was still holding on to him, completely by surprise. To Mika it felt as though Blart was possessed by some unnatural force, which twisted and turned and pulled Mika on to the bed.

Uri's dagger connected.

'Aaarrrggghh!'

There was a howl of pain as it thrust straight through Mika's arm. Surprisingly sensitive to the sight of blood for a murderer, Mika fainted, but the noise of his anguished cry had penetrated into Blart's dream. He woke up and sat up in the same moment, his head crashing into Uri's, who had been bending over Blart to check for signs of life after his strange fit.

Blart did not have many outstanding physical qualitites but he did have a particularly thick skull. The force of the blow was so strong that Uri was knocked unconscious to the floor.

Blart blearily rubbed his eyes.

A moment ago he was leaping back to avoid a dangerous boar, and now he was sitting up in bed with one man lying unconscious on the floor, while another lay beside him with a dagger through his arm.

Blart sighed. He'd only just finished saving the world for a second time yesterday. You would have thought that he could have been allowed one decent night's sleep.

But before he could even begin to work out what had just happened in his bedroom, from the diamond tower the emergency bell began to toll.

Chapter 2

The bell had been tolling for less than a minute and already the palace was alive with activity. Blart stuck his head into the corridor and saw guards with torches rushing up and down passageways. Courtiers caught up in the confusion barged into each other. Blart had never seen such a scene in Illyria. Normally it was a peaceful place, where everybody was relentlessly nice to each other and all they ever did was eat fruit.

A courtier rushed past, muttering to himself.

'What's happening?' asked Blart, but the courtier didn't even bother to turn round. It was almost rude. It was most unIllyrian.

A guard ran past in the opposite direction.

'There are two strange men in my bedchamber and one of them has got a knife in his arm,' shouted Blart after him.

The guard stopped.

Finally, thought Blart.

The guard turned round and glared at him. An angry-looking guard in Illyria! Normally Illyrian guards were the ones with the biggest smiles.

'Why are you wasting my time with such trivia?' demanded the guard. 'Can you not hear the Gigantic Bell of Disaster tolling?'

Blart was taken aback.

'How was I supposed to know it was the Gigantic Bell of Disaster?' he said. 'It could have been just telling the time.'

'The Gigantic Bell of Disaster has not tolled in Illyria since the dreaded Toxic Satsuma Blight of five centuries ago,' the guard informed him angrily. 'It tolls only in times of national emergency.'

'You were nearly invaded by three other countries last week and it didn't sound then,' Blart reminded him, referring to his previous quest.

'Its clapper was being serviced,' replied the guard haughtily. 'Now detain me no more. I must away to the throne room.'

With no desire to return to a bedroom containing two would-be assassins, and with nothing else to do, Blart rushed down the passageway after the guard.

Chapter 3

The vast golden throne room was already thronged with worried Illyrians by the time Blart reached it. Above them, the Gigantic Bell of Disaster continued to toll out its warning of impending doom. Courtiers whispered, servants speculated and guards muttered. But nobody whispered, muttered or speculated to Blart. Even though last night he had been recognised as the official husband of Princess Lois of Illyria (their wedding having taken place in a cold cave on the side of a mountain in order to fulfil a prophecy) and accepted into the Illyrian royal family as Prince Blart, it seemed that he was not yet regarded as trustworthy.

So, taking matters into his own hands, Blart stamped, barged and elbowed his way through the crowd to the thrones at the far end of the room, where he felt sure there would be someone who could tell him what was going on. Instead, he found in front of these thrones, pacing back and forth, his jaw grimly set, Illyria's newly appointed knight, Sir Beowulf. He had been a knight for just one evening (most of which he had spent drinking flagons of ale and eating numerous large succulent pies) and so, with bleary red eyes and stale breath, had not yet attained the gravitas that comes with knighthood, still resembling more the simple warrior who cheerfully cleaved people in two. But together with Blart, Sir Beo the Knight had succeeded in twice defeating the evil Lord Zoltab and saving the world from destruction.

Beo caught sight of Blart as he emerged from the throng.

'Where have you been?' he demanded. 'Lying in again?'

But before Blart could think of a suitably indignant reply, the Gigantic Bell of Disaster ceased to toll. The sudden silence had a sobering effect upon the crowd gathered in the throne room and they too fell silent.

At that moment the King and Queen entered, their subdued subjects stepping aside to let them pass. They ascended the royal dais and Beo knelt with a flourish at their feet.

'Sir Beowulf the Knight reporting for duty, sire.'

'It isn't necessary to say Sir Beowulf the Knight,' the Queen told him. 'Sir Beowulf is quite sufficient.'

'Thank you, Your Majesty,' said Sir Beowulf. 'Now do you have any orders for me?'

'You could just stand there and be quiet,' suggested the King. He was already beginning to regret his rash act at the banquet the night before when he had touched each of the warrior's shoulders with his sword and fulfilled Beo's dream by transforming him into a knight. And also an officious nuisance.

'Good people of Illyria,' the King addressed the anxious crowd. 'I have ordered the Gigantic Bell of Disaster to ring out across our land because a calamity has befallen us.'

'Is it the satsumas again?' shouted a voice from the crowd.

'No,' said the King.

'The pears?' cried another.

The King shook his head.

'The bilberries?' cried a third.

'No, no and no,' answered the King. 'My good people, the tolling of the bell is not fruit related.'

The crowd seemed to relax a little, but then another voice cried from amongst the muttering throng.

'If not a fruit blight then what catastrophe could be so dire as to require the tolling of the Gigantic Bell?'

Those close to the thrones noticed the Queen dab away a tear. The King swallowed to find the courage to speak, then raised his hand for silence and addressed the crowd once more.

'All of us here today are aware of the dread curse on Illyria,' said the King.

'I'm not,' said Blart.

'Know, then,' said the King, 'that for countless epochs and numberless ages and lots of other time, Illyrians have lived in fear of a terrible prophecy.'

'Is there any other kind?' groaned Blart.

16

'The Chilling Prophecy of Endless Torment!' exclaimed the King.

There was a horrified gasp from the courtiers, servants and soldiers. No longer could the Queen maintain a controlled demeanour and tears ran freely down her cheeks. Sir Beowulf the Knight realised too late that the closest thing he had to a tissue was a dagger, which was not appropriate for the task of wiping a regal visage.

'Let me remind you of its words,' said the King.

'Beware this time, a time of joy,
A time of nuptial bliss,
For endless torment will plague the land,
If the newly-wed bride be missed.

If she be fine when one month's passed,
This prophecy's naught but air,
But if she be gone at dead of night,
Illyria BEWARE!'

'I don't understand,' said Blart.

'The Queen was awakened by a noise from Princess Lois's bedchamber not an hour ago,' the King said solemnly. 'She rushed in to find the Princess gone and a torn piece of paper lying on the pillow where her head should have rested. On it were written four terrible words: *I have been taken.'*

Low groans and cries of 'No!' echoed through the throne

room as the significance of the message was understood by all. Well, all but one. One person still stood with the same puzzled expression that he had before.

But soon Blart stopped trying to work out what the prophecy, in conjunction with the disappearance of Princess Lois, might mean. For he noticed something different. Every pair of eyes in the chamber, from the King to the lowliest servant, seemed suddenly to be trained upon him.

'What?' he demanded.

'Perhaps I should read the rest of the prophecy,' said the King.

'I don't know why,' said Blart defensively. 'I didn't understand the first bit – I don't see how I'll get the rest.'

But the King ignored him and read once more:

'If these grim tidings come to pass,
Your land's for ever cursed
With endless suffering and pain
And maybe even worse,

Unless the husband of the bride
Return her ere full moon is high,
Then all Illyria will be saved,
Except her husband – he must die!'

The King stopped. All eyes remained trained on Blart. Most of the prophecy didn't make any sense to him, but the last line seemed clear enough, so he decided to confine his remarks to that.

'No, no, no.' Blart shook his head violently. 'Not again.'

'It may be your destiny, Prince Blart,' said the King.

'I've always had a rubbish destiny,' said Blart. 'I want another one. And stop calling me Prince Blart. I'm Blart the Pig Boy. I want nothing to do with princesses.'

His words had no effect on the crowd in the great chamber, who continued to stare impassively at him.

'Stop looking at me!' Blart told them.

But one person in the throne room was not looking at him impassively. One person was advancing towards him with murder in his eyes. Sir Beowulf the Knight had a great respect for the institution of marriage and he was not about to let Blart slide away from his responsibilities.

'Listen here, pig boy,' he began. 'I don't care if you're only fifteen. You are going to save your wife and you are going to die in the attempt or you are going to die right here and right now when my sword cleaves you in two.'

The Illyrians, who were not accustomed to violence of any sort, took a collective step backwards.

Blart looked at Beo – he was already reaching for his sword. Blart didn't want to die now, any more than he wanted to die later. He thought desperately of a way out and his mind chanced upon the one person who had always been able to stop Beo from cleaving him in two before: the great wizard who had led them on two previous quests …

'Capablanca!'

Beowulf paused in his advance just long enough for everyone to hear a shout from the rear of the chamber.

'Harken to my tidings of woe.'

All those in the throne room swung round. Standing in the doorway was Lowenthal the Court Physician.

'I have news,' he announced. 'Capablanca the Great Sorcerer is dying.'

Chapter 4

The King, followed by the Queen, followed by Sir Beowulf the Knight, followed by Lowenthal the Court Physician, followed by Blart, rushed up the steps of the castle to Capablanca's bedchamber.

In the dim light of a solitary candle, the great wizard lay motionless on his bed.

'He's not breathing,' observed the King.

'He's terribly pale,' observed the Queen.

'He keeps his socks on at night,' observed Blart.

Lowenthal the Court Physician hastened to his patient's side. He felt the wizard's wrist for a pulse, he felt his chest for a heartbeat and he leant over his mouth to feel the lightest of breath, but he could sense nothing at all.

Turning to the four onlookers, he told them, 'It is as I feared. The fever was too strong and it has overcome him. Capablanca the Greatest Sorcerer in the World is no more.'

There was silence in the room as the enormous import of the doctor's words sank in.

'He was a great friend to Illyria,' said the King.

'The whole nation feels his loss,' added the Queen.

'I was proud to cleave people in two for him,' attested Beo, and there was a lump in the ex-warrior's throat as he cast his mind back to the numerous body parts he had lopped off.

'He was a very good friend of mine,' said Blart solemnly, somewhat to the surprise of the others, as he was not known for his ability to strike the right tone in times of seriousness and grief.

'We will give him a state –' began the King.

'I hadn't finished,' interrupted Blart. 'I was going to add that in a private talk I had with him last night, Capablanca told me I was never to go on another quest even if I wanted to, especially if it could risk me dying.'

'You're a disgrace,' bellowed Beowulf, forgetting Blart's royal rank and shaking him forcibly.

'It's all right for you,' said Blart, slipping free and bouncing nimbly, if somewhat disrespectfully, over the deathbed of Capablanca the Sorcerer, giving his corpse an accidental kick as he did so. 'Nobody said you had to die.'

'Really, Prince Blart,' said the King. 'There are certain standards that you must live up to.'

He felt he could talk more freely now Blart was family.

'I never asked to be a member of the royal family,' said Blart. 'And I never asked for your standards. I was happy being a pig boy.'

'You shame the Royal House of Illyria,' said the King sadly.

'I agree,' said the Queen.

'So do I,' said Capablanca.

'You will go on that quest or I …' Beo stopped.

Along with everybody else he turned to look at Capablanca the Wizard.

'You're supposed to be dead,' said Blart.

'Am I?' said Capablanca, looking surprised.

'Yes,' nodded Lowenthal the Court Physician. 'I did all the tests. You've no pulse or breath and your heart has stopped. I'm afraid you are dead.'

'Couldn't you break it to him more gently?' asked the Queen.

'I've never had to diagnose death to the corpse before,' answered Lowenthal defensively.

'I'm sorry to disappoint you,' said Capablanca weakly, 'but I appear to be still alive, though I confess I do not feel well. I felt as though I was slipping away. My strength was ebbing and I felt ready to die. Then a sudden shock to the chest restarted my heart.'

'I kicked you when I was running away from Beo,' Blart told him. 'I must have saved your life.'

'Thank you, Blart,' said the wizard.

'And that means you have to save mine by stopping them sending me on the quest.'

'Quest?' said Capablanca, looking puzzled. 'What quest?'

23

Quickly the King outlined what had happened.

'I must get up,' said Capablanca. 'Pass me my cowl.'

But the wizard was too weak and he could not even raise himself into a sitting position, never mind get up. He lay back, exhausted.

'I cannot account for this inability to get out of bed,' he confessed.

'It happens to me all the time,' said Blart sympathetically.

'Disgraceful,' said Beo, glowering over the bed at Blart. 'You should be thinking of others and not yourself – your wife being kidnapped or Capablanca nearly dying.'

'I was nearly dying before,' Blart snapped back, 'when two men tried to murder me in my bed.'

'What?' roared Beo. 'Why didn't you say so before, you fool?'

'I forgot,' said Blart.

'Forgot?'

'It's been a busy night,' said Blart. 'But they were still in my room unconscious last time I looked.'

'Forward,' cried Beo, dragging Blart along. 'There's no time to lose.'

And so saying he charged out of the wizard's bedchamber.

Chapter 5

Through the passageways of the palace raced Beo, tugging Blart behind him.

'You'd be quicker without me holding you back,' pointed out Blart, but Beo didn't seem to hear him. Instead he began to climb the dimly lit stairs of the west turret that led to Blart's bedchamber. He was a big burly man, but due to a great fondness for succulent pies and flagons of ale he was not in the prime of physical condition, and halfway up the stairs his breathing became deep and heavy. But Beo would not stop, in spite of his shortness of breath. Up and up they went, faster and faster. They reached the top of the stairs. They charged down the final passageway. They flung open the door to Blart's room and saw ...

An empty bedchamber.

Were they too late?

Not quite.

'Look.' Blart pointed to the window at the far side of the chamber. The shutters were open and moonlight was pouring in, silhouetting two figures.

'Stop by order of the King!' roared Beo.

Uri and Mika whirled round in surprise.

'Surrender or die!'

'Surrender or die?' replied Uri calmly. 'We'll do neither.'

And so saying he turned and leapt from the window.

Beo and Blart were stunned. Uri's action was suicidal, for Blart's bedchamber was high up and all that lay below was hard stone. And then Blart looked at his bed.

'Where are my sheets?' he cried.

'This is no time to worry about bed linen,' said Beo in exasperation.

But there Beo was wrong. Upon awakening, Uri and Mika had swiftly torn Blart's sheets into strips and then tied them together to make a rope which, even now, Uri was descending.

Beo and Blart realised what was happening just as Mika prepared to follow, but the assassin had dropped out of sight by the time they reached the window. Undaunted, Beo leant out of the window as far as he could. His outstretched hands touched the top of Mika's head, but before he could grab hold of his hair and yank him up, the intruder slipped out of reach.

'Curses!' yelled Beo. 'If only I was taller.'

Without pausing for breath, he reached behind him and grabbed Blart.

'Whoa!' cried Blart.

Ignoring his cry, Beo thrust Blart straight out of the window.

'Grab him,' instructed Beo and, switching his grip to hold Blart by his ankles, he leant out as far as he could again.

'Aaargh,' said Blart as he was suddenly turned upside down.

'Grab him,' repeated Beo.

The extra distance was just enough. Blart found himself face to face with Mika.

'Hello,' said Blart.

The assassin's look of surprise was quickly replaced by one of delight.

'An unexpected opportunity to complete our mission and kill you,' he remarked with pleasure. And then he hit Blart as hard as he could in the face.

'Ow!' cried Blart.

'Ow!' cried Mika, remembering too late that his attacking arm had been stabbed during the first attempt to kill Blart.

'What's going on down there?' demanded Beo. 'Just grab him, boy, and I will haul you both up.'

Thwack!

Mika hit Blart in the face once more and again their cries rang out over the courtyard, across which Uri, having slithered down to the ground safely, was already scampering to make good his escape.

Crack!

Another fierce blow connected with Blart's chin.

'Hurry, boy,' instructed Beo, 'for I cannot hold you much longer.'

In the bright moonlight Blart could see the hard stones that would smash him to pieces were Beo to let go. Avoiding another glancing blow, he grabbed Mika's head.

'At last,' cried Beo and immediately he began to haul them up.

'I can't hold him,' Blart shouted.

'You drop him and I'll drop you,' threatened Beo grimly.

Blart gritted his teeth and kept his hands clamped firmly to Mika's head. Above them, Beo, his great muscles growing weaker with every passing moment, kept pulling, but the pace of their ascent was slowing. Beo felt his strength ebbing away. He could pull no further. Blart and Mika stopped and hung a small but significant distance from the safety of the window.

'What's happening?' cried Blart.

For a second he felt himself go down rather than up. At any moment he expected his descent to accelerate a hundredfold as the knight let him go. But though his strength was ebbing, Beo's will was strong. With one gigantic heave he hauled Blart and Mika through the window and on to the floor of Blart's bedchamber, where they all collapsed in a heap.

Mika was first to react. He tried to prise himself free from Blart's grip, but Beo thwarted his desperate escape bid by simple means. He sat on him.

'He hit me,' panted Blart.

'You can wear those scars with pride,' answered Beo in

between deep breaths. 'For they are the marks of bravery and courage.'

'They are the marks of a coward,' spat Mika. 'But I know what you do not. I know that there will come a time when Blart will wish he had died this night rather than face what the future holds.'

'Cease your foolish prattle,' Beo ordered his prisoner. 'We will take you to Capablanca and there we will find out what you know.'

'I'll never talk,' insisted Mika. 'Never, never, never.'

'I wager you will,' said Beo with the cheerful confidence of a man who had changed many a prisoner's mind in the past. Pulling Mika up, he dragged him towards the door.

Blart did not follow immediately. Instead he lingered for a while in his chamber, wondering what Mika could have meant when he said that there would come a time when Blart would wish he had died that night. There was something about the way he had said it that chilled Blart's heart.

Chapter 6

By the time Blart caught up with Beo outside Capablanca's bedchamber, Mika had been informed of what the knight felt should happen to sneaky Styxians who tried to murder people in their sleep rather than wake them up and engage them in a fair fight. The bloody details Beo had included had resulted in Mika rethinking his policy of never talking, 'never, never, never' and altering it to: 'I'd like to talk, now, now, now.'

'Come on,' said Beo. 'We will hear what he has to say in front of Capablanca so that we don't have to make him repeat it.'

'I'll repeat it if you like,' said Mika quickly. 'I like to talk.'

'Be silent until I tell you,' ordered Beo gruffly. 'Knock on the door, Blart.'

Blart could not even find the energy to ask Beo who he was to go round giving orders, and did as he was told.

The door opened a crack and a head stuck out. It belonged to Lowenthal the Court Physician.

'What do you want? I am treating my patient. He lapsed into a trance after you left. He mumbles occasionally but none of the things he says makes any sense.'

'We must see him,' insisted Beo.

'I have a duty of care to him,' answered Lowenthal. 'As his physician I forbid it.'

'As someone who would quite happily crush the skull of his physician I unforbid it,' said Beo menacingly.

On reflection, Lowenthal decided that in this case his duty of care could be laid to one side for a short period. He opened the door wider.

'But you can only see him for a short time,' he cautioned.

Beo pushed Mika into the room ahead of him.

The chamber was almost dark. One weak candle flickered by the side of Capablanca's bed and an intangible yet unmistakeable feeling of sickness hung in the air.

Keeping a tight hold on Mika, Beo and Blart approached the bed. The great wizard lay in a trance, his breathing shallow and rasping.

As they got nearer their eyes spied movement on the wizard's body. Fascinated, they edged closer. There seemed to be little dark things crawling all over him.

'Ugh,' said Blart.

'What's going on here?' demanded Beo.

Lowenthal allowed himself a smile.

'Obviously you are not men of science,' he said.

'No, I'm a boy of pigs,' answered Blart.

'Not being men of science,' said Lowenthal, 'you are of course not up to date with the latest medical advances.'

'You mean amputation?' said Beo.

'I beg your pardon?' said Lowenthal.

'I thought amputation was the latest in medical science,' said Beo. 'Chop off the infected bit and then stick a red hot sword on it to stop the bleeding.'

Lowenthal looked disdainful.

'We are not in the dark ages,' he told Beo.

'Aren't we?' said Blart.

'We are in a new advanced age,' answered Lowenthal. 'With new advanced medical treatments. Gone are the crude amputations of the past. Today we are curing illness and disease without chopping off bits of the patient, thanks to a revolutionary new treatment known only to me and a few other doctors operating at the very cutting edge of science.'

'You can't get more cutting edge than amputation,' protested Beo.

'What is it?' asked Blart.

Lowenthal paused for maximum effect

'Leeches!'

'Ugh!' said Blart.

Blart and Beo looked closer at the dark things crawling all over Capablanca's body.

'Evil bloodsuckers!' said Beo in disgust. 'What do you think you're doing to him?'

'I'm curing him,' maintained Lowenthal. 'Amputation is a

crude solution. The patient may survive but he is often left impaired and, not to put a fine a point on it, considerably stumpier than he was before. Whereas with leeches, only a small incision is needed to suck out the infection. The result is that the patient is cured with no loss to his stature or increase in his stumpiness. It is potentially the greatest medical breakthrough in history.'

The Court Physician looked expectantly at the faces of Beo and Blart.

'I suppose it's worth a try, if you say so,' acknowledged Beo grudgingly.

'You will see the results yourself,' said Lowenthal.

'We need results quickly,' said Beo. 'For soon we will be setting off on a quest and we will need Capablanca's wisdom if we are to succeed.'

Mika scoffed derisively.

'What?' demanded Beo.

'Nothing,' said Mika.

'I thought you said you wanted to talk,' said Beo, 'but if you want me to remind you …'

Mika remembered.

'The wizard will be going nowhere. We arranged for some tarsatz to be placed in his food last night.'

'Tarsatz?' said Beo. 'What is –'

'Poison,' interjected Lowenthal. 'One of the most lethal toxins known to man.'

'He should be dead already,' said Mika. 'Along with him.'

Mika indicated Blart.

'Why did you want to kill me?' Despite being the veteran of two quests where people regularly tried to kill him for no apparent reason, Blart still couldn't get used to it.

A low moan came from Capablanca's bed and the wizard's eyes opened.

'Tell us,' said Beo, 'and tell us quickly before Capablanca lapses into a trance again.'

The wizard gave a half-nod to show he was listening.

'There is little to tell,' said Mika, 'and you knowing it can change nothing, so I may as well –'

'Hurry,' urged Beo.

'Do you remember Prince Anatoly the Handsome, son of King Gregor the Grizzled, who was a suitor to Princess Lois of Illyria?'

'Always bringing her flowers and comparing her face to things,' remembered Blart.

Mika nodded.

'He is my master. His father, King Gregor the Grizzled, was approached by a seer who had discovered a prophecy …'

Blart groaned.

'This prophecy,' said Mika, 'foretold that the Kingdom of Gregor the Grizzled was doomed to suffer a great revolution and that the people of Styxia would rise up and slaughter Gregor and all his family and declare the land a republic. Only one thing could save the royal house: if Gregor's son married the heir to the Illyrian throne.'

'Princess Lois,' interjected Blart.

'King Gregor was delighted when he heard this news,' said Mika without pausing to agree, 'for Prince Anatoly was known to be the most eligible bachelor in the whole world, having the most noble features, the most winning personality and an expectation of the vastest fortune. And so Prince Anatoly crossed the Eastern Ocean, confident that he could woo the Princess – for what maiden in all the world could resist him? Unfortunately it turned out she could. But he was determined to persist until – disaster – she was already married to a man of no fortune, a repulsive personality with the face of a halfwit.'

'Do you mean me?' said Blart.

Capablanca groaned quietly, either in pain or exasperation.

'Of course he does,' said Beo impatiently. 'Do you see anybody else in the room with the face of a halfwit?'

'This was terrible news,' said Mika. 'For if the Princess was already married then Anatoly could not marry her himself. No longer could we rely on looks and charm and money if the Styxian throne was not to fall. Now we had to rely on something else.'

'What?' asked Blart.

'Murder,' answered Mika. 'The only way for Anatoly to marry Princess Lois was if her previous husband was out of the way. Therefore it was decided to murder him and kidnap her.'

'What about Capablanca?' Beo wanted to know. 'Why poison him?'

'The seer assured the King that there would be no chance of our plans succeeding unless we could stop Capablanca from intervening.'

'The seer is a wise man . . .' the wizard croaked.

'What about me?' demanded Beo. 'Why didn't you think it was necessary to kill me?'

Mika had not expected to have to justify not killing someone. He picked his words carefully.

'You were not seen to be quite as big a problem as Capablanca.'

'That is an outrageous insult,' said Beo. 'I am a very big problem indeed. I insist that next time you have a list of people to murder you put me on it.'

'As you wish,' said Mika.

'Your plan has failed, then,' whispered Capablanca weakly.

'Not completely,' answered Mika. 'For Princess Lois has been successfully abducted and you, the great wizard, have been poisoned. Only the killing of Blart has been entirely unsuccessful.'

'We must act without delay,' said Beo, suddenly realising the seriousness of the situation. 'Now we know the identity of the Princess's kidnappers I will go after them, kill them and bring her back.'

Mika laughed derisively.

'Do you think we are amateurs?' he demanded. 'We have arranged the fastest horses to get the Princess to the harbour at Arcadia, where lies the fastest ship ever built, ready to carry her to Styxia.'

'As a knight, I will still try,' insisted Beo, 'though I may die in the attempt.'

'No, Beo,' said Capablanca, managing to invest his voice with a little of its old authority. 'The Styxians have long been masters of the seas – such a chase would be hopeless. I must have time to think of a better plan.'

'What are we to do, Capablanca?' asked Beo. 'They will marry the Princess against her will.'

Capablanca shook his head.

'They cannot,' he wheezed, 'since Blart is still alive. Any such marriage would be invalid and would not satisfy the prophecy. But the Styxians must be notified. Send Pig the Horse with a message to the Styxian kingdom saying Blart survived.'

'What else?' asked Beo.

Capablanca was about to answer when a leech moved on to his face. Until now the wizard had been unaware of the presence of the bloodsuckers.

'What's that?' he cried in horror. 'Get them off me!'

'They are sucking out all the infection,' Lowenthal assured him.

'They're sucking all the blood out too,' protested Capablanca. 'Look how fat that one is.'

'I told him to amputate something,' said Beo, 'but he wouldn't listen.'

'Get them off me!' repeated Capablanca.

'But …' protested Lowenthal. 'I'm convinced that leeches are the answer to every medical problem. They are a panacea for all human ills – plague, ague, warts and bunions. In years to come, mothers will tell their children, "A leech a day keeps the doctor away."'

'Do as he says,' instructed Beo.

Reluctantly, and with the aid of some salt, Lowenthal complied.

'Come on, Bile,' he said, pulling one leech off and placing it gently in a glass bowl filled with water. 'And you, Mucus.'

'You give the foul bloodsuckers names?' said Beo in disbelief.

'I give my pigs names,' said Blart, for the first time feeling a little kindred spirit with the doctor.

'A creature that may soon prevent all human illness for ever deserves a name,' said Lowenthal defensively. 'There you go, Ooze.'

Capablanca closed his eyes.

'I do not know how long it will be before I can travel again,' he said. 'I am too weak to cast spells and so I cannot use magic to rid my body of this terrible poison.'

'What are we to do while you recover?' asked Beo.

The wizard opened his eyes. It was obvious to anybody that the conversation had drained the last of his strength.

'It is very important …' he began, 'that you … puddle … custard … fork …'

'Puddle, custard, fork,' repeated Beo mystified.

'Trousers … pillow,' continued Capablanca and his open eyes were wild and glassy.

'He is delirious,' diagnosed Lowenthal. 'The sucking of the leeches was keeping the poison at bay, but now they have been removed the poison has once more taken hold of his body. If we do not immediately put them back on he could die.'

'Soup … earwig … promise … suitors,' continued Capablanca.

'Are you sure there isn't a bit of him that you could chop off?' asked Beo.

Lowenthal shook his head.

'The poison is everywhere. Only leeches can help him now.'

'Hamster,' said Capablanca.

Blart looked at the wizard and remembered the quests they had gone on together; he remembered the risks Capablanca had made him run; he remembered the pigs that he would never see again because of this wizard; but he remembered something more important – a king somewhere wanted Blart dead, and kings tend to get what they want. Blart needed all the friends he could get.

'Put the leeches back on,' he ordered the physician.

Beo looked a little surprised at Blart issuing an order, but he made no attempt to countermand the decision and Lowenthal acted immediately. Capablanca's wild eyes closed and he lapsed back into the fog of a trance, his harsh breathing rasping around the bedchamber as he fought for his life.

Chapter 7

'And is there any news on Capablanca?' asked the King dolefully the next morning, still coming to terms with the attempted murder of Blart and the Styxian prophecy which required Princess Lois's marriage to Prince Anatoly, thus spelling the destruction of Illyria. He really felt as if he could do with some good news.

'He is still delirious, my liege,' answered Beo.

The throne room had been cleared overnight but outside they could hear the great crowd which had gathered during the morning.

'But my people need guidance,' said the King. 'Did he not say anything that might lead us in the correct course of action?'

'The last words he spoke,' Beo informed the King, 'were "soup, earwig, hamster".'

'Is that a code that we might decipher?' asked the King.

Beo shook his head.

'This is terrible,' said the King. 'Capablanca is the person

Illyrians have always turned to in times of need.'

'And me,' Blart reminded him.

'We must be prepared to act without him,' said Beo. 'For his recovery may take a long time or … he may not recover at all.'

'I must be decisive,' said the King. 'I must lead my people in this time of crisis. What should I do?'

Kolkis, the King's steward, entered the room.

'Would you speak to the crowd, sire?' he asked. 'Things are starting to get out of hand. There's been some mumbling and muttering.'

'Mumbling and muttering?' said the Queen in surprise.

'And quite a lot of head shaking.'

'Head shaking?' repeated the Queen.

The steward nodded. 'And there are reports that in some parts of the city there have been spontaneous outbursts of queue jumping.'

The King's countenance paled.

'The orderly queue is the foundation of Illyrian society.'

'You must calm your people, sire,' said the steward.

'But how?'

'You were wrong,' said Blart suddenly.

'I beg your pardon,' said the King.

'I wasn't talking to you,' said Blart, showing scant respect for his father-in-law. 'I was talking to Beo.'

'What are you talking about?' demanded Beo.

'When you said that Capablanca's last words before he

fell into a trance were "soup, earwig, hamster" – you forgot he said "promise" and "suitors" as well.'

This news seemed to jolt the King's memory, and his face lit up.

'Capablanca, how could I forget?' he proclaimed joyfully. 'Illyria is once again in your debt for having a cunning plan in readiness for such an occasion.' The King's eyes gleamed with hope as he turned to Blart and Beo.

'Before he became ill,' continued the King, 'Capablanca discussed with me a plan he had concocted in readiness for when the prophecy should begin to unfold. It's …' The King stopped suddenly.

'You haven't forgotten it, have you?' asked Blart.

Outside, the discontented noise was growing louder.

'Throw open the windows!' the King cried. 'I will tell my people of the plan that will save them.'

The steward threw open the balcony windows.

'Come, my dear,' said the King to the Queen. 'Stand on my right as I speak.' Then he looked at Blart. 'And as Prince of the realm you must stand on my left.'

The King was already stepping out on to the balcony. Dragging his feet, Blart followed.

'Don't pick your nose,' said the steward as Blart stepped into the light.

Chapter 8

The trumpets blared as the King, the Queen and, a few moments later, a surly-looking Blart appeared on the balcony. In truth, the trumpet playing that greeted the King and Queen was not quite as impressive as that which announced the arrival of other sovereigns. It was felt in Illyria to be unfair if only the best trumpet players got to play for the monarch, because it discriminated against those who tried hard but just weren't very good. So it was decreed that all trumpet players of any ability could play when the King appeared. Which meant that when the King stepped out there was a cacophony of trumpet notes in every key known to music, and some that were yet to be discovered.

'Hello, everybody,' said the King. 'The Queen and I and Prince Blart are very grateful to you for coming to see us today. We are never happier than when we see our subjects.'

'I'd rather see some pigs,' muttered Blart.

There was a shout from the crowd.

'Tell us about the Gigantic Bell.'

The King was taken aback. Heckling in Illyria is unheard of.

'Yes, tell us,' demanded another voice.

Quite unbelievable. In the panic of last night it was reasonable for some licence to be granted – it was dark, confusing, frightening – but now, in the bright light of day … To the King it felt as though the whole of Illyrian society was breaking down in front of his eyes. But for the sake of the nation he controlled his consternation.

'What a good idea,' he said to the crowd. 'Thank you for reminding me. That's exactly what I wanted to do, but I must warn you that I have some good news and I have some slightly less good news. The slightly less good news, as some of you may already know, is that my daughter, heir to the Illyrian throne, has been abducted.'

Discontented murmurings in the crowd turned to cries.

'She's been married less than a week.'

'That fulfils the prophecy.'

'We're doomed.'

'Peace, good people!' cried the King. 'For now that the slightly less good news is known I can move on to the good news. The good news is that we have a plan.'

There were mutterings of approval. Whenever things go wrong people like to know that there is a plan, even if they don't know what the plan is.

'All of you,' continued the King, 'will have heard of the great sorcerer Capablanca, who has been a friend to Illyria and has recently saved it from destruction. Thanks to

Capablanca, with the assistance of Sir Beowulf the Knight and our own noble Princess Lois –'

'And me,' Blart reminded the King.

'– Illyria remains the kindest and happiest kingdom in the world. And so it will continue. For Capablanca, who is, er … indisposed just at the moment with a fruit-related stomach upset . . .' The crowd murmured sympathetically. Fruit-related stomach disagreements were common in Illyria. 'For Capablanca anticipated this problem,' the King went on. 'And he foresaw that Illyrians, as the most peaceful people on earth, would be at a loss as to how to act should the prophecy begin to unfold. Seeing the numerous suitors for Princess Lois's hand in marriage, he wisely advised me to make every potential suitor give a solemn vow before they were allowed to press their suit: that if they were unsuccessful and Princess Lois married someone else and that marriage was ever threatened, they would do all in their power to defend it.'

There was confusion in the crowd as they tried to understand exactly what it was the King was saying. He wasted no time in making it clearer.

'Princess Lois rejected seventy-five suitors. This means that there are seventy-five noblemen all sworn to defend her marriage. Messengers will be despatched to each and every one of them, asking him to bring a ship fully loaded with armed men to the main Illyrian harbour at Arcadia. There will be gathered the greatest fleet ever seen. This armada will set sail for Styxia, where Princess Lois has been taken. It will land at Yort, the grim fortress capital where she is imprisoned. There the troops will lay siege until the Styxians return the Princess to us. Before the moon is full again and the dread prophecy comes true the Great Armada will bring her back and Illyria will once more be a happy and peaceful land.'

The words of the King captured the hearts of the people. The questioning minority began to shrink as rounds of applause and cheers echoed through the square. The King was delighted that he had had such an effect on his people and determined to tell them even more good news.

'Let it be known,' he cried, 'that these princes and nobles from kingdoms all over the globe will be led on their voyage by our own new flagship. This ship will be named and launched any day now and I declare that day to be a day of national celebration.'

More cheers and applause echoed through Elysium Square as the image of a great new ship gripped the crowd and filled them with pride. Overcome with a love for his people and with his faith in their ability to see the good in all things, the King decided to reveal one more piece of news.

'And furthermore,' he announced, 'let it be known that the Great Armada will be led by none other than our own adopted son, Prince Blart.'

The cheers dwindled to mumbles, the applause slowed and then stopped. Blart looked about him at the thousands of doubtful eyes that trained their gaze on him.

'What?' he demanded.

Chapter 9

The country was a fever of activity. Messages were dispatched all round the world to suitors near and far, summoning them on their oath to come and join the Great Illyrian Armada. Each day more noblemen docked their ships in Arcadia and led their troops into Illyria to pay homage to the King. The population of Elysium swelled dramatically as the Illyrians tried to house and feed all the extra bodies, and fruit supplies ran dangerously low. In the palace, extra servants were taken on and the passageways were jammed full of them, rushing hither and thither. All these noblemen required rooms to be found for them and all needed feeding. It was a mammoth undertaking. And everywhere there was the talk of war. In every corner, excited young men earnestly discussed the coming campaign, considered possible routes, debated tactics and wagered on who would achieve the most glory.

There was only one place where this feverish anticipation was absent.

Blart's bedchamber.

While all around him there was hustle and bustle, Blart sat grumpily staring out of his window, thinking about how unfair life was as he watched the moon slowly diminish. Every night less of it was visible. At some point it would disappear entirely. But then it would return. Little by little, night by night, it would grow again until it hung high and full above the world. And the prophecy said if Blart did not have Princess Lois back by then, Illyria would be destroyed. And if he didn't go to save her, Beo would cleave him in two. But if he did go to save her, as her husband he was doomed to die anyway. The only options Blart had were to die now or when the moon was full once more. He didn't think it was much of a choice.

'What's the matter with you?'

Blart turned round. Sir Beowulf stood in the doorway to his bedchamber. He was under strict instructions from the King to cheer Blart up.

'Don't you know about knocking?' said Blart sullenly.

'Tis times like this,' said Beo, ignoring Blart's question, 'when a man stands on the verge of a great quest, that he takes a moment or two to think of the things that matter to him most.'

Beo paused. Blart said nothing. Beo wasn't finding this cheering-up thing particularly easy. Nobody ever tried to cheer him up when he was a young page. The youth of today were all pampered and spoilt, he thought. Why, when he was a stripling he'd longed for the opportunity to die on a quest. But young people these days. Give them a perfectly good opportunity to die and they sat around sulking. What they needed was a good … but then Beo remembered the King's orders.

'I normally think about pies,' he continued. 'I think to myself that when I return from the quest I will sit me down in a comfortable tavern with a flagon of ale and treat myself to the largest most succulent pie that a cook could make.'

Still Blart said nothing.

'It would do you good to think of what you will reward yourself with when this task is done,' Beo went on.

'I'll be rewarded with my death,' Blart reminded him. 'It says so in the prophecy.'

'Oh, yes,' said Beo awkwardly. 'I'd forgotten.'

'So don't be asking me to think of what I want when I come back from this quest, because I won't be coming back, will I?'

'Well, best not to dwell on these things,' said Beo, trying to inject a cheery tone into his voice. 'Have you done your packing?'

But before Blart could answer, Kolkis the Steward rushed in, red-faced.

'The King requests that Prince Blart and Sir Beo attend on him in the throne room at once – Pig the Horse has returned from Styxia. There is news!'

'Do you hear that, Blart?' repeated Beo. 'There is news!'

'So what?' said Blart.

Beo decided he had had enough of the gentle approach.

Minutes later the King and Queen were startled when the throne room door burst open and Sir Beo marched in, carrying Blart over his shoulder.

'Is he cheered up?' asked the King with concern.

'Well, he's up,' said Beo.

'It is good to see you happy again, Prince Blart,' said the Queen.

'I'm not …'

But Blart's objections were lost as the steward entered, leading a massive black horse, its flanks still steaming. The great beast seemed bigger and more powerful than ever in an enclosed space, even one as large as the throne room.

'Pig!' cried Blart.

It was a name that Blart himself had bestowed on the horse and was considered by almost everybody else to be inappropriate, being neither noble nor inspiring. But Pig the Flying Horse would answer to no other name.

'What's that in his bridle?' said Beo.

'It's a dispatch,' answered Kolkis. 'It bears the seal of King Gregor the Grizzled.'

'Bring it to me, please,' requested the King.

The steward did as he was bid. The King broke the seal and unrolled the parchment and read, '*So-called King Philidor …*'

'That's not a very friendly start,' observed the Queen and then, feeling annoyed with herself for having rushed to judgement, she added, 'but then again, perhaps he is not a natural letter writer.'

'*I wish you were here …*'

'A much more pleasant sentiment,' said the Queen more cheerfully.

'*… for then,*' the King continued, '*I would rip out your heart and feed it to my dogs, and for pudding I would stuff them full of the bloody entrails of your adopted son, Blart, which I would tear with my own bare hands from his still living body …*'

'He does have quite a turn of phrase,' said the Queen. 'Very visual.'

'What are entrails?' asked Blart. 'Would I miss them?'

'Not for long,' said Beo.

'*Know that I have your daughter. She has an ill nature …*'

'He's right there,' agreed Blart.

'*… but that will be beaten out of her when she is married into my family. Sadly the wedding will have to be delayed, for the foul pig boy, her husband, still lives – a fact confirmed by my servant Uri, who paid for his failure to kill him with his own life. But know, O feeble monarch, I am a true king. I am not used to delay and inconvenience and I will not tolerate it. Know that I have opened the coffers of the Styxian treasury and withdrawn gold sufficient to pay the Guild of Assassins. Blart will be dead before the month is out and your daughter will be dragged up the altar to marry my son whether she says "aye" or "nay". Give my regards to your wife.*'

'Well, at least he's finishing in a civilised fashion,' said the Queen.

The King coughed.

'*Give my regards to your wife, who I would happily watch die in a pool of her own blood. Yours sincerely, Gregor.*'

The room fell silent as they pondered these grim tidings. It was Blart who spoke first.

'Does that mean someone else is trying to kill me?'

The others were saved the task of having to admit this was true, because Lowenthal rushed into the throne room.

'Capablanca has recovered consciousness,' the physician announced, 'and demands to see Blart alone immediately.'

'He must still be delirious,' said Beo.

'Possibly,' said Lowenthal, 'but he is most insistent.'

Soon afterwards, Blart gingerly entered the chamber of the sick wizard.

'Come closer, boy,' said Capablanca faintly. 'Let me look at you.'

'Why?' said Blart.

'Because I am weak and my eyesight is failing.'

'I look just like I always did.'

'Just come here when I tell you to,' said the wizard with a touch of his old exasperation.

Reluctantly, Blart obeyed.

'Blart, my boy,' said Capablanca, and there was something approaching tenderness in his voice.

'What are you calling me "my boy" for?'

'Because,' said the wizard, 'tomorrow you will become a man.'

'Are you going to tell me about the pigs and the bees?' demanded Blart.

'You mean the birds and the bees,' corrected Capablanca.

'I know what I mean,' said Blart. 'Well, you don't need to. I know where piglets come from.'

'That was not why I summoned you here,' said Capablanca peevishly. 'But if you will just listen for a moment I will tell you why.'

Blart listened.

'I say you will become a man tomorrow,' repeated Capablanca, 'because it is then that you will lead the Great Armada from the port of Arcadia in pursuit of your bride and to save this beautiful country. It is a noble quest.'

'I've been on quests before,' countered Blart. 'Why is this one different?'

'Because …' Capablanca paused. 'This time I will not be there to guide you. You will be the leader.'

It took a few moments for Blart to comprehend what the wizard was saying. And then there was panic.

'What do you mean you're not coming?' cried Blart desperately. 'What do you mean I've got to be the leader? I don't know where I'm going. I'll get lost.'

'The burden of leadership is heavy,' agreed Capablanca gravely, 'and I confess that I would have hoped to have been there at your side, for the task you face is filled with peril. But, alas, I am too weak.'

'You don't look so bad to me,' said Blart.

'Blart,' said the wizard, 'after you depart I have my own enemy to face in this very room. My battle with death.'

'Perhaps the sea air will do you good,' suggested Blart.

'It is no good,' said the wizard. 'You must go without me. But I have something to give you, the most precious thing I own. It may help you in this quest.'

Though Blart tried not to show it, he was excited. What could this thing be?

'Reach under the bed, Blart,' instructed the wizard, 'for it is there that you will find it.'

Blart did as he was told. He reached under the bed. His hand touched something cold. He pulled out the wizard's chamber pot.

'Eeeeuurghh,' said Blart.

'Not that,' said the wizard angrily.

Blart shoved the chamber pot back under the bed. He felt again, this time more carefully. His hand touched something soft. He pulled out a small black bag.

'That's it,' said the wizard. 'Pass it to me.'

Blart handed it over. The wizard took out a small mirror. He held it up in front of Blart.

Blart's face looked blankly back at him.

'It's me,' he observed.

'Now it is you,' said the wizard, 'but know that this is no normal mirror. This is the Misty Mirror of Miracle. Sometimes it mists over. When it clears it will show you somewhere else entirely.'

Blart shook the mirror vigorously and looked in it again.

'Still me,' he informed Capablanca.

'Stop shaking it,' ordered the wizard. 'It's not a toy. This mirror was made long, long ago by the elves in the hidden forests of Mysteria. Those elves have long departed from this world and with them the ancient lore that allowed its creation. Look into it, Blart, and sometimes it will show you things that will help you.'

'But how do I make it show me?' persisted Blart.

'Puddle,' answered the wizard.

'Puddle?' repeated Blart.

'Puddle … lettuce … bunion … earwig …' The wizard lapsed back into delirium. Blart was on his own.

Chapter 10

All too soon, as far as Blart was concerned, it was morning and he found himself behind Beo, riding on the back of Pig the Horse as they approached the port of Arcadia, where the Great Armada lay waiting for them. He could feel the Misty Mirror of Miracle nestled in his pocket. Last night, he had looked at it many times, but it had shown him nothing but his own face. Blart decided it was broken.

'Remember,' said Beo, 'when we get there, you're going to stay sitting on Pig's back to make your speech so that you're high enough for people to see. You name the new flagship the *Golden Ray of Hope* and you smash a bottle of ale against its side to make its launch official.'

As they got closer to the harbour the streets became more and more crowded. All the inhabitants of the port had thronged down to the wharf to cheer the great fleet as it departed. Children caught the air of anticipation and ran giddily about, women chatted noisily and men halloed greetings.

Through them all, Pig the Horse trotted down towards

the quay, where a spectacular sight greeted the questors.

Seventy ships, each commanded by a failed suitor of Princess Lois, choked the harbour, every one fully manned and ready to sail. There were ships of all different shapes and sizes. There were tall ships and small boats, slim skiffs and stout galleons, every one ready and waiting for the leader of the armada to join his flagship.

And there was Blart's flagship, tied to the harbour, her mast reaching higher into the sky than that of any other ship, a grand vessel built for speed. And her colour added to her impressive appearance, for sides, deck and mast were all painted in a shimmering gold.

'Tis a fine sight,' cried Beo. 'Anyone who considers himself a man would yearn to sail on her.'

'But I'm not a man,' protested Blart. 'I'm a …'

He remembered Capablanca's words. No longer was he a boy.

Every possible vantage point was filled. Men stood on walls and fences, women crowded into windows, boys stood on other boys, often without their consent, to get a better view. There was a noisy hubbub until Blart and Beo approached. Word spread faster than fire through the crowd and it turned as one to watch the approach of Prince Blart, who was to lead the greatest armada ever assembled. The King and Queen rose from their travel thrones at the gangway to greet him. And so the news spread out from the land on to the sea where the ships lay ready to weigh anchor, and from the ships arose shouts of approbation. Their leader was coming. The huge figure on the back of the great black horse. That was a leader and no mistake, thought the fleet as they caught what they thought was the first sight of their commander.

And then Pig the Horse stopped and the great hulking figure got off, revealing the slight weedy frame of Prince Blart. If Blart did not rise to the occasion now, then the quest might be doomed before it began.

'Say something,' hissed Beo from below. 'Name the ship the *Golden Ray of Hope* and smash this bottle against her side.'

Beo passed up a bottle of ale.

All Blart wanted was for these eyes to no longer be upon him.

'Inamethisship the *GoldenRayofHope*,' he said as fast as he possibly could and threw the bottle.

It was unfortunate that in his nervousness Blart threw the bottle rather harder than necessary. It sailed over the side of the ship and smashed straight into the head of the captain, knocking him unconscious to the deck.

'Oh,' said Blart.

There was a silence. And then there was laughter. Laughter from the harbour and laughter from the fleet. But no laughter from Beo.

'Was it so hard?' he shouted.

'I think they like me,' said Blart, gulled like so many before him into mistaking mockery for approval.

'They're not laughing with you,' Beo informed him. 'They're laughing at you.'

The knight pulled a spare bottle of ale from his jerkin, which he had been reserving for his own personal use, and passed it up to Blart.

'Name the ship and this time get it right or I'll pull you off that horse and throw you into the harbour, prince or no prince.'

Kolkis the Steward rushed over from the King's side.

'His Majesty says you must call it something different. If the bottle fails to break then the original name is unlucky.'

'Make it good,' ordered Beo.

The laughter subsided. Everyone waited to see what Prince Blart would do next.

Blart tried to think of a good name for a ship. He needed more time. Maybe if he started to speak then a name would come to him. And before he knew it he was speaking to more people than he had ever spoken to in his life.

'Hello,' he said. 'My name is Blart. And I am going to be the leader of the quest. And I don't think you should be laughing at me. Anyone can miss the side of a boat with a bottle. It's not like I'm a bottle thrower. Or a ship namer. Or a prince.'

Sir Beo put his head in his hands. They would never follow him if he told them that.

'I'm a pig boy,' Blart continued. 'If that ship had been a pig, I would have known what to do. So you shouldn't laugh at me. Just because my body is that of a feeble pig boy it doesn't mean that my heart isn't just as big as a prince's. So there.'

There was a moment's silence as everyone took in what he had said.

And then there were cheers. Loud ringing cheers which echoed around the quay. Sir Beo lifted his head out of his hands in amazement. Instead of the moans of a sulky boy, the crowd had heard a young man nobly acknowledging his humble origins while proudly announcing that despite them he could still lead the quest as well as any prince of royal birth. It was an inspiring, revolutionary statement. It also wasn't what Blart meant. But who cared? Certainly not Blart. With the cheers ringing in his ears he raised the bottle of ale high.

'I name this ship the *Golden Pig*!' he cried, and so saying, smashed the bottle against the hull.

The crowds cheered wildly. The great voyage had begun.

Chapter 11

Blart and Beo stood on the foredeck, looking out on the vast expanse of the Great Eastern Ocean. Above them the last of the gulls which had followed them out of the harbour were beginning to disappear. They were now on the high seas.

'The *Golden Pig*?' said Beo for the hundredth time. 'The *Golden Pig*?'

'It's a great name,' said Blart.

'I still can't believe the armada followed you.'

But, whatever Sir Beo could or couldn't believe, follow him they had. The Great Armada now lay stretched out behind the *Golden Pig*, its crisp white sails billowing in the noon-day sun.

'This leading thing is much easier than I thought,' boasted Blart. 'Capablanca always used to act like it was a terrible burden but it's very simple.'

Sir Beo was not sure that he could listen to Blart lecture him on the simplicity of leadership without surrendering to the urge to pick him up and hurl him overboard, and so, mindful of his Illyrian knight's vow to use violence only when all other means had been exhausted, he decided to go and find his cabin.

Blart was left alone. He looked at the sea. The sea had been bothering him ever since they left the port. Every sea that he'd seen before was blue, but this sea was green. Not even a bluey green. Just green. He wondered if there was something wrong with it. But his speculation was halted by something banging against his foot. A mop.

'Watch it,' said Blart.

The mop banged against his foot again.

'Oi,' said Blart indignantly.

The mopper was a small fresh-faced boy, wearing a neat blue and white stripey T-shirt and trousers that stopped just below his calves. He had his hair in a pony tail as seemed to be the fashion among sailors. He was mopping vigorously. And he was getting Blart's shoes wet in the process.

'What are you doing?' Blart demanded.

'Cap'n told me to swab the foredeck,' said the boy.

'To what the foredeck?' said Blart.

'Swab it.'

'But you're mopping it,' Blart pointed out.

'That's what swabbing means,' the boy replied.

'What's your name?'

'I'm Tigran the Cabin Boy.'

'I'm Prince Blart,' said Blart. 'But really I'm Blart the Pig Boy.'

'Whichever you are,' said Tigran, 'your feet are in the way of my mop and I'd be obliged if you'd shift 'em or the captain will have me picking weevils out of the ship's biscuits until a quarter past six bells.'

Blart thought about asking Tigran to translate this strange sea talk but then decided that he didn't really care. So instead he moved his feet and Tigran the Cabin Boy swabbed past him and onwards across the rest of the foredeck. There was something strange about Tigran the Cabin Boy, Blart thought, but he couldn't decide what it was. Thinking about it was too much trouble, so he went back to staring at the sea.

He had been contemplating its unnatural greenness for a while when suddenly he felt a tap on his shoulder.

Blart turned round.

Standing behind him, straight and tall, with an open friendly smile, stood a young man a few years older than Blart.

'Prince Blart, I presume,' said the stranger, extending his hand. 'Good to meet you at last. The successful suitor. I'm one of the failures – too cheerful apparently. That's what the Princess said. But no hard feelings, of course. The best man won and all that. Delighted to make your acquaintance.'

'Who are you?' said Blart suspiciously. People weren't usually pleased to meet him.

'Who am I? Fair question,' said the youth. 'I am Olaf. Count Olaf to be precise. Heir to the something or other. Can never remember what it is. Father tells me about it but my mind glazes over. Don't you find your mind goes all blank when your parents start to talk about money?'

'I haven't got any parents,' said Blart.

This revelation in no way embarrassed Olaf.

'Murdered were they?' he asked cheerfully.

'I don't know,' said Blart.

'Lots of people's parents are.'

'Are they?'

'Oh, yes,' said Olaf. 'Tribal feuds account for a lot of them where I come from. Parents lying dead wherever you look. Children who haven't got at least one murdered parent tend to get bullied at school. Still, got to look on the bright side, eh?'

'What's the bright side?' said Blart, noticing a second sailor, wearing a red bandana and carrying a mop, join Tigran to swab the foredeck.

Olaf looked momentarily puzzled as he searched his mind for a bright side to the death of your parents, but then his countenance cleared once more.

'Don't know what it is,' he said. 'But I'm sure there is one. Always is. Look on it when it turns up, eh? That's what I do.'

Being told to look on the bright side made up Blart's mind once and for all about Olaf. He wanted nothing to do with him.

'Why haven't you got your own ship?' demanded Blart. 'All the other suitors have.'

'Terribly good question,' agreed Olaf. 'Truth is that I had a bit of a groat-flow problem. Don't understand money, never have. Still I did bring something.'

'What?' asked Blart.

'The Longest Rope in the World,' said Olaf. 'It's coiled up in my cabin.'

'A rope?' said Blart. 'Everyone else brings a ship and you bring a rope?'

'A long rope,' Olaf reminded him. 'Bound to come in handy. I knew everybody else was bringing ships, so thought I'd bring something different. Can't wait to get to Styxia and show the Styxians a thing or two. I'm sure we'll all be home by Christmas. Awfully decent of you to give me a berth on board the *Golden Pig*.'

'I didn't give you one,' Blart pointed out.

'No, of course not,' said Olaf. 'Too busy with plans and strategems and whatnot, I suppose.'

'Strata-what?' began Blart, but he was interrupted by a mop swabbing into his feet.

''Scuse me, sir,' said a rough voice. 'I'm mopping –'

'I know,' said Blart. 'But this part has already been done. You don't need to do it again.'

'I think the cabin boy missed a bit,' said the sailor, keeping his head respectfully down. 'If you could just move a bit closer to the rail, then I'll have it spick and span in a second.'

Blart sighed but he moved closer to the rail as instructed. Obviously the captain of the *Golden Pig* felt very strongly about deck cleanliness.

'Almost got it,' said the sailor, scrutinising the deck intently. 'Just move right back to the rail.'

'I can't see any dirt at all,' said Blart.

'Not to the untrained eye,' said the sailor. 'But it's there. Just one more step back.'

Still looking at what appeared to him to be a perfectly swabbed deck, Blart took a step back.

'There it is, sir,' said the sailor. 'There it —'

Suddenly the sailor jerked his mop up and thrust it hard into Blart's chest.

'You're not supposed to swab me,' said Blart. 'I had a bath last month.'

'Steady on,' Olaf cautioned the sailor.

'I'm not mopping you,' announced the sailor, and his voice had a cold steely quality that Blart had not noticed before. 'I'm killing you. I am Vetro the Assassin. The Guild of Assassins always completes its missions.'

'No,' cried Blart, realising he was pinned against the rail by a mop-wielding killer.

Vetro forced the mop harder into Blart's chest so that he began to tip backwards over the rail.

'Olaf,' he shouted. 'Help me.'

But Olaf had vanished.

Below Blart could hear the slap of the waves against the

ship's hull. Any moment now he would tip over the side into the ocean below.

'Help,' cried Blart, but his voice didn't travel very far above the wind and the waves.

'Nobody can help you,' said the assassin. 'Prepare to fall, Blart. Prepare to –'

Vetro's words were cut off by a harsh clunk on his head. He turned round to see Tigran the Cabin Boy brandishing his mop.

'Get back,' shouted Vetro. 'I have no fight with you, cabin boy.'

'But I have one with you,' replied Tigran. 'Put up your mop or I will swab you once more.'

'Don't go anywhere,' said Vetro grimly to Blart. 'This won't take a moment.'

He pulled his mop away from Blart's chest and brought it down with tremendous force. It crashed into the spot where a moment before Tigran had been standing, but the cabin boy had leapt speedily to one side, avoiding the sickening blow. Vetro raised his mop and struck again. Again Tigran slipped aside at the very last moment. Could Tigran keep dodging the mop? Could his luck hold out?

No.

For the deck had been swabbed, but the sun had not yet dried it. So it was slippy. And as Tigran skipped nimbly to one side to avoid another blow, he skidded … slipped … and fell, his mop clattering across the deck.

'Now I have you,' said Vetro, advancing on the defence-less cabin boy. 'And I will be dispatching you next,' he added in Blart's direction.

Vetro the Assassin towered over the squirming figure of the cabin boy. He raised his mop. 'There is no escape.'

But Tigran wasn't squirming to escape. He was squirming towards his bucket. And just as Vetro prepared to land the fatal blow with his mop, he stretched out a thin arm, grabbed the bucket and flung its scummy contents at the assassin.

'Aargh,' cried Vetro, rearing back as the soapy water splashed into his face. 'My eyes!'

Tigran leapt to his feet.

'But I can still see enough to kill you,' the assassin growled. He charged at Tigran.

But though Vetro could vaguely see Tigran through his blurry eyes, what he could not see was that the cabin boy had retreated closer to the ship's rail. At least he couldn't until Tigran stepped elegantly out of the way and Vetro found himself with too much momentum to stop. He toppled over the rail and plunged, screaming, into the sea below.

Blart and Tigran looked over the side. Vetro's head bobbed up from the swirling water.

'I am only one of many,' he shouted. 'The Guild of Assassins never gives up. Your death has not been cancelled, Blart. It has just been delayed. The Guild apologises for any inconven—'

And then his head disappeared below the water again. This time it did not reappear.

'Wow,' said Olaf, emerging from behind a barrel.

'Where have you been?' said Blart. 'I shouted for help and you'd gone. I thought you couldn't wait to get to Styxia to show the Styxians a thing or two.'

'Quite right, quite right,' agreed Olaf. 'Thing is: training. Combat training. I've trained with swords, trained with spears, trained with daggers. Never trained with mops. I hold my hands up. Out of my depth. I'll take a mop down to my cabin and start practising straight away.'

And immediately Olaf picked up the mop that had fallen from Vetro the Assassin's hands and headed below deck, making parries and thrusts as he went.

Blart turned to Tigran.

'You saved my life. Did you know that the Guild of Assassins is trying to kill me?'

'No,' said Tigran. 'But I knew something was wrong when he said "mop" rather than "swab", you see, and so I was already suspicious.'

'I'll tell the captain if you like,' said Blart. 'He might give you a better job.'

Tigran's face flushed with enthusiasm.

'What I'd really like is to go all the way on this quest. Not just stay on the boat when we get to Styxia. I'd like to be part of the army that rescues the Princess.'

'Why?' said Blart.

'I can't explain,' said Tigran. 'It's just something I feel I must do.'

Unusually for Blart, whose affinity with pigs had always been stronger than that with his fellow man, he felt a twinge of understanding and nodded sympathetically.

'I'm like that with pigs,' he explained. 'I try to tell people what it's like to be a pig boy but I can never find the right words.'

Tigran looked as though he doubted if this was exactly what he meant.

'But if you want to go, then I'll see what I can do. Although I bet you change your mind about rescuing Princess Lois once you meet her.'

'Thank you,' said Tigran.

'That's all right,' said Blart, blithely ignoring the fact that it was *he* that owed his thanks to the cabin boy for saving his life. 'Oh, one more thing.'

'Yes?' said Tigran.

'Does the sea look too green to you?' asked Blart.

Chapter 12

'Gentlemen. This is first mate Polo. I am Captain da Gama. You are all welcome at my table. Let us eat.'

The tall captain in the smart blue uniform of the newly formed Illyrian navy sat down next to his short first mate. The rest of the table consisted of Count Olaf, Sir Beo and Blart. Since knocking him unconscious, Blart had avoided the captain of the *Golden Pig*. An angry purple bruise on his forehead suggested this was a wise idea.

'Someone's missing,' observed First Mate Polo.

'Who are we waiting –' began Sir Beo, but he didn't finish the question because the answer came through the door.

'I haf made a great discovery,' announced the new arrival. 'The name of Herglotz the Scientist vill be known across ze world.'

The soon-to-be-famous scientist was an alarming sight. He had long tousled grey hair, a messy beard and an assortment of clothes in a variety of colours which somehow all managed to clash with one another. One of his eyes was half closed while the other gripped a large monocle through which he glared at the world.

'We were just going to have some soup,' said the captain.

'Soup?' said Herglotz dismissively. 'What time haf I for soup? Let me tell you of my most important discovery.'

Such was the intensity of Herglotz's words – emphasised by his monocled eye, which seemed to grow as he spoke – that all at the table waited expectantly to hear what he had to say.

'This day,' announced Herglotz proudly, 'I haf discovered that ze world is flat!'

Herglotz paused, waiting for the gasps of astonishment. There were none.

'I'm afraid that has already been discovered,' the captain explained.

'Vot?' demanded Herglotz. 'You try to steal my discovery by pretending that there are others who know zis? Yes, I know zis trick. You tell ze world my discovery and take all ze credit and it is Captain da Gama who is suddenly ze famous scientist. This happened to me before when I voz a youngster and I invented ze wheel.'

'The wheel?' said Beo. 'But the wheel has been around for ages.'

Herglotz sat down moodily at the table.

'Where is the cabin boy with the soup?' said First Mate Polo, who seemed very anxious for his supper.

Just as he spoke, Tigran appeared at the door, carrying a

72

large silver tureen. The ship lurched forward as he came into the room and he staggered slightly.

'Careful, boy,' said the first mate harshly. 'Any spillage of the soup and I will be spilling your blood with a lash.'

'You don't sound like an Illyrian,' said Sir Beo, noticing the gratuitous threat of violence.

'I'm not,' answered Polo.

'But this is an Illyrian ship.'

Polo laughed.

'So it is,' he agreed. 'But you will not find an Illyrian on it. None of them would be suitable to come on a voyage where there was the possibility of war. And so the ship is now staffed entirely by mercenaries hired from the different countries of the world.'

'It is true,' said the captain. 'We had very little time to recruit. Why, Polo himself was not hired until the final day. I was very lucky to find someone with his experience on the wharf.'

Polo smiled modestly as Tigran the Cabin Boy managed to manoeuvre the huge tureen into the centre of the table.

'With your permission, sir,' said Tigran to the captain. 'The bo's'n asked me to tell you that we're a heading into a nasty squall.'

'A squall, eh?' said Captain da Gama.

'Pah,' interjected Polo. 'The bo's'n thinks every cloud is a squall. There'll be nothing to worry about, mark my words.'

'I will come up to check on the situation after the first

course,' said the captain. 'Send a message to the bo's'n to hold his course steady until I arrive.'

'Aye, aye, sir,' said Tigran. And he left the dining room briefly but was back in a trice to await further orders.

'At last we can eat,' said Polo, lifting the lid of the tureen and passing it to Tigran. The soup was green with purple lumps in it. And it stank.

'Euurgh,' said Blart. 'I'm not eating that.'

'You must eat it,' said Polo. 'It is kelp and crustacean soup. A speciality of the sea.'

'What's kelp?' asked Sir Beo.

'It is seaweed,' replied the first mate.

'Seaweed?' repeated Blart. 'You want us to eat seaweed?'

'It is perhaps an acquired taste,' conceded Captain da Gama. 'I confess to having slight misgivings when you suggested it for the first meal, Polo.'

'These landlubbers must learn to appreciate their sea grub,' insisted Polo. 'We have a long voyage ahead of us and the day will come when they're picking weevils out of ship's biscuits and dreaming of kelp and crustacean soup.'

'I'm not eating it,' repeated Blart.

'But you must,' said Polo.

'Let him starve,' said Beo. 'A man at war must eat what he is given. Sir Beowulf the Knight will not be scared by a meal, no he won't. Give me a ladleful and let us set to.'

And so saying Sir Beo served himself a large portion. He was followed by all the others around the table, who set to with varying degrees of enthusiasm. All except Blart.

'I sink,' said Herglotz, scrutinising a crustacean that he had extracted from his portion of soup and that now lay on his spoon, 'that zis creature may be entirely new to science.'

The captain looked puzzled.

'The shell-less mussel,' continued Herglotz. 'I haf never seen one before. Ze question science vill ask is why it does not haf a shell when all ze other mussels do.'

Tigran the Cabin Boy coughed.

'Begging your pardon, sir, but the cook removed the shell in the galley prior to cooking.'

Herglotz gave Tigran a fierce glare. Meanwhile Polo had left his seat and approached Blart.

'I do have some Tasty Powder,' said Polo. 'It is very rare, for it is made from a secret mixture of the most precious herbs and spices from all the corners of the world. Perhaps if I added some of it to your soup, you might find it more palatable. I would so like you to try it.'

In truth Blart was beginning to feel very hungry and, seeing that everyone else around the table seemed to be eating the soup with apparent relish, he decided that this might be a way to give it a try without people thinking that he was changing his mind.

'All right, then,' he said.

From his pocket Polo pulled out a jar of powder and shook a number of grains from it on to the soup.

'What about the rest of us?' demanded Beo. 'Don't be

giving that boy special flavours that you're not going to give us all.'

'Of course,' agreed Polo. 'There will be Tasty Powder for all, but let Prince Blart try it first. Afer all, he is the leader of this quest.'

Blart thought that this was a most appropriate sentiment. Nobody had referred to his leadership role for ages. He lifted the spoon to his lips.

The ship lurched.

Blart's soup spilled out of his spoon and back into his bowl.

Blart refilled his spoon and raised it to his mouth once more.

The ship rolled.

Blart's soup slopped out again.

'Perhaps the bo's'n was right about that squall after all, Mr Polo,' observed the captain. 'It seems to have some strength in it.'

But Polo did not seem to hear the captain's words. Instead he watched as if hypnotised as Blart once again dunked his spoon into the purple and green soup and raised it to his mouth. He blew on it.

'It's not that hot,' insisted Polo.

'I burnt my mouth very badly on soup once,' replied Blart. 'And ever since I have been careful.'

This was a rare example of Blart learning from experience, but the first mate was not impressed.

'Get it down you, lad.'

Blart opened his mouth.

There was a rumble of thunder. The ship pitched violently. Blart's soup flew from his spoon.

'I say, Polo ...' began the captain, concluding that they had both better head aft immediately. But the captain was doomed not to head aft immediately, for the gob of soup which jumped from Blart's spoon flew across the table and landed in his open mouth.

He swallowed it.

'That powder really adds something, doesn't it?' he observed. 'A piquancy, a —'

Suddenly the captain clutched his chest. Then he clutched his throat. The other diners watched in horror as his face went pinker and then scarlet and then purple and then, with a desperate choking wheeze, he slumped forward, dead, on the table.

There was a vicious hiss as a dagger of lightning stabbed into the sea outside.

In the dining room there was chaos as the diners all jumped from their seats and rushed to assist the captain.

'What's happened?'

'The soup has killed him.'

'Ze killer soup. It is entirely new to science.'

'It wasn't the soup,' shouted Beo. 'We've all eaten of the soup. It must have been the Tasty Powder.'

They all turned to look at Blart, the only person not to

have rushed to the captain's aid. Along with the first mate. Polo stood directly behind Blart's chair. In his hand he gripped a gleaming sharp knife.

'What are you all looking at?' demanded Blart of the five horrified faces that looked in his direction. 'He's the one that's dead.'

'First Mate Polo,' cried Sir Beo.

'Acting Captain Polo, if you don't mind,' replied Polo. 'I believe recent events have given me an unexpected promotion. But my true allegiance is to the Guild of Assassins.'

Chapter 13

Blart's face froze in horror at these dread words. But it was too late. He was armed with only a soup spoon while his adversary held a vicious knife. Though Polo was outnumbered, the others were all too far away to prevent the one deadly blow that would end Blart's quest for ever. And members of the Guild of Assassins did not miss. Polo gripped his knife and prepared to strike.

Sir Beo, Count Olaf and Herglotz looked on helplessly. But Tigran the Cabin Boy reacted. He still held the lid of the soup tureen, handed to him by Polo. In a flash he had swung his arm back and skimmed the lid across the room. Polo drove his knife down towards Blart's neck. The lid tureen arced its way towards him. Which would hit its target first?

Knife. Lid. Knife. Lid.

Crash.

The lid scythed into Polo's neck a moment before his knife plunged into Blart. The first mate's head was jolted backwards. The deadly knife dropped harmlessly to the floor.

Blood began to pulse from his neck as he slumped against the far wall.

Sir Beowulf rushed across the room.

'We mustn't let him die,' he cried.

'Why not?' protested Blart.

'If we can keep him alive then he can give us answers,' said Beo. 'There may be others from the Guild of Assassins on board. He might be able to tell us who they are.'

'That's a good reason,' agreed Blart.

But it was too late. Polo was fading fast. Through the bubble of blood he found the strength to speak once more.

'The Guild ... of ... Assassins ... are ... everywhere.'

And with these final words he slumped back dead on the dining-room floor.

'Do you know I've lost my appetite?' observed Count Olaf. 'Normally I can eat like a horse, but right now I don't even fancy a morsel.'

But Blart wasn't listening. He was looking suspiciously at Tigran the Cabin Boy.

'Did you just save my life again?'

Tigran the Cabin Boy nodded.

Blart's face assumed an expression of superior wisdom. Well, that was the expression he intended to assume anyway.

'You look like you've just swallowed a lemon, old chap,' remarked Count Olaf.

'I have not swallowed anything,' Blart said. 'And I have a few ideas of my own about what has been going on.' He adopted the air of a man who had noticed things that all others had missed.

'Now you look like you've swallowed a frog,' said Olaf.

Blart ignored the count.

'Isn't it strange,' he demanded of Tigran, 'that whenever I'm near you, somebody tries to kill me?'

Tigran looked perplexed.

'Not got anything to say?' observed Blart with a knowing nod. 'I thought not. Some people would say it was a coincidence, but I don't think so.'

'But I saved you,' pointed out Tigran.

'Exactly,' said Blart. 'And that was where you made your first mistake.'

'There'd be many who'd agree with that,' confirmed Sir Beo.

'I see what you're doing,' Blart continued.

'I'm saving your life,' insisted Tigran, more mystified than before.

'It is a shame Capablanca isn't here,' Blart said to Beo. 'He's the only person clever enough to understand what I have spotted.'

'Which is what?' cried Beo, infuriated by Blart's continued delay.

'Twice today I've been nearly killed,' Blart told him, 'and both times this cabin boy has been on hand to save me. What does he think will happen when he does that?'

'You'll carry on living,' answered Beowulf.

'That's what anybody could spot,' said Blart smugly. 'But only I could see that something else would happen too.'

Beo looked blank.

'I would start to trust him,' Blart explained. 'And once he had got me to trust him I would no longer be on my guard, and then he would strike.'

'Strike?' repeated Beo.

'Exactly,' said Blart. 'He is planning to kill me. We must arrest him at once.' Blart jabbed his finger accusingly. 'Tigran the Cabin Boy is a member of the Guild of Assassins.'

There was a silence.

'But,' said Beo, 'if the boy wanted you dead, why didn't he just let either of the other two assassins kill you?'

Blart's accusing finger held straight for a second. Then it began to wobble. Then it dropped to his side.

'Oh,' he said.

'In science ve say that there is a flaw in your hypothesis,' observed Herglotz.

But there was no time for Blart to apologise. Outside the storm was beginning to take hold.

Chapter 14

It was pitch-dark as Blart forced his way out on deck against a howling wind. He was instantly soaked as he stepped into the driving rain. Huddled figures scuttled up and down the main deck, banging into each other and shouting things Blart didn't understand.

'Splice the main brace!'

'Lash the foc's'le!'

'Hard a starboard!'

'I've dropped an oar on my foot.'

Actually, Blart understood the last one. Someone careered into him. A sudden flash of lightning lit up the face of Tigran the Cabin Boy.

'What's happening?' shouted Blart as a huge wave crashed against the side of the *Golden Pig*, sending gallons of water cascading over the rail. He desperately grabbed a nearby rope as his feet slipped beneath him.

'We're running too much sail,' cried Tigran. 'If we don't get it down, it'll tear the ship apart and we'll all be drowned.'

'Why aren't the crew doing it?' demanded Blart, understanding that his own safety was an issue and reacting accordingly.

'There's nobody to give orders,' answered Tigran. 'The captain and the first mate are dead.'

A fearsome crack above them.

'The mast could come down any moment,' cried Tigran.

'Why don't you tell them what to do?' said Blart.

'I'm a cabin boy,' cried Tigran. 'They won't listen to me.'

'Who will they listen to?'

Suddenly Tigran gripped Blart's arm.

'They'll listen to you!' he shouted. 'You're the leader of the quest.'

'But I don't know what I'm doing,' said Blart.

'I'll tell you,' cried Tigran. 'Follow me to the poop deck.'

Another huge wave crashed over the side. Water slewed everywhere. A sailor skidded past them, his hands clawing wildly at nothing. The ship lurched forward suddenly and he was catapulted over the side. A terrible cry rent the air as he fell.

'Quickly,' said Tigran.

But watching the sailor had had a profound effect on Blart and he gripped the rope he was holding tighter than ever.

'It's easier than it looks,' encouraged Tigran. 'Nothing bad will happen to you if you don't think it will.'

'Bad things have been happening to me ever since I can

remember, whether I thought they were going to or not,' shouted back Blart.

There was another sickening crack from the mast.

'If the mast falls then we'll capsize,' said Tigran. 'We must go now.'

Simultaneously there was a crash of thunder and a flash of lightning. The storm was directly overhead.

'Hold on to me!' shouted Tigran. 'I'll lead the way.'

Blart grasped the cabin boy's soaking jersey, and the agile lad led as together they slipped and skidded their way towards the poop deck.

There was a huge thud behind them.

Blart turned round just as a helpful bolt of lightning lit up a thick hawser that had crashed on to the main deck in the spot where, only a moment ago, Blart had been standing. It appeared that Tigran the Cabin Boy had saved Blart's life for a third time. It was just too suspicious, thought Blart.

'We're nearly there!' Tigran shouted, as they barely avoided the barrels that with each roll hurtled murderously from one side of the ship to the other.

They pulled themselves up the rail on to the poop deck, where the helmsman was fighting to control the great wheel that steered the ship. His muscles stood out with the effort.

Cupping his hands together, the cabin boy shouted with all his strength into the helmsan's ear.

'This is Prince Blart! He's in command now!'

The helmsman leant towards Tigran to try and make out what he was saying, which was unfortunate because otherwise he might have heard the desperate cry from the deck below.

'Lower heads! Boom's a swinging!'

But he didn't. Which sadly meant that the swinging boom cracked him firmly on the back of the head, knocking him across the poop deck and leaving him slumped unconscious against the rail.

'Ooops,' said Blart.

The wheel spun wildly.

'The storm's turning us,' shouted Tigran. 'We have to stop it.'

But the cabin boy's strength was not enough to hold the great wheel.

'Prince Blart!' he cried. 'The *Golden Pig* needs you.'

The magical word 'pig' stung Blart into action. *Yes*, he thought, *this is a ship, but it is also a pig and I am responsible for all pigs, be they ships, be they horses or be they simply pigs.* Blart rushed to join Tigran and pushed the wheel with all his might.

'The other way,' shouted Tigran.

'Oh,' said Blart.

Together they strained and struggled against the storm, which wanted to send the ship twisting off to its destruction. The great wheel fought for freedom. Blart and Tigran doubled and redoubled their efforts to hold it. Just as they felt their strength about to yield to nature's ferocious power, the wheel submitted. A brief lull in the gale gave them the time to take control.

'I think the storm is getting weaker,' gasped Blart.

But Tigran shook his head.

'It's only the eye of the storm,' he informed Blart grimly.

Blart looked at the cabin boy as though he was an idiot.

'Wait and see,' said Tigran, fiddling with some rope that hung from the wheel.

'Where are the crew?' shouted Blart, looking desperately around him and seeing only the unconscious body of the helmsman.

'The cowards have fled below deck,' said Tigran. 'But if the *Golden Pig* is to survive the second half of the storm, I must lower the sail. I'll climb the mast to the crow's nest and release as much of it as I can. You stay here and steer the ship.'

'It took two of us before,' cried Blart. 'I'll never be able to hold it on my own.'

'It was out of control before,' answered Tigran. 'Now we are its master and if you keep a firm hand on the wheel the wind will not be able to take it.'

'But …' protested Blart.

'And I have done something to help you,' said Tigran. 'You will be able to concentrate solely on steering and not have to worry about being driven from the wheel because I have lashed you to it.'

Tigran moved away. Blart attempted to do the same but

he found he could not. He had not paid enough attention when Tigran was fiddling with the rope. Now he was tied to the wheel. And tied to the wheel with some of the biggest, most complicated knots he'd ever seen.

'I can't remember what side starboard was,' Blart shouted.

But it was too late. Tigran was already high in the rigging, stepping coolly from rope to rope, and never once doubting that he would reach the top.

Down below, Blart was certain he didn't know what way to turn. 'Port' and 'starboard' were lousy directions, he concluded. There was a port on neither side of him and there were stars on both. How was he supposed to know what was right?

While he was puzzling over this, the strength of the wind grew and the hail begun to dash into his face once more. He picked a direction at random and turned the wheel that way and held it.

The sea, churning and swelling, tore at the ship, demanding that Blart bow to nature's power. The hail stoned his audacity in defying the power of the elements. But Blart did not give in. Not because he was particularly determined. Not because he was heroic. But because he didn't have any other choice. The knots that Tigran had tied were tightening the wetter they became. Blart had to keep control of the boat or go down with it. He felt the strength leaking out of his muscles. The wheel began to move the other way. It was now obeying the orders of the wind and the sea. Blart was losing control of the *Golden Pig*. The ship was spinning to its doom.

He looked up, hoping to see Tigran climbing down the sails to his rescue.

But he saw nothing. Nothing except the moon between the scudding dark clouds. Blart thought glumly about the prophecy — how he would happily have taken that extra month of life rather than die in this storm.

He straightened his head. Was that a figure he could see climbing the steps to the poop deck?

A hulking figure. A hulking, singing figure.

Sir Beowulf the Knight singing defiantly into the gale:

'*We set out on our voyage with sails in fine trim,*
But the weather forecast was awfully grim,
There was rain from the west and hail from the east,
And wind all around us which howled like a beast.

The tempest it drove us so far off our course,
I would have much rather been riding a horse,
But no, I was sailing with very wet socks,
Then, with a crunch, we were dashed on the rocks.

Most of the crew were instantly drowned.
When I heard this had happened I certainly frowned,
So I swam to the island, dragged myself on the shore,
My body and bones they were soaked to the core.

As the sun rose it showed me one other survivor,
Our jolly fat bosun, luckily called Ivor,
All others consigned to a watery grave.
I agreed with Ivor we'd had a close shave.

We were hungry and cold, we were dead on our feet,
We had searched the whole island for something to eat,
But no fruit could I find, nor animals neither,
So in desperation I ate my friend Ivor.

And now as I chomp on his leathery hand,
I hope that you listeners will understand.
Should I have eaten him? That is the question.
I'm not so sure now for I've got indigestion.'

Sir Beowulf caught sight of Blart, who was by then spinning helplessly round on the wheel, and he stopped singing immediately.

'What are you doing?' he demanded. 'This is no time for fairground rides.'

'Help!' cried Blart. 'We've got to steady the ship!'

Suddenly the *Golden Pig* pitched forward and Beo was thrown across the poop deck. A huge mass of white sail crashed on to the wooden boards of the deck below.

'Our sails are falling down,' said Beo. 'Do you think we should try to put them back up?'

Blart looked at him as if he was an idiot.

'We're carrying too much sail for a storm like this,' he said grandly. 'I've ordered Tigran to take down more of it so that we can ride this storm out without being torn to pieces by the wind.'

In spite of himself, Beo was impressed with Blart's knowledge.

'I'm no sea dog,' he said defensively. 'The life of a knight is spent on land and steed. What use have I for sails?'

Blart was not used to being treated with such deference and unsurprisingly let it go straight to his head.

'After he's done that, I may order Tigran to climb up to the owl's nest to give an accurate weather forecast.'

'The owl's nest?' Beo looked puzzled. 'I thought it was the crow's nest.'

Blart was momentarily discomforted.

'Only during the day,' he answered. 'It's night now so it's the owl's nest. I thought everyone knew that.'

There was a crash as another sail fell.

'You must help me ride out this storm,' commanded Blart imperiously. 'Grasp the wheel and help me steer a course for safety.'

And so, through the hail and wind and with sails crashing around them, Blart the Pig Boy and Sir Beo the Knight steered the ship through the tempestuous darkness.

'Do you know which way starboard is?' asked Blart.

Chapter 15

It was dawn. The storm had raged through the night but when the first hint of light glinted on the horizon it had abated. As the sun climbed, the sea adopted such a tranquil lapping calmness that it was impossible to believe it was the same raging dark torrent which had tried to sweep so many mariners to their dooms the night before.

Rubbing his wrists where the rope that had tied him to the wheel had chafed, Blart walked to the rail of the ship. There was a movement in a barrel beside him. A head emerged.

'Morning,' said Count Olaf cheerily. 'A tip for you chaps. Never try to sleep in a barrel. It doesn't work.'

'Where were you last night when I was lashing myself to the wheel and risking my life?' demanded Blart.

Olaf didn't answer straight away.

'Well?' said Beo.

'Fair question,' agreed Olaf. 'The thing is, I ran on deck when the storm struck, ready for anything – best foot forward to Death or Glory and all that – but I had the same old problem. No training. Trained on land, me. Ready for anything.'

'Except mops,' Blart reminded him.

'Except mops,' acknowledged Olaf. 'And storms. I decided to leave it to the professionals. I didn't want to get in the way.'

'So you hid like a coward in a barrel?' said Beo with contempt.

'I can see how it seems like that,' said Olaf. 'Me, barrel. Everyone else, storm. I see what you're thinking. But I had a plan. I thought to myself, *What if the ship goes down?* Comrades in sea. Situation dire. No one to alert the rest of fleet. But if I'm in a barrel, I can float off, find other ships and get everybody rescued. The only problem was . . . the ship didn't sink.'

Olaf looked very sincere.

Beo was unsure. Could it be that what seemed an act of craven cowardice was in fact an act of great courage?

'Excuse me,' interjected Tigran, 'but do you know your chances of finding a ship in the dark in a barrel?'

'Not a clue,' answered Olaf.

'No chance at all,' said Tigran.

'What a good thing that Blart saved the ship, then,' said Olaf. 'Now, whatsyourname, how about rustling me up some breakfast? A man gets peckish sitting in a barrel all night.'

Each moment that passed the sky grew lighter and the sea, which had been a dark green, slowly turned to a light green, but much to Blart's annoyance it refused to turn blue.

Behind him, Herglotz the Scientist clambered on to the poop deck.

'I haf made a very interesting discovery,' he announced.

'Where did you disappear to last night?' demanded Beo.

'I voz at the front of ze ship, doing research.'

'Now, now,' said Olaf shamelessly. 'Research is all well and good in its place, but when there's a flap on, when comrades are in danger, it's action that is required.'

'You sat in a barrel,' Blart reminded him.

'I haf made a most interesting discovery,' insisted Herglotz. 'It is a major breakthrough for science. I voz struck by an idea in ze storm last night. At first it voz raining, but then as ze wind grew stronger ze rain turned into hail. I thought about zis problem all night. For many years scientists haf thought that water becomes ice when it gets colder, but I haf a new theory. Remember – ze rain became hail as ze wind became stronger. Vot does that tell you?'

It didn't seem to tell anyone anything.

'It tells you that if water is propelled at a great velocity, then it vill solidify and become ice,' continued Herglotz. 'All I haf to do now is to prove it.'

It so happened that two buckets which had filled up with water during the storm stood conveniently at Herglotz's feet. He picked up one and threw the water – straight at Blart.

'Eurgh!' said Blart as it drenched him.

'Hmm,' commented Herglotz. 'It seems that ze water did not gain enough velocity. I must simply ensure that ze water is propelled faster.'

'What do you think –' began Blart.

Herglotz picked up the second bucket and hurled the water twice as hard.

'Eeuurrgghh!' cried Blart as the water hit him.

'Tsk,' said Herglotz. 'I do not sink zat I can call zis experiment a success.'

'Why did you throw water at me twice?' demanded Blart.

'In science it is very important that ze second experiment is done under ze same conditions as ze first one. You are vot ve call a *control group*.'

'I'm a pig boy,' insisted Blart fiercely.

Tigran returned carrying a plate of biscuits. He put it down next to the ship's wheel.

'Breakfast is served,' he announced.

Beowulf was fond of his food, as his more than ample belly demonstrated. But the ship's biscuits looked hard and unappetising. The good mood that he had been put in by seeing Blart unnecessarily doused with water twice swiftly evaporated.

'What's the meaning of this, lad?' he demanded, wagging his finger. 'Do you think that great knights like me can do valiant deeds on an empty stomach? A knight must begin the day with a hearty breakfast.'

'The cook is unable to work, sir,' explained Tigran. 'He was preparing dinner when the storm struck and a large saucepan fell on his head. He is confined to his hammock.'

'Don't give me your trifling excuses, lad,' said Beowulf. 'A cabin boy is like a page. He should be resourceful. He should not be appearing on deck with lame reasons and stale biscuits. If I was still a mere warrior, I would strike you hard for your insolence, but as I am now a knight I will content myself with no more than a playful cuff of rebuke.'

The playful cuff that Sir Beo attempted to mete out to Tigran would have knocked him clean across the deck. But it did not land, for Tigran elegantly avoided the blow.

'You're as nimble as a pig on market day,' said Blart.

Tigran looked confused, not realising that he'd actually been the recipient of one of Blart's rare compliments. Then he looked behind Blart and a frown of concern wrinkled his brow.

'I'm afraid, sir,' he told Blart, 'that I have bad news.'

Fearing that the bad news might turn out to be another killer from the Guild of Assassins, weapon in hand and poised to strike, Blart turned round quickly. But there was nothing to be alarmed about. He could see far across the smooth untroubled sea.

'I don't see anything,' said Blart.

'Aye, sir,' agreed Tigran.

'Why should I worry about nothing?' said Blart.

'With respect, sir,' said Tigran, 'where's the rest of the fleet?'

There was a pause.

And then Blart and Beo and Tigran and Count Olaf and Herglotz each looked north, and then east, and then south, and then west, and saw nothing but ocean. The fleet had vanished.

'Oh,' said Blart.

'They can't all have sunk, can they?' said Count Olaf.

The tranquil sea yielded no answers.

''Tis terrible,' said Beo. 'To die because of a puff of wind and a drop of rain is not a noble end. I would rather they had died with their swords in their hands and a dagger in their guts.'

'Or maybe that they had not died at all,' suggested Herglotz.

'If the ships had sunk,' commented Tigran, 'I'd have thought we would be able to see more wreckage. And bilge.'

'Vot is *bilge*?' asked Herglotz.

While Tigran was explaining what bilge was, Blart was reaching a conclusion.

'As leader of this quest,' he announced. 'I have decided that as we have no fleet we will have to go home.'

'What?' said Beo, Olaf, Tigran and Herglotz at the same time.

'We set out on this quest with seventy-five ships,' pointed out Blart. 'We've been gone less than a full day and seventy-four of them are already lost.'

'I don't believe what I'm hearing,' spluttered Beo angrily. 'Are you telling me that because of a minor setback you would abandon this noble cause?'

'It's not a minor setback,' said Blart.

'Tush and pish,' said Beo. 'I never believed that we need-ed all those ships. It didn't smack of a proper chivalric deed. Where were the overwhelming odds ranged against us that is the hallmark of a proper quest?'

'How owervhelming do ze odds haf to be?' inquired Herglotz. 'Zis could be an entirely new area for science. I vill call it *game theory*.'

But before Herglotz could develop his theory or Blart could explain that overwhelming odds were overrated, there was a shout from Tigran.

'Ship ahoy!'

The cabin boy picked up the eyeglass and was about to look into it when Blart decided that it was time he asserted his authority as leader of the quest and commander of the ship.

'I should get to do that first,' he said, grabbing it and pointing it in the direction of the approaching ship. 'Dwarves,' he announced confidently.

Tigran took the eyeglass out of Blart's hand and turned it round.

Blart surveyed the advancing ship once more.

'The dwarves are much taller now,' he informed his com-rades. 'And they're running about a lot.'

He raised his eyeglass to focus on the approaching ship's mast.

'That's not the Illyrian flag,' he observed. The Illyrian flag was blue with an apple in the middle. 'It's got some kind of bones and … What's that? … Oh, yes – a skull.'

'No!' cried Tigran.

'What?' said Blart, displaying a previously hidden interest in design. 'It's on a black background. It's quite striking.'

'You'll be stricken in a minute,' shouted Beo. 'The skull and cross bones can only mean one thing.'

'Pirates!' cried Tigran.

Chapter 16

The word 'pirates' struck dread into the crew of the *Golden Pig*. Those who had not been injured or swept overboard in the previous night's storm rushed up on deck. Desperately they tried to hoist the sails again, but the storm had left them sodden and torn. The sailors pulled frantically to no avail as the pirate ship bore down on them. Cries of despair echoed from stern to prow and chaos threatened to overcome the boat.

'You must take control of this ship or it will be lost,' Tigran told Blart.

'How?' said Blart.

'Just shout out what I tell you,' said Tigran, 'and we may yet continue our quest to Styxia.'

The cabin boy whispered a stream of orders into Blart's ears for him to relay to the crew. Their pursuer loomed ever larger. They could see the pirates' cutlasses shining in the sun and hear their bloodthirsty curses. They would be alongside the *Golden Pig* in minutes unless Blart could command his men and lead them to safety. Tigran nodded encouragingly.

Blart raised his head high and shouted as loudly as he could.

'Man your trousers. Tack the fo'c'sle. Set course for gybing. Trim the anchor. Close-haul the broaches. Reef the cringles. Star a hardboard. Drink the port. Dredge the crow's nest.'

Tigran stared at Blart in disbelief.

'That wasn't what I said.'

'There was a lot to remember,' said Blart. 'They'll get the idea.'

But the crew did not get the idea and already the pirate ship was smoothly drawing alongside, its dread name visible to all: *Bloody Cutlass*.

'We must organise our defences,' counselled Tigran, his blue eyes shining brighter and brighter. 'There is still time if we can just rally the men.'

A volley of arrows was loosed from the pirate ship.

'Look out!' cried Tigran, spotting that each arrow was connected to a rope.

A mighty roar sounded from the *Bloody Cutlass* as a number of the arrows embedded themselves firmly in the deck of the *Golden Pig*. Urged on by the terrifying cries of their comrades, and with their daggers clenched between their teeth, the pirates began to slide expertly across.

'Slash the ropes,' cried Tigran, leaping from the poop deck and pulling out his dagger. In a moment, the first rope was severed and there was a cry as a pirate plummeted into the water.

Blart and Beo were quick to follow Tigran. With a strike

from the knight's sword another rope was cut and another pirate tumbled helplessly into the sea.

'Faster!' cried Tigran. 'Faster!'

Seeing what they were doing, the crew joined in, desperately severing the ropes as arrows rained down on the decks. But some of the arrows were landing in the mast, which would allow the pirates to swing across, and already some pirates were preparing to take advantage of this swifter route.

Beo saw the danger. As the first pirate swung across, the knight stood in his path. The pirate's swing ended with a squelch on the end of Beo's great sword. Blood dripped on to the deck.

A second pirate swung across. Beo pulled his sword free and, moving faster than he had since the days when he was a page, reached the forecastle, where the pirate was about to land.

Squelch.

Fearsome threats of vengeance came from the *Bloody Cutlass*, followed by more arrows, followed by more ropes, with more pirates slithering and swinging their way across. The crew rushed again to stop them, but with no clear orders their attempts to prevent the boarding of the ship were chaotic. More and more pirates attacked.

Beo swished his sword left and right, scything into swinging pirates with every slash, while Blart, Tigran and Herglotz hacked at the ropes that stretched across the two vessels.

Two pirates swung across simultaneously. Beo saw them

coming. He lunged to his left. A satisfying squelch. But he had no chance to lunge right too, and …

The first pirate boarded the *Golden Pig*.

Beo spun round to deal with him.

But already two more pirates had boarded.

Beo parried a deadly blow from one, then another. Behind those two came two more, cutlasses out and ready to fight. They couldn't be stopped. Hordes of pirates were dropping on to the deck.

The disorientated crew were no match for them. They were hacked, skewered and stabbed. Blart, Beo, Tigran and Herglotz were driven back towards the navigation room under the poop deck.

'What are we going to do?' shouted Blart.

'If we barricade ourselves in the navigation room then we might hold them off yet,' Tigran suggested.

The four comrades rushed across the deck into the cabin.

'Block the door!' Tigran cried.

Maps and charts slipped on to the floor as Beo picked up the table and slammed it into place, just before the pursuing pirates charged. For the moment they were safe.

Admittedly, it was not safe in the way that word is normally understood: they were surrounded by angry pirates filled with bloodlust, who rained threats and curses upon them from outside the cabin.

'Don't kill me,' said a voice from the far corner – a voice they all recognised.

'Olaf?'

'For shame, man!' cried Beo. 'The ship is under attack and you run and hide under a bench.'

'Ah,' acknowledged Olaf. 'I can see how it looks like that, but let's not jump to hasty conclusions we might all regret. You see, I wanted to fight with you. Nothing would have given me greater pleasure. The cut and thrust. The jab. The parry. One for all and all for one. Who would say no?'

'You,' Blart pointed out.

'Comrades,' Olaf said. 'Once again, events have shown up gaps in my training.'

'Training again, is it?' scoffed Beo.

'It is,' agreed Olaf. 'I've been badly let down by my combat trainers. They never mentioned enemies on ropes. In all my training the enemy was stationary. Right in front of you, weapon out, fair fight. In that situation, I'm your man. But an enemy on a rope – what to do?'

'You get your sword out and start hacking,' shouted Beowulf.

'That's what I wanted to do,' Olaf told him. 'But I didn't want to get in the way. So I sacrificed my desire for glory for all of you.' Olaf wiped a tear from his eye at the thought of his own self-sacrifice.

There were three swift cracks on the door.

'This is Babel the Butcher of Barca, first mate on the *Bloody Cutlass*,' rasped a terrible voice. 'Open this door now.'

'Aha,' said Olaf. 'Now we are in a situation for which

104

I have had extensive training.'

'Hiding in a cabin?' said Blart.

'No,' answered Olaf. 'I am an expert in negotiating a surrender.'

'Why doesn't that surprise me?' growled Beo.

'Get out here now or I'll make shark feed of you,' rasped Babel. 'My cutlass is eager for your blood.'

'The key thing about negotiating a surrender is not to be hasty,' said Olaf. 'Don't let your enemy know he's got the advantage.'

'Our enemies just took over ze ship and massacred ze crew,' pointed out Herglotz. 'It is possible that they may already know zis.'

This news did not seem to concern Olaf. He went to the door.

'I would like to speak to your official siege negotiator,' he said.

'Our official what?' rasped Babel from outside the door.

'Siege negotiator,' repeated Olaf. 'In siege situations such as this, one should always speak to the official siege negotiator. This leads to a successful parley – reassurances and undertakings given, justifiable fears and concerns allayed, give and take on both sides and a non-violent resolution to what could otherwise have been a very unpleasant outcome.'

'Let me tell you somethin',' growled Babel. 'We don't 'ave no siege negotiator. We 'ave me. And here's my assurance: if you ain't out here on deck, face down in front of me and beggin' for your lives before I count to three, then I'll flay you with the cat until you be dead.'

'Why's he going to hit us with a cat?' asked Blart.

'One …' said Babel.

'It's not a real cat,' explained Tigran.

'He's going to hit us with an imaginary cat?' said Blart, even more perplexed.

'Two …' said Babel.

'Perhaps ve should consider surrendering,' said Herglotz. 'He appears to be counting in integers.'

'He's bluffing,' explained Olaf airily. 'These early threats are all part of a rather simplistic negotiating strategy. We'll let him get it out of his system and then get down to business.'

'Three,' shouted Babel. 'Right, I'm fed up with this.'

Olaf laughed.

'I think we're outmanoeuvring him.'

A slither of smoke crept under the door of the cabin.

'Now, according to my training, this is where he will ask for our demands.'

The slither became a plume.

For the first time, Olaf looked a little concerned.

'I'm beginning to think that our friend Babel is unaware of the proper negotiating procedures.'

The plume became a thick haze.

Suddenly Olaf's face fell.

'I've just spotted a flaw in my training.'

'What?' demanded Beo.

'You see,' said Olaf, 'I am an expert in negotiating in siege situations. But only siege situations when one holds a valuable hostage. You can see how it could have happened. Understandable mistake. They're similar in lots of ways: surrounded by the enemy, faced with death threats, seemingly hopeless. Just one minor difference. No valuable hostage.'

'That might be an important difference,' said Tigran.

'Suppose so,' agreed Olaf. 'I'll remember next time.'

'Couldn't I be a hostage?' asked Blart.

'You need to be on the pirate's side to be a hostage,' said Olaf.

'I could join,' said Blart.

But it was too late to join. The smoke had filled the cabin, making their eyes water and their throats burn. Blart decided the situation required the kind of leadership only he could provide.

'We surrender!' he shouted between coughs.

'Too late!' rasped Babel. 'You can all choke in there.'

This was an unexpected setback.

'You don't want to kill us,' shouted Blart. 'I'm a prince!'

'I've killed princes before.'

'But I'm worth a huge ransom!'

There was moment of silence which seemed to last much longer. Then they heard Babel's voice.

'Well, why didn't you say so before? Bring me some water! Put that smoke out!'

Chapter 17

The questors had been locked in the brig of the *Bloody Cutlass* for some time when they heard Babel thumping down the steps. He was a terrifying sight, as broad as he was tall, with a shaven head that was deeply gashed and scarred. His upper body was covered with tattoos: a mermaid on one arm, a shark on the other, golden treasure on his back and a vicious scimitar dripping blood down his chest.

'I 'ave informed the cap'n of your claims to be worth a fine ransom,' he rasped, 'and he tells me that he 'as a mind to be hearin' what you 'ave to say on the morrow, for tonight he will be busy a-counting his plunder – which he can't do very fast on account of him never 'aving been to school. But if you've been lying about being worth a fortune in ransom then he'll 'ave you flogged. So make yourselves comfortable for the night and don't mind the rats.'

'Any chance of supper?' asked Olaf.

But Babel was already stamping back up the stairs. Moments later the hatch clanged down and the brig was plunged into darkness.

'I'll take that as a no, shall I?' said Olaf.

Babel had not lied about the rats. As night descended on the *Bloody Cutlass* the scurrying began in the straw . . . slowly, cautiously, at first retreating at a shout or stamp, but each time returning bolder than before, rustling nearby and running over a foot or a hand.

'Ow!' cried Herglotz as a particularly bold rat nipped his hand.

'I will not sleep this night,' announced Beo. 'No rat will make a morsel of me for its supper.'

They all agreed to keep each other awake throughout the night by talking non-stop.

And then nobody could think of anything to say. Heads hung, eyes closed and slowly, one by one, the questors fell asleep. Beo's snores reverberated through the brig. Herglotz's breathing was deep and heavy. Olaf sniffled and talked. Blart found himself in a land of pigs – dwarf, pot-bellied pigs that capered around, running over his feet and up his legs, tickling, nipping and . . .

Ow!

Blart woke up in the dark and a rat scuttled away. A shaft of moonlight shone through the grille above them. The moon would be almost half full by now. Time was running out if they were to rescue the Princess. But even if they did rescue her, Blart was her husband, and the prophecy said her husband must die. Even by Blart's standards, it was quite a run of bad luck. He wanted to hide from these awful thoughts, but just as he was about to try to sleep again the moonlight caught the face of Tigran the Cabin Boy sitting nearby. Except … except Tigran was different. His hair, which was normally kept in a jaunty ponytail, was loose and hung down either side of his face, changing it somehow, making it softer and smoother and … with a jolt, Blart realised what the difference was.

'You're a girl,' he said.

Alarm creased Tigran's features as the cabin boy swiftly and silently retied the escaped hair back into a jaunty ponytail.

'Ssssh,' said Tigran.

'You're a girl,' repeated Blart.

'Stop saying that.'

'Why?'

Tigran motioned for Blart to be silent, but he was too surprised to remain silent for long.

'But you saved my life,' he said.

Tigran looked back at him. 'And why shouldn't a girl save your life?'

That wasn't quite what Blart meant.

'I don't mind who saves my life,' he said, 'so long as somebody does. It's just not normally a girl, that's all.'

'That's not a girl's fault, is it?' said Tigran.

'Isn't it?' said Blart. His head was fuggy with lack of sleep and this new turn of events had left him confused.

'No,' said Tigran. 'It's Society's.'

'Whose?'

'Sssh,' said Tigran, hearing a muttering in the brig.

'Damsel … snort … Distress … snort … Pies …'

'It's only Beo talking in his sleep,' explained Blart.

And sure enough, just a few moments later the regular trumpet-like snores of the knight resumed. It was a good thing they were so loud, because they drowned out the sound of Blart and Tigran's conversation. Satisfied that only Blart was awake, Tigran continued to explain.

'I don't like having to pretend to be a boy.'

'Then why do it?' demanded Blart bluntly.

'Because I wanted to have adventures.'

Blart shook his head.

'I've had adventures,' he said. 'They're overrated.'

'I don't believe you,' answered Tigran, eyes shining through the gloom. 'All through my childhood my grandfather used to sit by the fireside on cold winter evenings and tell me and my brothers stories of great adventures on the high seas. Tales of bravery and skill and glory. I was determined that when I was grown up enough I'd go on them myself.'

'Those stories never mention all the bad bits,' said Blart. 'Never trust stories.'

'But,' said Tigran, 'when I was fourteen and ready to leave home and seek adventure, my grandfather laughed at me and told me I couldn't because I was a girl. Yet I could climb a tree as well as any boy and tie a knot as strong. And I more than matched them in speed and agility. But I couldn't use any of these skills, all because I was a girl. My grandfather told me I should take up sewing and cooking so that one day I might attract a husband.'

Blart didn't say anything.

'But I hated sewing and cooking,' explained Tigran.

'Did you think about pig farming?' asked Blart.

'No,' said Tigran. 'I ran away. I travelled to the nearest port, found a ship that was looking for a crew and asked if I could join.'

'What happened?'

'They mocked me,' said Tigran. 'They said a girl was not fit for a life on the high seas – that girls were weak and lacking in seafaring skills. So in front of the first mate I tied a knot faster and stronger than one any man could tie. I climbed up the rigging more nimbly and I showed them I could unfurl a sail and secure it again better than any boy.'

'What did they do then?'

'Then,' said Tigran. 'Then, they stopped laughing. And they started grumbling. They didn't like it that a girl could do the tasks so well. All of a sudden, they said that it was unlucky to have a girl on a ship. That if there was a girl on the ship then the ship was doomed never to find good winds. It would be caught in violent storms and get hopelessly lost.'

'Is that true?' said Blart.

'Of course not,' said Tigran in frustration. 'It's not really that girls are unlucky – it's just Society's way of stopping us from going on adventures. And then boys get all the glory and all girls get is burns from our cooking pots and pricks from our sewing needles.'

'I'm not stopping you going on adventures,' said Blart, feeling that he was being criticised unfairly. 'You can go on as many adventures as you like. Next time someone wants me to go on one you can have my place.'

'You are not like most people,' observed Tigran.

'I know,' said Blart. 'I'm worse. Everyone's always telling me.'

'And so,' said Tigran, 'I tied up my hair, dirtied my face, learned to spit and changed my name to Tigran. The next ship took me straight away. It turns out that being a girl wasn't that unlucky after all.'

'Well …' said Blart.

'What?'

'You've been quite unlucky for me,' said Blart.

'I've saved your life three times already.'

'But perhaps if you hadn't been on board, nobody would have tried to kill me,' said Blart. 'And after that we were caught in a storm and now we've been captured by pirates.'

'I don't believe this,' said Tigran. 'I saved your life and then I saved the ship. You're just doing what men have been doing for centuries – blaming their bad luck on women because they can't admit that it's their own fault that they get into stupid situations in the first place!'

Blart, showing unusual sensitivity, decided to change the subject.

'What's your real name?' asked Blart.

At first Tigran appeared too angry to answer, but when Blart asked the question again there came the grudging reply, 'Tigrana.'

'That's not very different,' said Blart. 'If I got to change my name I'd change it to something much more different, like … Pig.'

'Pig?!'

Blart nodded.

'But then you'd be Pig the Pig Boy?'

'Vot's that?' Herglotz's voice, slurry with sleep, came out of the gloom of the cell.

'Don't tell anyone,' Tigran whispered urgently to Blart.

'Don't tell anyone vot?' said Herglotz, demonstrating extremely good hearing.

'That I would like to change my name to Pig the Pig Boy,' said Blart.

'Vot?' said Herglotz. 'Why do you vant to change your name to Pig?'

'It's private,' insisted Blart.

'Science has a name for a person like you,' observed Herglotz.

'Does it?' asked Blart.

Herglotz nodded.

'Nincompoop.'

Chapter 18

The heavy iron hatch clanged open and a pair of booted feet descended the stairs, followed by the tattooed body and the scarred face of Babel the Butcher.

'Comfortable night?' he enquired with a leer.

The bleary-eyed, dirty questors dragged themselves to their feet.

'Tis easy to mock a man who has had no sleep or food,' retorted Beo. 'But were there a sword in my hand you would not mock so easily.'

Babel laughed.

'You 'ave plenty of pies stored in that fat belly of yours,' he said, insolently prodding Beo's stomach with his sword. 'I 'ave a mind to recommend to the cap'n that he maroon you on some island of cannibals. They would eat well for a year.'

Beo's face flushed at this insult, but he was unable to do anything to avenge it.

'Now, move!' ordered Babel savagely. 'Captain Kozali will see you now. And if you 'ave lied about your value, then you'll find yourselves tied to the mast and lashed to within an inch of your lives.'

'To within an inch of your life is a very precise calculation,' interjected Herglotz. 'How do you get so close?'

'We 'ave a wide margin of error,' answered Babel. 'And we err on the side of death. Now move! Captain Kozali ain't the kind of man who likes to be kept waitin'.'

Four pirates armed with vicious scimitars herded the captives up the steps. They emerged on the deck to a hail of jeers and taunts from the pirates of the *Bloody Cutlass*, and to the sight of the *Golden Pig*, now crewed by pirates, cruising majestically alongside.

'They be sharks' meat,' shouted one pirate.

'They be orca food,' cried another.

'They be octopus breakfast,' insisted a third.

The questors were hurried through the jeering pirates.

'Back, you scum,' rasped Babel, waving his sword at his fellow pirates. 'Captain Kozali wants these prisoners unharmed.'

At the mention of Kozali's name the kicks and punches stopped immediately. Blart wondered what kind of man could be so terrible that simply the mention of his name could cower a crew of cutthroats and murderers such as these.

'Faster,' ordered Babel. A thwack from the flat side of his cutlass stung Blart's back. Moments later the questors found themselves face to face with the pirate captain himself.

Captain Kozali wore a three-pointed admiral's hat he had taken from the corpse of the commander of the last ship he had captured. A deep scar from a cutlass wound ran from his forehead down his cheek to his chin. A patch covered an empty eye socket – the eye in question having been gouged out in a tavern brawl after a disparaging remark about his parrot – and from one ear dangled an earring fashioned from the tooth of a killer whale, while the other ear was missing, having been chopped off during a bloody dagger fight over a vast treasure chest.

He wore a bloodstained captain's overcoat and the left hand which emerged from it had been replaced by a deadly claw. Below one knee jutted a wooden stump, the lower leg having been bitten off by a shark after he was thrown overboard as a young pirate for cheating at cards. Despite being unable to swim, Kozali had somehow fought off the giant fish, dragged himself back on to the ship and, before collapsing unconscious on the deck, thrown his dagger with deadly accuracy into the throat of his accuser, leaving him slumped dead over a barrel.

In bloodthirsty pirate circles that was the kind of thing to get you respect. Word of Kozali's deeds soon spread. Pirates who once might have fought him chose to follow him. At that time the *Bloody Cutlass* was captained by Redbeard the Terrible. A month later Redbeard the Terrible was marooned on an island and left to rot, and Kozali was captain. Since then he had roamed the seas, attacking any ship he came across, killing its crew and taking all the money and goods he could find.

He studied them with his one good eye.

'So,' said Captain Kozali. 'You claim to be valuable booty. On the bones of my grandfather, you do not look like you're worth anything to me. Tell me quickly why I should not crack open the grog and glug back a dram every time I throw one of you overboard.'

'Just try it,' said Tigran.

The questors were dumbstruck by the cabin boy's words. Captain Kozali looked as though he couldn't believe his ear.

'What did you say?' he roared.

'I said, just try it,' repeated Tigran. 'We're not afraid of you.'

'Aren't we?' wondered Olaf.

Captain Kozali propelled himself towards Tigran. He bent down so that his face was level with the cabin boy's. Despite his ferocious glare and the stench of his breath, Tigran held his gaze without flinching.

Kozali threw back his head and roared with laughter.

'"Just try it," the little boy tells me. Me. Kozali the Beast, whose name strikes fear into any man who sets sail across the high seas. Well, my little barnacle, I hope you can swim because I think you will soon be needing to. Not that swimming will save you from the sharks. Think about their teeth, little barnacle, their sharp teeth.'

But Tigran refused to give Kozali the satisfaction of quailing under his awful gaze.

'As for the rest of you,' said Kozali, turning abruptly

away from Tigran, 'I spared your lives because you claimed to be worth many doubloons in ransom. You had better not be lying!' The captain's bloodshot eye focused on Blart. 'I cannot see how this ignorant-looking dolt would be worth even a groat!'

'But I'm especially valuable,' said Blart. 'I'm the most valuable of all. I'm Prince Blart.'

'And I'm Count Olaf,' said Olaf.

'And I'm Baron Herglotz,' said Herglotz.

'And I'm Sir Beowulf the Knight,' said Beo.

'Hmm,' said Captain Kozali. His greedy bloodshot eye suddenly returned to Tigran.

'And you, my little barnacle?' he asked the cabin boy. 'What is your value?'

'I do not weigh my worth in doubloons,' answered Tigran confidently.

'Then how do you weigh it?' said Kozali, licking his lips dangerously.

'I weigh my worth in the deeds I have done and shall do,' said Tigran.

'What a pity for you that I do not,' commented Captain Kozali. 'So we have reached a disagreement, my little barnacle. And I cannot tolerate disagreement. For on my ship there can only be one captain. Perhaps on that we may at least agree?'

Tigran did not reply.

'I will take your silence as a yes,' said Captain Kozali. 'Now will you forgive me for killing you, my little barnacle?'

The captain placed the point of his cutlass on Tigran's throat. His eye was wild. Dribbles of sweat ran down the side of his scarred face. Blart realised that for the first time in his life he was in the presence of a person who was utterly and completely insane. And it was just his luck that this person had the power to kill him.

'Give me a sword and let me fight for my life and I will forgive you,' said Tigran.

'Ah, but that would be fair,' said Kozali. 'And I don't believe in fair.' And so saying, he raised his cutlass, ready to strike.

Tigran glared with fierce pride, and Kozali started laughing.

'Still you show no fear,' he roared.

'I have none,' Tigran answered boldly.

'Ah, that will come, my little barnacle, that will come,' said the pirate captain and he abruptly stopped laughing, his good eye looking away into the distance. 'Not in the day. Never in the day, my little barnacle. But alone at night. The faces of the dead. They rise up in my dreams. They rise up and live once more. And I have to kill them again and again and again and …'

Captain Kozali paused, realising that even his own pirate crew were looking at him doubtfully. He shook himself back to sanity.

'A pirate's ship loses many men,' he said. 'It is always in need of fearless new recruits. And you, little barnacle, are the right sort to join. You are not like these scabs of wealth and privilege,' Kozali waved his cutlass dismissively in the direction of the other questors, 'born into a life of luxurious ease, whom I will ransom to the highest bidder. I offer you the chance to be a pirate. Will you join us?'

Kozali's eye bored into Tigran.

'I go wherever there is adventure,' the cabin boy answered clearly.

'I can promise ye that,' said Kozali with a leer. 'There'll be booty and plunder and doubloons by the score. Take yourself up to the crow's nest. I'm in sore need of a new lookout.'

'Traitor,' muttered Beo as Tigran sprang expertly into the rigging.

Kozali turned to Blart.

'You did not tell me where you were prince of.'

'Didn't I?' said Blart innocently.

'No,' said Kozali. 'So tell me now.'

'Illyria,' whispered Blart.

'Speak up!' ordered Kozali.

'Illyria,' admitted Blart.

A tired smile flitted across the lips of the pirate captain.

'Illyria,' he repeated. 'I have never heard of the treasures of Illyria.'

'Haven't you?' said Blart. 'It's unusual treasure.'

'Unusual how?' demanded Kozali.

'It's mainly fruit.'

'Fruit?' yelled Kozali. 'What do I want with fruit?'

'I sink fresh fruit could be very useful on a boat such as

121

zis,' said Herglotz excitedly. 'I voz at a gazzering of scientists where the theory voz advanced that regular fresh fruit could prevent scurvy.'

'Prevent scurvy?' shouted the captain in high indignation. 'Why should I prevent scurvy? Sure a pirate is nothing but a milksop washerwoman until he's seen the teeth rot in his mouth from a dose of scurvy.'

'Perhaps they would be fitter,' suggested Herglotz tentatively.

'They would be spoilt,' screamed the captain. 'Grog, scurvy and the lash – these are what a make a true pirate. That and doubloons. Does the King of Illyria have any doubloons?'

'He might have a few lying around,' said Blart.

'A few doubloons,' cried the captain, his one eye rolling crazily·in its socket. 'I should throw you overboard now.'

'Terribly sorry for butting in,' said Olaf. 'But I've got some estates. I think they might be worth something.'

'Where are they?' demanded the captain, flecks of foam appearing at the sides of his mouth.

'I'm not quite sure,' admitted Olaf. 'Always meant to find out.'

'You are a pile of useless bilge,' Kozali told him. 'I shall kill you all.'

'I haf been working in my laboratory on alchemy,' said Herglotz urgently. 'Ze great goal of science – to turn lead into gold.'

Kozali's eye stopped rolling.

'And can you do it?' he asked eagerly. 'Can you turn lead into gold?'

'Not quite,' admitted Herglotz. 'But with ze aid of my forge I can turn it into hot lead.'

'Hot lead.' Kozali's eye began rolling once more, but this time twice as fast. 'What use is hot lead? You have lied to me. Accept a ransom of fruit? I would be a laughing stock. You are all worthless. A bottle of grog to the pirates who throw you overboard first.'

Before the questors could do anything they were surrounded by pirates, all desperate to earn a bottle of grog by pitching them into the green sea.

'Get off,' cried Sir Beo, punching the first two pirates to try to subdue him and sending them reeling. But without a weapon he was soon overpowered and dragged towards the rail. Herglotz and Olaf were carried after him, protesting all the way. Finally Blart too was grabbed. All the questors seemed doomed. A vision of the future flashed across Blart's mind as he saw the foaming sea he would soon be thrown into. He would die. Princess Lois would have to marry Anatoly the Handsome and Gregor the Grizzled would have triumphed.

Gregor the Grizzled. Blart felt that there was something he should remember about Gregor the Grizzled.

'Drop them together,' shouted Kozali, his one crazy eye circling in its socket. 'I love a big splash.'

The questors were lifted into the air by dozens of eager pirate hands.

'I think I might have something important to tell you,' shouted Blart desperately.

Beo, Olaf and Herglotz's heads all swung towards Blart in hopeful anticipation. Could he save them?

'Say it quickly,' spat Kozali. 'I am eager to see the sharks feasting on your remains.'

'I can't quite remember what it is just now,' admitted Blart. 'It's hard to concentrate when you're about to be killed. But perhaps if you were to let me sit and think about it for a while, it would come back to me.'

The pirates groaned and jeered.

'Enough,' said Kozali. 'You will have all the time you need to think when your skeleton lies at the bottom of the ocean, its bones being picked clean by crabs.'

A wild cheer went up.

Blart closed his eyes and concentrated as hard as he could.

'After three!' ordered Kozali. 'One ... two ...'

'Gregor the Grizzled's got lots of doubloons and he'd give you them all for the chance to kill us himself!'

Chapter 19

The questors, with a last-minute reprieve, found themselves back in the brig of the *Bloody Cutlass* with nothing but each other and the rustling of the rats for company. But despite having narrowly cheated death, they were not happy. Instead, they dwelt on the fate that lay in store for them at the hands of Gregor the Grizzled. Beo felt that a song might lift their low spirits:

> '*My enemies captured me alive*
> *And wanted me to talk,*
> *But I was a bold warrior,*
> *Their purpose I would baulk.*
>
> *I shook my head to show that they*
> *Would get no words from me,*
> *They said foul tortures would ensue*
> *And laughed with fiendish glee.*

With a hey fol de rol. A fol de rol de rol,
And a fol de rol de ree.

They stuck me in the village stocks,
Threw cabbages at my head,
And various other vegetables,
But still no words I said.

They took my burly soldier's hands
And put them in thumb screws,
But even when they tightened hard
I issued forth no news.

With a hey fol de rol, a fol de rol de rol,
And a fol de rol de ree.

So then they put me on the rack
And stretched till my bones broke,
I may have grown a foot or two
But still no words I spoke.

At last the iron maiden closed
Her spikes so sharp and grey,
But even though they punctured me
I would not say "Good Day!"

With a hey fol de rol, a fol de rol de rol,
And a fol de rol de ree.

But, I must admit, I might
Have had a change of heart,
Had not the fools a-torturin' me
Cut out my tongue at the start.

With a hey fol de rol, a fol de rol de rol,
And a fol de rol de ree.'

Beo looked about him expectantly, but the faces of the other questors suggested their spirits had been lowered rather than raised. Perhaps a song about the various methods of torture was not the cheeriest choice of subject matter.

Trying not to think about being stretched on the rack, Blart remembered the Misty Mirror of Miracle. He shuffled over to a corner of the brig and secretly pulled it out. At first it was hard to see in the gloom, but gradually his eyes became accustomed to the darkness and he was able to make out … his own face.

Some miracle, he thought scornfully and gave it a dismissive shake. Immediately his face disappeared and the mirror grew misty.

It's broken, thought Blart.

But just as he was about to drop it into the fetid straw that was strewn round the floor, the mist in the mirror began to clear. And this time the image it showed was not Blart's face.

It was the face of Princess Lois. Her freckles were burning red and her nose was wrinkled in fury. Next to her, Blart saw the soppy face of Anatoly the Handsome, still imploring the Princess to love him. But Blart's gaze was drawn away from the pleading features of Anatoly to a dark brooding figure which loomed behind him, dressed from head to toe in dark grey and glaring with hatred at the Princess. Blart had his first sight of Gregor the Grizzled.

The mirror seemed to sense Blart's fascination and closed in on the glowering figure, revealing a ferocious brow, dark eyes and a mouth set in cold fury. Even though he knew that the mirror was showing things far, far away, Blart flinched at the sight of the man who, if Captain Kozali had his way, would soon hold Blart's life in his hands. Then the mirror showed Princess Lois again. As Blart watched he saw the Princess catch sight of Gregor herself and, for a fleeting moment, fear registered on her face before she resumed her usual expression of defiance. Blart had never seen her look so scared.

But before he could see what happened next, the mirror misted up once more.

Blart shook it. The mist parted.

Now the mirror showed Capablanca. The great wizard did not move, and for an awful moment Blart thought that he was dead. But as the mirror grew closer to Capablanca's face, Blart's sharp eyesight spotted a slight fluttering in the wizard's eyes. So little strength did Capablanca have, it seemed he was unable to open them fully. He was even weaker than when Blart had last seen him. Blart remembered the wizard had said that the mirror showed pictures of things that were happening at the same time in different places. If this was Capablanca's physical state at this moment, then it was futile to believe that he could come to their rescue.

Once more the image misted over. And then cleared again. This time it showed the sea. And a ship. Then another. And more stretching out in a line. With a start, Blart recognised the Great Illyrian Armada. It could not have been destroyed by the storm as they had thought. By some ill chance only the *Golden Pig* had been separated. The rest of the armada had regrouped and was continuing on its voyage to Styxia without its flagship. Blart was filled with sudden hope. If the armada could intercept the *Bloody Cutlass*, then they could be rescued and would no longer have to face the awful prospect of Gregor the Grizzled and his tortures. But then he saw the armada's sails had been torn in the storm and required repair, whereas the sails of the *Bloody Cutlass* were bulging with wind as it zipped over the waves towards Styxia. The armada would never catch it before it anchored in Styxia and yielded up the questors into the grip of Gregor.

The Magic Mirror of Miracle might work, thought Blart, *but it is showing me nothing that I want to see.* He tapped it disapprovingly with his finger and, almost as though it sensed his disapproval, the mirror misted over once more. The next time it cleared it showed Blart his own face, like any other mirror. Disappointed, he shuffled back over to the other questors.

'I tell you what surprised me,' Olaf was saying. 'That cabin boy joining the pirates. Rum do. One thing you can say about Count Olaf is that he sticks by his friends.'

'It is understandable,' said Herglotz. 'Ze cabin boy veighed up his own chances of survival against that of ours and made a choice. I suppose mathematically one could say that he made ze correct decision.'

'But there is more to life than maths,' insisted Beo. 'There is honour and chivalry and duty.'

'I haf a problem with these things you speak of,' said Herglotz, 'for I haf never been able to successfully represent them on a graph.'

'There is more in heaven and earth than you can fit on a graph, Herglotz,' said Beo.

'I am not so sure,' said Herglotz. 'Perhaps if one were to add extra axes.'

'Pssst.'

The questors turned round. Standing outside the brig, his eyes shining with excitement, was Tigran the Pirate.

'Traitor,' spat Olaf.

'Listen,' whispered Tigran desperately. 'I thought if I pretended to join the pirates, I might be able to discover a way to help us all escape.'

Beo was unconvinced.

'Sounds like a sneaky way to do things to me.'

'Have you found one?' Blart asked.

'No,' conceded Tigran.

'What's the point of coming to tell us that?' demanded Blart.

'I came to warn you,' said Tigran, looking nervously over his shoulder. 'After Babel brought you back down to the brig, the wind suddenly dropped and the ship was becalmed. Since it happened, Captain Kozali has grown strange. He paces the deck and mutters that the *Bloody Cutlass* is under some terrible curse. He shouted something about appeasing the Spirits of the Sea, and then he ordered all the pirates who were sailing the *Golden Pig* to leave that ship and come over here. He's issued a bottle of grog to each crew member. Now the mood on deck is becoming hostile. I fear that something bad will happen. Be ready to act in an instant,' he instructed them. 'I will do all I can but you must prepare yourselves for anything.'

The sounds of harsh singing drifted down from the deck.

'Now I must return before I am missed. But stay alert and listen out for my command.'

He disappeared up the stairs towards the deck. From above the questors heard the first angry words from the pirates. The grog was beginning to take effect.

'Come on,' said Beo sternly. 'You heard what the lad said. We must be prepared to act at a moment's notice. I want to see you all ready for action.'

Chapter 20

It turned out that being ready for action got boring quickly. The questors were extremely ready for a little while. Nothing happened apart from more raucous shouts and tuneless singing from above. Then they were quite ready for a little bit longer. And finally they were not ready at all when Babel and four pirates thumped down the steps and threw open the hatch.

'Cap'n wants you on deck now,' rasped Babel. 'You curvy scurs ... I mean scurvy curs.' Obviously, the grog was beginning to take effect. He waved his cutlass menacingly at the questors. 'You'll be mashed to the last and clogged with the fat.'

'I beg your pardon,' said Olaf.

Babel tottered dangerously at the top of the steps.

'What are you fatin' wor?' he shouted. 'Set up these gairs.'

Up the stairs went the questors. When they arrived on deck a terrible sight greeted them.

Every pirate was awaiting their arrival, each of them well lubricated with grog. There were boos, jeers and a crash as an empty bottle smashed at Blart's feet.

'Landlubbin' scum!'

More insults rang out as the questors were hustled to the mast and then tied tightly to it.

It was dark by now. The half-moon shone down, reminding each of the questors of the dread prophecy and their ever diminishing chances of rescuing the Princess. Captain Kozali was silhouetted on the poop deck. He waited until all the pirates had quietened down before addressing his captives.

'What have you done with my wind?' he screeched. And from his voice the questors could hear that he had drunk more grog than any other member of the pirate crew. He was drunk with anger.

'Where is the wind?' he wanted to know.

None of the questors replied.

'Nothing but ill luck from the moment you came on board.'

Olaf decided to take this opportunity to use his hostage negotiation skills.

'We'd be quite happy to leave again.'

'Silence!' cried Kozali.

Olaf changed his mind.

'You have offended the Spirits of the Sea!' shouted Kozali, waving the hook that stood in for a hand. 'They demand a sacrifice!'

'Sacrifice,' echoed the pirates with a bloodthirsty cheer.

'We will offer one of you to the spirits and in return they will give us a breath of wind.'

Cheers rang out from the pirates.

'Babel,' commanded the captain. 'Let them draw lots to determine which one of them the spirits want. The one who draws the short straw will walk the plank.'

Swaying slightly, Babel approached the questors. He held four straws. All appeared to be the same length but, concealed in his hand, one was shorter.

'Who wants to go first?' said Babel.

'Surely we can't pick properly unless you untie us,' said Beo cunningly. *At least*, thought the knight, *if I pick the short straw I will die fighting rather than being torn apart by the serpents that lurk in the ocean.*

'You think you can trick me into loosening your bonds, fat man,' rasped Babel. 'You'll choose with your mouths. You first.'

Beo leant forward, grabbed a straw between his teeth and pulled it out.

It was long.

'I vill go next,' said Herglotz speedily. 'I calculate that ze odds are still in my favour.'

Herglotz leant forward and bit on a straw. The laws of probability held good. It, too, was long.

Next it was Blart.

'Hurry up and pick,' instructed Babel, thrusting the remaining straws into Blart's face. Reluctantly, Blart bit. And pulled.

The straw was long.

At least it was when Blart first gripped it. But unfortunately he had gripped it with a little too much bite. As Blart began to pull it from Babel's hand it split in two.

Now it was the short straw.

'Ha!' shouted Kozali. 'We have our sacrifice.'

'That's not fair,' protested Blart. 'I bit it in half.'

'Awfully decent of you,' said Olaf, who would have been due to get the real short straw.

'Prepare the plank,' ordered Kozali.

'Wait!' shouted Blart. 'I demand a remeasure. My straw was long.'

'It ain't long any more,' rasped Babel.

'But I'm the most valuable,' shouted Blart. 'I'm the Prince. I'm the one he wants dead the most. Gregor the Grizzled will pay more doubloons for me than all the others.'

Captain Kozali gripped the rail of the poop deck. In the dark his one good eye shone with madness.

'You don't understand, do you, boy?' he raved. 'This is more important than doubloons. The Spirits of the Sea demand appeasement. A stinking landlubber like you has never heard on calm nights the dread cries of mariners who did not appease them. Mere doubloons are nothing when compared to the wrath of the Spirits of the Sea. Feel how they have taken the wind from us.'

Babel and the others untied Blart and dragged him towards the plank he had to walk.

'Couldn't it just be that it's not very windy today?' cried Blart.

'Accept your fate, boy,' ordered Kozali. 'I have been at sea for thirty years and I know when the sea needs to taste blood. It's almost as if there's a woman on board.'

'A woman?' repeated Blart.

'Aye!' said Kozali. 'Any female on a ship brings nothing but ill luck. Now to the plank with you!'

'You have lived like a pig boy, Blart,' Beo called out in support. 'But there is still time to die like a prince.'

And before Blart could say anything else, he was bundled on to the plank which jutted over the edge of the *Bloody Cutlass*.

All of a sudden he found it difficult to stand up straight. It's strange. Put a plank of wood on the floor and stand on it and it's the easiest thing in the world. But put that plank over the dark churning waters of the sea and it becomes a much trickier task. Blart had to concentrate hard to stop falling off. Below him the sea swelled against the side of the boat and then ebbed away before rushing up once more. It was almost as though it knew he was coming.

Don't look down, Blart told himself. *Don't look down.*

He looked in front of him.

He could just make out the shape of the *Golden Pig*, lying crewless in the still waters close beside the *Bloody Cutlass*. But apart from the shape of that once proud flagship there was nothing but the blackness of night and the ocean, eager to envelop him in its deadly grip.

He looked behind him. There was Babel, cutlass out, and behind him the leering mass of the pirates.

'Any last words?' taunted Kozali from the poop deck.

Blart looked up at the mad pirate captain and tried to think of something rude to say. But just as his mind was framing a suitable insult, his eye was taken by a movement high above the pirate captain's head. Atop the mast, framed against the bright half-moon, hanging on to the crow's nest with an easy grace and looking down at the murderous scene about to be enacted on the deck below, stood the slender figure of Tigran the Cabin Boy.

Or Tigrana the Cabin Girl.

And isn't, thought Blart, *a girl basically the same thing as a woman?*

If Blart revealed to Kozali that there was a girl on his ship, then he would be spared and Tigrana would be forced to walk the plank in his place.

'I haven't got all night,' ranted the captain. 'If you wish to speak, say it now.'

Blart opened his mouth. Was he about to betray Tigrana or was he about to utter one last final insult and die the death of a pig boy?

In the event, it turned out he did neither. Instead, Blart's last words were, 'What's that smell?'

As he spoke them, Tigrana loosed her hair from its tight ponytail and slid unnoticed down the mast, a stolen cutlass gleaming in her hand.

Chapter 21

'What's that smell?' mocked Kozali. 'We waited all this time for "What's that smell?" Force him …'

But before Kozali could finish, he smelt it too. As did all the other pirates. Their noses detected the worst smell that one can encounter on a boat.

Fire!

The *Bloody Cutlass* was burning.

And not just in one place. Or two. Several little fires had been started below deck and were now beginning to take hold. Who could have lighted them?

The answer was the nimble figure sliding gracefully down the mast, her long hair trailing in her wake.

'Water!' ordered Kozali. 'Put out the fires!'

Blart stood on the plank, open-mouthed in astonishment, as Babel and the pirates rushed off in all directions, their bloodlust swallowed by the fear of the fire.

Tigrana the Cabin Girl reached the bottom of the mast, and leapt carelessly on to the deck.

'You're a girl!' observed Beo in amazement.

'Not just a girl,' said Tigrana, her eyes shining with excitement. 'I'm Tigrana, the girl who's going to save your lives.'

And with three elegant flicks from her cutlass, the ropes that bound Beo, Olaf and Herglotz fell to the deck.

'Follow me!' said Tigrana. 'We must climb to the crow's nest.'

'Help,' shouted Blart.

The other questors, who had momentarily forgotten Blart, turned to his cry.

And saw a terrible sight.

For though Babel and the rest of the pirates had rushed to put out the fires, one member of the crew was not distracted by the threat that the *Bloody Cutlass* would soon be transformed into a floating inferno.

Captain Kozali.

Showing amazing speed for a man with his many disabilities, he had hobbled to the plank where Blart stood transfixed.

'The Spirits of the Sea will have their sacrifice,' he raved, stepping out on the plank towards Blart. One of his hands was a deadly claw and the other held a razor-sharp cutlass. His eye rolling in its socket faster than ever, he jabbed out a deadly thrust.

Blart jumped backwards.

Beo, Tigrana, Olaf and Herglotz gasped.

For Blart had landed at the very edge of the plank. He

had to struggle desperately to keep his balance.

'Thwart the Spirits of the Sea, would you, you lice-ridden cur?' cried Kozali. And he held his cutlass like a spear and threw it straight at Blart's head.

The moonlight glinted off the blade as it sped through the night sky. Its aim was unerring. At the last moment, though, Blart swerved to one side. The cutlass missed and disappeared into the darkness with a faint splash. But Blart's sudden lurch had left him off-balance. A leg in the air, he tipped wildly to one side. At any moment he was surely going to tumble off.

The other questors held their breath.

Incredibly, Blart righted himself. But Captain Kozali was not to be denied. He advanced further down the plank and, using his claw like a deadly cleaver, swung at Blart's chest. Blart couldn't go backwards, couldn't go forward and couldn't go sideways. The only way was up.

Captain Kozali lunged. Blart, using all the bending plank's springiness, jumped. Captain Kozali's deadly claw missed Blart's heart by a hair's breadth. Now the captain overbalanced. He toppled forward, out of control. Would he become his own sacrifice to the Spirits of the Sea?

But Kozali was a survivor. As he fell from the plank he sank his claw deep into it.

Above him, Blart had dropped safely back down.

'Babel!' bellowed Kozali, dangling helplessly from the plank like a deranged pendulum. 'Pirates! Come to the aid of your captain! Our prisoners are escaping!'

Hearing the desperate cry, Babel rallied the crew.

'Leave the fires!' he cried. 'Our cap'n needs us.'

The pirates rushed back to rescue Kozali and prevent the questors' escape, though how the questors were going to escape was not immediately apparent. Blart got himself off the overhanging plank fast and ran to join his comrades.

'I'll boil you all in oil, d'you hear?' screeched Kozali after him.

'Follow me!' cried Tigrana. And she began to climb. Up the rigging she went, as surefooted as if it had been a simple set of steps. The other questors did not find the climb as easy. Still Olaf and Blart rose steadily with Herglotz just behind them. But Beo struggled.

'Blast this rope,' he shouted as he lost his footing. 'What kind of idiot invented ropes that won't stay still?'

Meanwhile, Tigrana had reached the crow's nest. She looked down at the questors clambering after her.

'Faster!' she urged them.

And they did need to go faster, for down below Babel was dragging Captain Kozali back on deck. The captain was purple with rage.

'A bag of gold to any pirate who brings one of the prisoners to me,' he bellowed.

Never had the captain offered such a reward before. The pirates leapt on to the rigging in pursuit.

'Hurry!' shouted Tigrana. 'They're gaining on you.'

Olaf and Blart discovered a previously unknown talent

for climbing. Breathless and panting they joined Tigrana in the crow's nest. They looked down. The pirates were swarming towards them.

Herglotz reached the crow's nest next. But the lookout post was only built for one and, with four people squashed inside it, it began to creak and splinter.

Blart looked down at Beo. He was barely past halfway and the pirates were gaining on him rapidly. Blart decided the knight needed some encouragement.

'They're after you,' he shouted. 'They're catching up. They've all got cutlasses in their mouths.'

'Blast you, boy, and blast this rigging,' shouted back Beo.

Closer and closer came the pirates.

'If we consider the progress of ze knight to be x and the speed at which he is being captured by ze pirates to be y,' said Herglotz, 'then put both figures into a simple equation, I am able to conclude that he vill soon be chopped to pieces.'

'Shall we call the pieces z?' asked Blart.

'We must think of a way to hold the pirates back!' said Tigrana, her eyes gleaming with excitement.

'Pull my leg, would you?' cried Beo over his shoulder.

The first pirate eager for his bag of gold had caught hold of the knight's foot with both hands. He was perhaps a little overzealous though, for Beo placed his other foot firmly in the pirate's face and kicked down hard. The force flung the pirate off the rigging, his body arcing through the air before landing with a thud on the deck.

'And there's more where that came from,' Beo shouted.

But the knight's threats were nothing compared to the pirates' hunger for gold. Six more swarmed up the rigging towards him. Beo did not have enough feet to kick them all away.

'Come on, Beo,' encouraged Tigrana.

The first pirate climbed alongside the knight and received a massive fist in his mouth as a reward. But another was close behind. And another.

'We need a weapon to use against them,' said Tigrana.

'Don't mean to be rude,' said Olaf, 'but isn't that a bow behind you?'

'Yes,' Tigrana replied, 'but we need that for our escape. Look for something else.'

All four questors looked around the crow's nest. It didn't take long.

'Nothingk,' announced Herglotz.

'Shoes!' said Blart suddenly.

'What?'

'When I was a pig boy,' explained Blart, 'I used to hide in a tree, and when someone passed by I'd throw a shoe at them. They used to think they'd fallen out of the sky. It made me laugh.'

'You're rather strange, aren't you?' observed Olaf.

'It might work,' agreed Tigrana. 'Can you still throw?'

'I could hit the blacksmith at fifty paces,' said Blart proudly.

'Get back, blast you!' Beo was fighting and kicking as hard as he could, but there were too many pirates. He wouldn't be able to hold them off for long.

'Give me your shoes,' ordered Blart, pulling off his own.

'Euurggh!' said Olaf. 'Do you wash your feet?'

'Regularly,' said Blart. 'Every year.'

He leant over the dizzying edge of the crow's nest, took aim and threw.

The first shoe hit Beo solidly on the head.

'Ow!' shouted Beo, looking up angrily. 'What d'you think you're doing?'

'Helping,' shouted back Blart.

Unbeknown to Beo, a pirate was behind him, cutlass at the ready. Blart picked up a second shoe and threw once more.

This one caught the pirate full in the face. Instinctively, he tried to protect himself with his hand. One hand held a cutlass, one hand protected his face. No hands clung to the rigging any more.

'Aaarrgghh,' cried the pirate. He plummeted to the deck below.

'Fine shot,' complimented Olaf. 'If only I'd been trained in shoe warfare.'

'Keep throwing,' shouted Tigrana and she leapt nimbly out of the crow's nest and sped down the rigging.

A pirate swung towards Beo, his dagger aimed at the knight's heart. A shoe in the face stopped him just in time and the pirate's confusion about what had hit him gave Beo the chance to land a terrible blow with his fist.

'Euurrghh.'

The pirate crashed on to the deck just like his comrades. Babel and the other pirates who were watching from below were now taking cover to avoid being squashed by falling bodies.

And they were right to do so. A combination of Blart's unerring throws and Beo's weighty blows meant more stunned pirates were sent flying back down to the deck. Only Captain Kozali declined to hide. He stood fearlessly, looking up towards the crow's nest as bodies rained down around him.

'There is no escape,' he cried.

Tigrana reached Beo the Knight just as the first wave of pirates had been dispatched. But there were more coming.

'Follow me!' said Tigrana.

'I take no orders from a woman in battle,' said Beo gruffly. 'It is a man's job to lead.' And, ignoring her, he began to climb, missed his footing and slipped back to where he had begun.

The second wave of pirates were getting nearer.

Tigrana eyes flashed with anger. Nothing the knight said could have enraged her more. But he was a comrade in danger.

'Of course it is a man's job to lead,' she said, humouring him with considerable effort, 'but climbing this rigging fast is just like dancing – it is a matter of foot placement. Surely you wouldn't refuse to dance with a maiden who had no possible partner other than a bloodthirsty pirate?'

'Of course I wouldn't,' said Beo, outraged by the thought. 'A maiden without a dancing partner. Tis a most ignoble thing.'

'Then let us dance,' said Tigrana.

Satisfied he was not taking orders from a woman but simply dancing with her, Beo followed Tigrana, putting his feet where she showed him with the result that he quickly reached the crow's nest.

'I just saved your life,' boasted Blart.

'You threw a shoe at my head,' snapped Beo. 'I should cleave you in two.'

'This is no time for arguments,' said Tigrana, her face alive with the thrill of danger. 'We must fly.'

'Er . . . not trained for flying,' said Olaf.

'We're not Pig the Horse,' pointed out Blart. 'We can't fly.'

Tigrana picked up the bow that Olaf had noticed earlier. Beside it were three arrows with long ropes attached. She fired the arrows in quick succession towards the *Golden Pig*, and the questors heard three heavy thuds as each arrow found its mark, high in the mast of the Illyrian flagship.

'You're attacking our own ship,' said Blart.

'I've never seen a man with an arm so keen,' exclaimed Beo.

'How about a girl?' said Tigrana, handing him the end of one of the ropes attached to the distant arrows.

'Follow me!' she commanded 'We've going to board the *Golden Pig*!'

'I don't follow –' began Beo.

'I mean escort me so I don't get into any trouble,' rephrased Tigrana swiftly.

'Always happy to escort a maiden,' said Beo. 'They can be dangerous places these pirate ships.'

An arrow whizzed past his head. Kozali had ordered his archers to attack. Arrows shot up all around them. The second wave of climbing pirates was getting ever closer.

Hastily, Tigrana handed one of the other ropes to Olaf and Herglotz, and the last one to Blart.

'Which theorum did you employ to vork out ze precise parabola required to fire ze arrow?' the scientist asked.

Tigranana shrugged. 'I rely on natural talent.'

'You are too boastful for a maiden,' said Beo, who felt it was his duty to advise Tigrana even though to the rest of the questors she was the one of them least in need of any help. 'Sure, you won't attract a husband if you trumpet your achievements. No man will marry a show-off.'

Tigrana looked at Beo.

'Ah,' she said. 'Then I won't mention that I knocked out the cook, stopped up all the ventilation in the galley and put as much wood as I could into the oven … It should be ready to explode just about …'

There was a tremendous roar from below deck.

'… Now!'

Below them there were cries of terror and shouts of anger.

'If you would be so kind as to escort me, good knight,' said Tigrana.

Beo and Tigrana swung themselves out into the dark towards the *Golden Pig*. A gentle breeze disturbed the dead air.

Olaf and Herglotz followed them on the second rope.

Only Blart was left. Rope in hand, he looked at the looming mass of the *Golden Pig*, now lit up by the fire from the galley, which was rapidly consuming the *Bloody Cutlass*. It seemed a long way away. He took a last look down at the fires and the slain pirates. Below, one figure was unmoved. Captain Kozali stared upwards, his face crazed with rage.

'Destroy my ship, would you, Blart the Pig Boy?' he bellowed. 'Well, remember my face, for you will see it again. And that moment will be the moment you die!'

The flames crept closer and closer but Captain Kozali did not move. Feeling oddly conspicuous with the mad rolling eye of the pirate captain upon him, Blart grasped the rope firmly in both hands and swung out into the darkness.

Chapter 22

'What do we do now?'

Blart asked the question as soon as the last flames of the *Bloody Cutlass* were swallowed by the night. Almost magically, the wind had risen just as they had dropped on to the deck of the *Golden Pig*.

'We must steer the ship for Styxia,' said Tigrana eagerly.

'Couldn't we have a rest?' said Blart. 'I'm tired.'

'Rest!' roared Beo. 'What's wrong with you, lad? Princess Lois has already spent too much time in the evil hands of Gregor the Grizzled. We must get on with rescuing her.'

'I thought I was in charge of this quest,' Blart said. 'If I want a rest then I can order one.'

'You're right,' acknowledged Beo surprisingly. 'It's up to you what I do next. Head for Styxia and Princess Lois or cleave you into two. The decision is all yours.'

'Maybe I'm not that tired,' conceded Blart.

'Good' said the knight. 'Now, which way should we sail? It's pitch-black and we can't see a thing.'

'I can navigate by the stars,' said Tigrana quickly.

'The stars?' said Olaf.

'Look,' she said, pointing to a bright star high above them. 'The North Star – that is the brightest star in the sky. Styxia is east. Therefore we should go that way.' She pointed confidently into the black night.

'Tcah!' said Herglotz dismissively. 'You are lucky to haf me here. I can save you from ze grave mistake of listening to ze claims of this girl, who as far as I can see has no scientif-ic qualifications votsoever.'

'I don't need –' began Tigrana, but Herglotz cut her off.

'Only last year I did intensive research into night-time navigation.'

'You mean you know which way to go?' said Beo.

'Indeed,' said Herglotz. 'I vill lead us there by sound.'

'Sound?' said Tigrana dubiously.

'I believe ze waves that lap against a shore return to the sea with a different sound from those that haf not. I vill therefore listen for ze way.'

Tigrana's mouth opened wide in disbelief.

'But I have never seen navigation done like this,' she protested. 'Why not trust the star method that all other sailors use?'

Herglotz shook his head.

'I had expected more from you,' he said. 'You are young and ze young should embrace scientific advance and ze future.'

'But you don't know that it will work,' Tigrana argued.

'It always vorked in my laboratory.'

'But this is a vast ocean,' said Tigrana. 'How big was your laboratory?'

'If you must know,' said Herglotz peevishly, 'it voz about the size of my bath.'

'Your bath?'

'It is perfectly possible in science to extrapolate results from a small area of water, like zat in my bath tub, and apply it to large areas of water, like ze ocean.'

Tigrana turned to the other questors.

'You can't follow his navigation theory.'

'Sounds to me like he's had training,' said Olaf. 'I'm a great respecter of training.'

'Training?' Tigrana exclaimed, her eyes flashing with frustration. 'He's played with a toy boat in his bath.'

'Sounds like training to me,' said Olaf.

Tigrana allowed herself a screech of frustration.

'You see, don't you, lads?' observed Beo. 'Women always get emotional at times like this.'

Without saying anything else, Tigrana climbed furiously up the rigging to the crow's nest.

'And then it's the sulking,' Beo continued. 'Damsels. They're all the same.'

And so the skeleton crew determined to follow the course chosen by Herglotz the Scientist. Beo manned the wheel while Blart and Olaf did their best to control the sails.

Herglotz insisted on total silence so he could listen closely to the waves.

'Hard to starboard,' he began.

The ship set off in the opposite direction to that advised by Tigrana.

'Soft to port.'

The ship continued onwards into the night. Above them, Blart felt the moon was growing larger as he watched. Even though it was not cold, he shivered.

A few hours later, still in the pitch-dark, after numerous minute port and starboard adjustments, there was a tremendous crash. The ship shuddered dreadfully to a halt and the questors were thrown to the deck.

Herglotz was on his feet first. His confidence appeared to have deserted him.

'This is most unusual. We appear to haf schtopped.'

There was a terrible cracking sound.

'It appears that ze sea has broken,' concluded Herglotz.

'What?' demanded Beo, Blart and Olaf.

'It is ze only rational explanation,' said Herglotz.

A suggestion from the crow's nest descended through the darkness. 'Unless we've run aground.'

'Oh, yes,' said Herglotz. 'That is ze other explanation. I voz just testing. I can now confidently assert that we haf run aground on ze coast of Styxia.'

There was a loud scoff from the crow's nest.

Chapter 23

In the weak light of the early morning, an official, escorted by six soldiers, approached the *Golden Pig*, creaking help-lessly on the rocks of what Herglotz continued to insist was the Styxian coast.

Beo reached into his jerkin and pulled out a small well-thumbed book.

'I didn't know you could read,' said Blart.

The official and his armed escort began to clamber over the rocks.

'This is my *I Spy Enemies* book,' explained Beo. 'I've had it ever since I was a young warrior. It has pictures of the uni-form of every enemy I might encounter on any quest I undertake. And when I've encountered them and killed them, then I tick them off.'

Beo scrutinised the uniform of the approaching soldiers.

'They're not Styxian uniforms,' he said.

'Perhaps they're in disguise,' said Herglotz.

Beo shook his head.

'This book lists official disguises as well.'

'Perhaps that's because we're not in Styxia,' said Tigrana, who had descended silently from the crow's nest. 'And we're not in Styxia because we steered the ship completely the wrong way, thanks to his stupid ideas and your ignorant prejudice about not listening to a girl.'

'Someone got out of the crow's nest on the wrong side,' Olaf commented.

Tigrana's eyes flashed angrily.

'Where are we, then?' Blart wanted to know.

'Hold your horses, can't you?' said Beo, flicking through the book. 'Blue trousers, red jerkin, black boots, sword with a slight curve ...'

The official and his armed escort reached the *Golden Pig* and, without waiting for permission, climbed on board.

'Welcome to Triplicat.'

Beo found the correct page and the matching uniform.

'Got it,' he announced. 'We're in Triplicat.'

The official approached the questors.

'My name is Caylus and I am a representative of the Triplicatian government,' he said. 'Who's in charge of this ship?'

'I am,' said Blart, 'even though you wouldn't think it most –'

Caylus cut Blart off peremptorily. 'Have you anything to declare?'

Blart looked blank.

'Contraband, untaxed goods? All non-Triplicatian goods must be accounted for and any duty paid upon them.'

Blart understood the idea of paying.

'We've nothing to declare,' he declared.

'Customs parchment!' Caylus called out.

A massive soldier rushed forward and handed him a parchment.

'Quill!'

Another hulking soldier proferred a quill pen.

'Ink!'

A third giant soldier produced an ink holder.

'Desk!'

A fourth soldier came forward and bent down. Caylus, using the soldier's back as a desk, rapidly wrote on the parchment.

Beo watched in disbelief.

'What is this?' he muttered. 'These are men. Fighting men. Men who should be sacking and pillaging, and they are ordered about by this pipsqueak.'

Caylus signed the parchment with a flourish, folded it and tore it neatly into two. He handed one part to Blart.

'Your copy.'

'My what?' said Blart.

'Your copy of your statement that there is nothing on this ship to declare. Should anything be found subsequently which should have been declared, then you will be held liable by the appropriate authorities and subject to a fine or, at the discretion of a judge, a term of imprisonment commensurate with Triplicatian law.'

'Is that a good thing?'

'It is neither a good thing nor a bad thing. It is simply administration,' said Caylus briskly. 'Now, may I see your visas?'

'What?' said Blart.

'Your visas,' said Caylus. 'Before entering Triplicat it is necessary to write in advance to the Foreign Ministry requesting a visa which, if approved, will be sent to you before your visit.'

'I don't think we did that,' said Blart.

'Parchment!' shouted Caylus. 'Quill! Ink! Desk!'

The four soldiers rushed forward again.

'But you don't understand,' said Blart. 'We didn't know we were coming. We were on a quest, you see, and –'

'The reason for your visit is immaterial,' said Caylus imperiously, already writing a new parchment on the soldier's back. 'You have docked without the correct documentation. This will have to be recorded.'

Beo, already outraged by watching soldiers treated like serfs by the weedy-looking specimen, could keep silent no longer.

'What is all this nonsense, Quillpusher?' he demanded of Caylus. 'My name is Sir Beowulf. I have travelled all over the world. My name and my rank are all I need to enter a country.'

'How very quaint,' said Caylus dismissively. 'We, in Triplicat, like a little more than a man's name.'

'My name should be enough.'

'Your copy,' said Caylus, tearing another parchment expertly into two and handing half of it to Blart. 'It details that you and your comrades have entered Triplicat illegally. This is a crime under Triplician law and you are hereby arrested. This is your notification.'

'Arrested?' shouted Beo in outrage.

'But we don't want to stay,' said Tigrana. 'If we could just wait for the tide to rise it will lift the boat off the rocks and we'll sail away.'

Caylus didn't appear to have heard. Instead, he eyed Beowulf quizzically.

'Do you have a permit for that sword?'

'A what?'

'A permit,' repeated Caylus. 'Under Regulation Forty-two, subsection eight, clause seventeen, all swords must be registered with the Triplician authorities and an official permit issued which the bearer of said arms must carry with him at all times.'

Beo could not believe what he was hearing.

'Could I see your permit?' said Caylus coolly.

'No,' said Beo, reaching for his sword. 'But I'll show you your insides if you like.'

'Are you threatening to disembowel a Triplician official?' asked Caylus.

'I am,' said Beo. 'So let's have less of this talk of permits and visas. You take your men and you get off this ship.'

'Parchment! Quill! Ink! Desk!'

'I'm warning you,' said Beo. 'You write one more thing and I'll –'

'You'll kill me, will you?' said Caylus calmly. 'That would be most unwise. The killing of a Triplicatian representative would leave you filling in forms for the rest of your life.'

'I don't care about –'

'And what is more, the spear thrower who currently has a spear aimed at your heart would kill you before you had time to swing your arm.'

Beo looked at the spear thrower Caylus had mentioned. He held his spear expertly. Beo decided not to unsheath his sword.

'An excellent decision,' commented Caylus. 'And now we just need to deal with the matter of the litter and I think we'll be finished.'

'Litter?' said Blart. 'What's litter?'

'Litter,' explained Caylus, 'is unwanted rubbish left on public land rather than in a designated waste disposal facility.'

'But we haven't dropped any litter,' said Tigrana.

'You have littered the beach,' Caylus informed her.

'Don't see how,' said Olaf. 'We haven't even been on the beach.'

'Parchment! Quill! Ink! Desk!' ordered Caylus.

Moments later he handed Blart a copy of his citation for

beach littering. The item of litter in question was the *Golden Pig*.

'But it's a ship,' protested Blart.

'It's litter,' insisted Caylus. 'So, to sum up, you are guilty of illegal entry into the Kingdom of Illyria, bearing deadly weapons without a permit, and serious littering.'

'Would it help if we said sorry?' suggested Olaf.

'Not really,' said Caylus cheerfully. 'It would help if you decided to follow me to jail.'

Chapter 24

The Triplicatian jail was very different from the brig on the *Bloody Cutlass*. It was clean, it was orderly and the questors had to sign for everything.

'But I don't know how to spell my name,' Blart explained.

'Don't know how to sign your name?' said Caylus. 'That's most irregular.'

'I can make a mark,' offered Blart helpfully.

'Is it a neat mark?'

'Yes,' said Blart, picking up the quill and making a mark at the bottom of the parchment.

Caylus looked pained.

'That's more of a smudge,' he said.

'I can never use these fancy quills,' said Blart. 'You should have let me stick my thumb in the ink like they do everywhere else.'

'I suppose it will have to do. Now come and join your comrades.'

Blart was the last questor to be processed. He was led

through the door from the reception area to the cell block. Beo, Olaf, Herglotz and Tigrana looked up from their respective bunks as he arrived. Caylus closed the barred door behind him.

'When are we going to get out of here?' Beo demanded.

'Your case is complicated by the fact that you are accused of three different crimes,' said Caylus, 'so the parchments will need to be prepared for three different courts. Still, you've all been charged with the same crimes and so your cases may be rolled into one batch instead of needing to be heard individually.'

'I don't need to know every detail,' said the knight. 'Just tell me when.'

'If the dates of your trials don't clash and nobody makes any spelling mistakes on the parchments, you could be out in two years.'

'Two years!'

'Things really move along under this new streamlined system,' said Caylus proudly.

'We don't have two years!' said Beo. 'I thought it would take a morning to sort out and we'd be back on our ship. That's why I didn't fight your soldiers.'

'Don't worry about your ship,' said Caylus. 'I have already issued an order for it to be removed from the rocks at high tide and taken to the port for safekeeping.'

'I'm not worried about the ship!' bellowed Beo. 'We're on a quest, man. There's a princess who is going to be married against her will. There's a country called Illyria that is going to be destroyed. We need to get out now.'

Caylus seemed to sympathise.

'Am I to understand that you're dissatisfied with your incarceration?'

'Of course I am.'

'I think I can help,' said Caylus. 'Wait here one moment.'

'He's hardly going to go anywhere, is he?' pointed out Blart. 'He's in jail.'

Caylus disappeared briefly and returned carrying a parchment and a quill.

'This is an official complaint form,' he said.

Beo's face darkened.

'I don't want a complaint form,' he shouted. 'I want to get out of here *right now*.'

'It's got tick boxes.'

'Here's what I think of your tick boxes.'

Beo reached through the bars, snatched the complaint form and tore it into pieces.

'I'll have to make a note of this behaviour,' said Caylus.

'Aaargghh,' shouted Beo in frustration.

Olaf decided that his hostage negotiation training might be transferable to unjust incarceration situations.

'Sorry about that,' he said.

'Don't apologise for me,' growled Beo.

Olaf quailed.

'Just wondering,' he said sheepishly to the official, 'if

there was any other way that we could get out?'

Caylus considered his query.

'There's bail,' he said.

'Bail?'

'If you can put up a hundred gold coins per person and fill in one short form, then you'll be released until the time of your trial.'

'Zat's five hundred gold coins altogezzer,' interjected Herglotz, delighted to have the opportunity to do some maths.

'And we'd be free?' said Olaf.

'Oh, yes,' said Caylus. 'You couldn't leave the country, but apart from that you'd be free.'

Olaf turned to the other questors.

'Any of you chaps got five hundred gold coins?'

'The pirates took all our money,' Tigrana reminded him.

'Hmmm,' said Olaf.

'You could get a Triplicatian householder to put up the money for you,' suggested Caylus.

'Anybody know any Triplicatian householders?' said Olaf hopefully.

It appeared nobody did.

'Ah, well,' said Caylus sympathetically. 'I'm sure the two years will fly by.'

And he turned to leave the cell block. And then he stopped.

'There is one thing,' he said.

'What is it?' asked Olaf.

'Under Triplicatian law you are entitled to one free letter.'

'What do you mean?'

'Normally when a person is arrested they want to let their family know,' explained Caylus, 'so they don't expect them for dinner for a year or two. And that's why everyone gets one free letter.'

'But none of us has got any family waiting for us,' said Blart.

'No,' agreed Olaf. 'But if we can write a letter to someone in Triplicat, then perhaps they will be moved by our plight and put up the bail – and we'll be released.'

'What?' said Blart scornfully. 'You think that you can just write to someone and they'll give us five hundred gold coins?'

'I have tremendous confidence in the power of the written word,' said Olaf. 'Caylus, my good man, could we have a quill and a parchment?'

'It will be a pleasure,' said Caylus. 'There's nothing a Triplicatian official likes better than the creation of more parchment.'

An hour later the letter was complete. All the questors had insisted on a say in its authorship and so it had a somewhat muddled style.

Olaf read out the final version:

My dear esteemed Triplicatian,

Greetings! We hope you are well and have not been cleaved in two recently. We also hope you are rich. If you are not rich, please stop reading now and pass this letter to the nearest rich person you see. Hurry up. Please. If we find you have not done this, you will be cleaved in two at a later date. The two parts however may not be exactly equal as the cleaving will not be performed under laboratory conditions. Thank you. Read on, rich person. We are unfortunate travellers who, through no fault of our own, find ourselves in jail. We all have busy lives and frankly it's a dashed inconvenience. We would be very grateful if you would come to the jail with five hundred gold coins (separated into piles of one hundred gold coins for convenience — this is done by dividing by five) and tell Caylus the Official that they are for our bail. We'll pay you back double the amount of money (the amount of money will be calculated using multiplication). We are very grateful. Hurry up.

Yours faithfully, exactly, in anticipation, menacingly and I'm bored of this writing now,

Olaf, Herglotz, Tigrana, Beo and Blart

P.S. Do you like pigs?

'I'm still not exactly sure it strikes the right tone,' said Olaf.

'I would like more science in it,' said Herglotz.

'I'd like more threats,' said Beo.

'I'd like more pigs,' said Blart.

'Let's just send it,' cried Tigrana. 'I can't bear being

locked up in this cell a moment longer. I long for the wuthering heights of the crow's nest.'

'What does "wuthering" mean?' said Blart.

'I don't know.' Tigrana frowned. 'I saw it in a book once.'

'Caylus!' shouted Olaf.

The official appeared.

'Letter for dispatch.'

'Excellent,' said Caylus, reaching through the bars and grasping the letter. 'Where shall I send it?'

'Bit of a problem there,' said Olaf. 'Don't really know the names of any people, or the numbers of any houses, or the names of any streets.'

'The Triplicatian postal system will not handle such a letter,' Caylus informed them.

'Oh,' said Olaf.

For a moment the questors were lost. 'I know,' said Blart. 'Send it to: *The Person with All the Gold, Big House, Rich Street, Triplicat.*'

'Will that work?' wondered Olaf.

'Oh yes,' said Caylus. 'If the Triplicatian postal system has an address, then I can guarantee the letter will get there.'

'Even if the address is made up?' said Olaf.

'The postal system is very resourceful.'

It appeared that Blart had come to the rescue once more.

'Now,' said Caylus. 'Does anyone have a stamp?'

Chapter 25

'I can't stand this any more,' said Tigrana, pacing up and down the cell.

'You said that yesterday,' said Olaf.

'And the day before,' added Blart.

There had still been no response to their letter.

'Take a break and sit down,' suggested Olaf.

Tigrana suddenly stopped pacing.

'I've got an idea,' she said excitedly. 'We could dig a tunnel and escape through it.'

'Afraid I haven't had any training in digging,' said Olaf.

But Tigrana wasn't listening. Desperate for activity, she slipped behind her bunk, where she was almost invisible, and began loosening a plank.

'Keep watch,' she said to the other questors. 'Cough three times if you hear someone coming.'

'I vill keep watch,' said Herglotz. 'As a scientist I am skilled in observation.'

Beo was in a quandary. He was sure that it was against the

chivalric code to assist a damsel in digging a tunnel as she would become grubby, and chivalry abhorred a grubby damsel. As Beowulf well knew, the correct behaviour for an incarcerated damsel was to stare out of the window and sigh periodically until a hero came to her rescue. And then she should live happily ever after.

'Ow!' cried Tigrana.

'What is it?' asked Beo.

'Splinter!' said Tigrana.

Suddenly it all seemed clear to the knight. He could not stand idly by while a damsel pricked her finger with splinters and dripped precious maidenly blood all over the floor, even if by coming to her aid he was actively condoning her behaviour. He lay down beside Tigrana to help her.

'We need a distraction,' said Tigrana. 'A noise that will hide the sound.'

'I could do my impression of a piglet,' offered Blart. 'It's quite loud.'

'Interesting idea,' said Olaf. 'But a person pretending to be a piglet for no reason might attract suspicion.'

'You should sing to drown the noise,' said Beo. 'Then if the official appears, we can tell him that we were trying to keep up our spirits.'

'I can sing!' said Olaf. 'La la la la la la.'

For once the questors worked as a team – Olaf singing, Tigrana and Beo loosening the plank, Herglotz keeping watch and Blart doing nothing.

Is this what it's like to be a leader? wondered Blart.

Herglotz coughed three times.

'Something go down the wrong way?' asked Blart.

Herglotz coughed another three times.

Blart slapped him on the back to dislodge anything that might be causing this worrying choking. Herglotz repaid Blart's concern with an angry look and coughed a further three times.

'Have you got flu?' asked Blart.

'It's ze alarm signal,' Herglotz reminded him in a voice hoarse from fake coughing.

Luckily for the questors, Tigrana and Beo were more alert than Blart. They had replaced the loose plank and by the time the door opened they were whistling innocently on their respective bunks.

Caylus appeared in the doorway.

'Just remember not to say anything which might attract suspicion,' cautioned Beowulf.

'Why all the whistling?' the official asked.

Blart felt that a speedy reply would attract least suspicion.

'We're whistling to keep up our trousers,' he explained.

'Your trousers?' Caylus looked puzzled.

'He means our spirits,' corrected Tigrana.

'Them too,' agreed Blart.

'I will make a note,' said Caylus.

'Did you want anything?' asked Blart casually.

'I am simply doing my job,' said Caylus. 'Every hour I am

169

required to complete a form stating that I have checked that you are still in jail. While I am here, do you have any complaints?'

'No,' said Blart immediately. 'No complaints at all. In fact we've got compliments.'

'Compliments?' said Caylus, sounding pleasantly surprised. 'I confess that I don't get many compliments from prisoners. Sadly they tend to focus on the slow pace at which time passes when incarcerated and the pointless waste of their lives.'

'We think it's great here,' said Blart with a little too much enthusiasm. 'What we like about this cell especially is how solid it is. Very well built and secure. When you're walking on the floor you don't for a minute think there's any chance a hole is going to suddenly appear below you and that you'll disappear without a trace.'

Suspicion creased Caylus's face. This seemed a very odd compliment indeed. Fortunately Olaf interrupted.

'Very impressed with all the record keeping,' he told Caylus. 'One example. Say I was wondering how many prisoners should be in this cell. I ask you. You look at your form and you can tell me ...'

Caylus consulted the appropriate form.

'Five,' he confirmed.

'Exactly,' said Olaf. 'Five. Very handy to be able to know that. Where I come from they just throw prisoners into dungeons, one after another. No counting. No forms. The whole system is chaos.'

'No forms?' said Caylus in horror.

'How do they know if there's been an escape?'

'Stop talking about escapes, Blart,' said Tigrana.

'I was just wondering,' said Blart defensively. 'Some prisoners could dig a –'

Blart stopped abruptly as he was hit on the head by a small object thrown by Tigrana.

'Go on,' said Caylus.

'I wasn't saying anything,' said Blart.

'You were talking about escapes.'

'Can't remember.' Blart looked blank.

'What a pity,' observed Caylus. 'I was enjoying our little chat. Still, talking of forgetting things reminds me there was something I wanted to ask you. I have received notification from the harbour master. Your ship the *Golden Pig* has been placed there until your trial, when it will be used in evidence against you. But apparently a man has appeared and said the ship is rightfully his.'

'What?' cried Beo. 'The *Golden Pig* is the flagship of the Illyrian people. It belongs to their nation.'

'Oh, I see,' said Caylus. 'I will inform the harbour master immediately. He has been shown various papers which suggest that two of you are in this individual's debt, and he insists on taking the ship as full and complete repayment.'

'That's outrageous,' said Beo. 'That ship is needed for a noble quest. You can't let it be repossessed.'

'I will communicate your displeasure,' Caylus assured him. 'But the individual in question does have a considerable amount of paperwork to back up his claim. And paper talks.'

Beo huffed his displeasure.

'Oh, and one more thing,' said Caylus, consulting one of the many parchments he carried with him. 'Blart, you have a visitor.'

Blart was taken aback.

'I didn't know you had any friends in Triplicat,' said Beo.

'I didn't know I had any friends at all,' said Blart.

Chapter 26

Blart's visitor, her face a mask of concern, leapt up as soon as he entered the visitor's room.

'Oh, my darling, what have they done to you?' she wailed. 'Your skin is discoloured, you're so thin and you have a wild look in your eye.'

'Er, who are you?' said Blart.

'My name is Zarzuela,' said the lady, who Blart noticed was wearing a large amount of expensive-looking jewellery. 'But who I am is unimportant. What is important is you and your suffering. How could they have let your physical condition deteriorate so? You are a pale shadow of your former self.'

Blart looked down at himself.

'I've only been here two days,' he said. 'I look pretty much the same as I did when I came in.'

'How brave!' Tears shone on her cheeks. 'You need to eat the finest food and to rest on the most comfortable bed. You need to be pampered and spoilt by a multitude of devoted servants.'

'Do I?' said Blart.

'I have your letter,' said the lady. 'Its words moved me to tears every time I read it. I would have visited you sooner but I was prevented by the need to be close to a ready supply of tissue.'

'Runny nose?' said Blart sympathetically.

'Tears for you, Blart …' Her tears seemed to cease momentarily. 'You are Blart, aren't you?'

Blart nodded.

'For you, Blart.' The tears were flowing once more. 'After reading this dear, dear letter, I had to come. To bring you some comfort. Some tiny crumb of hope.'

'Do you like pigs, then?' asked Blart.

The lady looked confused.

'It was in the letter,' Blart reminded her. 'The P.S. bit. I wanted it to be the first thing, but the others said that it would distract people from the main point.'

Blart looked at Zarzuela expectantly.

'Of course I like pigs,' gushed Zarzuela.

'Which bit of them do you like best?' Blart asked eagerly. He did not often get the chance to fully discuss the various merits of pigs with a fellow enthusiast.

'Er …' Zarzuela seemed unsure.

'Curly tails?' suggested Blart. 'Cute snouts? Little brown –'

'All of them,' said Zarzuela, cutting Blart off before he could reel off the full list of possible choices. 'But I'm not here to talk about pigs. When I received your letter seeking bail I came as soon as I could to release you.'

'And the others?'

'I haven't come to post bail for the others,' said Zarzuela. 'Only you.'

Blart was puzzled.

'But you said it was the letter that made you want to come,' he said. 'And we all wrote that. Why do you only want to put up bail for me?'

'Oh,' said Zarzuela quickly, 'it's not that I don't want to. Of course I want to. Nothing would make me happier than to post bail for you and your little friends. But I haven't got enough money.'

Blart doubted this. He looked questioningly at the large quantity of expensive jewellery that adorned Zarzuela's person – the gold and silver rings, the ruby earrings, the emerald brooch and the diamond necklace.

'Oh, these things,' said Zarzuela with a dismissive wave of her hand, which made the large number of chunky bangles on her wrist jangle. 'All worthless paste, I assure you.'

'Oh,' said Blart.

'I have provided the official with your bail. As soon as he returns with the appropriate form for us to sign, then we can take you away from all this horror and –'

The door to the visiting room opened before Zarzuela could finish speaking. Caylus put a parchment marked with three crosses in front of her.

'Sign here … here … and here … and then I can release him into your custody.'

Zarzuela took the quill Caylus offered and signed with alacrity. Caylus turned to Blart.

'You are lucky to have the richest woman in Triplicat as a friend,' he said.

'Richest woman?' said Blart.

'How people exaggerate,' said Zarzuela quickly. 'All paste, I tell you. All paste.'

'Your mansion isn't paste,' pointed out Caylus. 'Largest house in all of Triplicat.'

'My heating costs,' said Zarzuela. 'Positively crippling.'

'But you own your own forest,' Caylus reminded her.

'Thank you,' said Zarzuela. 'We really must be getting on. Just put your mark on the parchment, Blart, and we can leave this man and his nasty prison behind.'

'I've always wondered how you got so rich,' said Caylus. 'In the Triplicat customs office we often tried to work out who it was that sent you all that gold.'

'You must have confused me with someone else,' insisted Zarzuela. 'Hurry up, Blart.'

Blart held the quill in his hand. But mentions of mansions and forests and gold were giving him pause for thought. It sounded very much as if Zarzuela had enough money to bail all the questors. Could he just leave them behind? Blart was unexpectedly having an attack of conscience. His quill hovered over the parchment.

'The sooner you sign the sooner we can be talking about pigs,' Zarzuela reminded him.

The magic word 'pigs' had an immediate effect. Blart decided he could leave his fellow questors after all. Gripping the quill hard, he made his mark.

'You've smudged again,' observed Caylus.

Chapter 27

'Make haste!' said Zarzuela. 'We need to get you home to a delicious meal and a warm bed.'

Blart took a look back at the prison as Caylus clanged the great gate shut.

Zarzuela led the way towards a golden carriage. At first Blart walked quickly behind her, but as they got closer to the carriage he suddenly stopped. Four huge black dogs were padding round it, purple tongues lolling from their mouths.

'Er …' said Blart.

Zarzuela turned round.

'You're not scared of my puppies, are you?'

'They're not puppies,' he said. 'They're dogs.'

'Only half-dogs,' said Zarzuela.

'They look like full dogs to me,' insisted Blart. 'I can't see anything missing.'

Zarzuela laughed.

'No, no,' she said. 'I mean that only half their ancestors were dogs.'

'What was the other half?'

At exactly this moment, one dog caught sight of Blart and emitted a blood-chilling howl.

'Wolf,' said Zarzuela nonchalantly.

The three other wolfdogs had spotted Blart now. Their howls were equally blood-chilling.

'They don't seem to like me,' said Blart.

'Of course they like you. That's just their way. Terror, Killer, Bloodlust and Gore,' she called. 'Come to Mama.' The four wolfdogs bounded over to Zarzuela. She gave each of them a rough stroke. 'Go and say hello to Blart.'

At Zarzuela's command, the four slavering dogs loped towards Blart. They were huge beasts. Everything about them was big. Heads. Bodies. And teeth. Especially teeth.

'Nice doggies,' said Blart hopelessly, backing away.

Terror, Killer, Bloodlust and Gore proceeded to say hello to Blart. They did this by jumping up at him, knocking him down, standing on him, nosing him and finally licking him all over.

'Get off,' shouted Blart.

'They're only playing,' said Zarzuela with the oft repeated cry of pet owners everywhere. 'Sniff, sniff,' she urged the wolfdogs.

And obediently the dogs began to sniff inquisitively at Blart.

'I don't like being sniffed,' protested Blart.

With a piercing whistle Zarzuela called the dogs off.

'You need a bath,' she said. 'Let's go.'

Once they were settled inside the coach and away from the wolfdogs, Blart could relax. The coachman shook the reins and they set off at a speedy canter.

'Is now when we talk about pigs?' Blart asked.

An involuntary sigh escaped from Zarzuela. Blart wondered if she was that interested in pigs after all.

'Later.' She closed her eyes and appeared to drift off to sleep.

Blart stuck his head out of the window to see what Triplicat looked like. But the first thing he noticed was the great wolfdogs loping easily beside the carriage. One of them spotted Blart's head poking out and let loose an angry howl.

Trying to ignore it, Blart looked out at Triplicat. There wasn't much to see and what there was all looked the same. Each cottage they passed was grey and exactly the same size as the last. Each vegetable patch was of the same size too. And the Triplicatian people he saw walking on the road or working in the fields all wore the same clothes. The only hint of irregularity was the river in the distance, coiling its way erratically across the plain.

Blart sat back in the carriage to discover that Zarzuela was actually awake.

'Why is everything the same?' he asked.

'In Triplicat,' Zarzuela answered, 'we believe in everybody having the best life possible.'

'That doesn't explain why they're all the same.'

'It does. Triplicat's architects have designed the best possible cottage and Triplicat's government has built them for everyone to live in.'

'What if I wanted a different cottage?' persisted Blart.

'That would be unhelpful.'

'I am unhelpful,' explained Blart cheerfully. 'So how come you have a mansion when everybody else has these grey square cottages?'

'Everybody is equal, more or less,' explained Zarzuela. 'Myself being one of the former.'

'What?'

'Never mind,' Zarzuela sighed. 'Perhaps one day someone will put it better than I can.'

As she spoke there was a cry from the coach driver and the horses abruptly stopped. There were no cottages here, just dense green forest.

'Here we are,' said Zarzuela.

'I don't see any food for me or luxurious beds,' said Blart.

'I thought you could do me a little favour first,' said Zarzuela. 'After all the trouble I've taken to free you.'

'What kind of favour?' said Blart, who mistrusted the whole idea of favours.

'Just take my dogs for a walk,' she said.

'But they've been running along beside the carriage,' said Blart. 'They've had lots of exercise.'

'Sometimes a well-trained dog needs to go into the forest briefly,' said Zarzuela. 'Surely you wouldn't embarrass a lady by making her explain further.'

'You mean for a –' said Blart.

'Exactly,' said Zarzuela.

Grumpily, Blart got down from the carriage. The four wolfdogs surrounded him.

'I really don't think they like me,' he said, looking up at Zarzuela. 'Wouldn't it be better if someone else took them for a walk?'

'Oh no,' said Zarzuela, producing a small card and offering it to Blart. 'You're the perfect person.'

Blart refused the card.

'I can't read.'

'Oh,' said Zarzuela regretfully, 'that rather spoils the drama of the moment. I do like the victim to be dispatched in some style.'

'Victim?'

'Yes,' said Zarzuela. 'You would have seen that the card has written upon it: *Just for you, a swift and painful death. Best wishes, the Guild of Assassins.*'

Blart's face fell. Zarzuela smiled at him.

'Ah, well it's still quite dramatic after all.'

'How did you know where to find me?' protested Blart, eyeing the wolfdogs nervously.

'We had no idea,' said Zarzuela cheerfully. 'We had lost your trail after our two assassins vanished on board the *Golden Pig*. It was very kind of you to write to us and tell us where you were.'

'But I didn't write to you,' said Blart.

'No,' agreed Zarzuela. 'You wrote to a rich person in Triplicat. And because of all the money that the Guild of Assassins pays me to kill people, I happen to be very rich.'

Blart reflected on this revelation for a moment.

'I really am very unlucky,' he concluded.

'Not as unlucky as you're about to be,' said Zarzuela charmingly. 'Now it works like this. It's inconvenient to have you killed on the road as corpses tend to attract attention, and I wouldn't want any overzealous official deciding my dogs were dangerous and insisting on having them neutered.'

At the word 'neutered' all the wolfdogs howled indignantly.

'I'm going to wait for five minutes,' said Zarzuela. 'And you're going to run away into the forest and then they're going to hunt you down and kill you by tearing out your throat with their vicious fangs. Are you with me so far?'

'Er ...' said Blart.

'Excellent,' said Zarzuela. 'And do try to run a fair distance before they catch you, because otherwise I'll have to exercise them later to keep them in tip-top-victim-killing shape. Let me tell you, Blart, an assassin's work is never done. So, do we all know what we're going to do?'

An idea shot into Blart's head.

'Ha!' he said. 'What if I don't run? What if I stay on the road? Then the dogs can't kill me because it will attract attention and they'll have to be whatever that word was.'

'You mean "neutered"?'

The wolfdogs howled once more.

'That's the one,' agreed Blart.

Zarzuela regarded Blart with wry amusement.

'I said it would be inconvenient,' said Zarzuela. 'I didn't say it would be impossible. And when one considers the vast bounty that is on your head – the largest bounty in the history of the Guild of Assassins – well, I think it's worth the risk.'

'Oh,' said Blart.

'So, you have a choice,' said Zarzuela. 'Instant death now or five more minutes of life?'

He looked at the fearsome black beasts, their teeth bared, their hackles raised, barely able to wait for the order to attack him.

Blart ran.

Chapter 28

*f*ive minutes later Blart was still running.

Behind him he heard howling as the dogs were released. The terrible sound spurred him on. He sped over bracken and zipped through fronds of ferns. He leapt over branches and forced himself through patches of stinging nettles tall enough to kill a child. He squelched through mud and ignored the gashes inflicted on him by cruel brambles.

The wolfdogs were closer, crying to each other as they closed in on their prey.

'Come on, legs!' Blart urged. 'Faster!'

Helpfully, his legs responded by running faster. Unhelpfully, they also tripped over a fallen branch.

He crashed to the ground. Raising his head, he saw he had stumbled in the very place that a previous victim had fallen. A skeleton lay there, a corpse in the copse, its head forced to a horrible angle by a wolfdog's lethal lunge.

'Nooooo!' cried Blart, dragging himself to his feet and through sheer terror finding the strength to run faster.

But it was no good. Closer and closer they came. Their barks were behind him, to the sides of him, even in front of him. The wolfdogs had him surrounded. Blart came to an abrupt stop in a small clearing. He was a hunted animal with no chance of escape.

Unless …

Could wolfdogs climb trees?

Because Blart could.

He ran towards the nearest tree just as the first wolfdog nosed its way into view. Until now, the beast had been following Blart's scent, which Zarzuela had ensured they had become familiar with. Now, for the first time, the wolfdog saw its prey.

It barked the news to the others and then bounded after Blart, its fangs bared.

'Don't fall! Don't fall!' Blart told himself.

From behind he heard a snort from the chasing wolfdog – it was almost on him now. The tree was too far away, its branches too high. The wolfdog's jaws would have him first. He could almost feel teeth tearing into his body.

'Neutered,' cried Blart between gasps.

The wolfdog paused to howl.

Blart put on a final spurt and jumped for the lowest branch.

One hand slid off the mossy surface but his second hand held. All four wolfdogs had arrived. They ran, baying, towards the dangling boy. Blart used the last vestiges of his strength to pull himself out of their reach. He lay on the branch, panting. The wolfdogs prowled underneath.

Slowly Blart recovered his breath and glanced down. The wolfdogs were circling the tree. Sooner or later someone would come looking for them and it would be best for Blart if he wasn't around when they did.

Which meant only one thing – he was going to have to go up.

He peered up into the green swaying canopy. The trees rose to dizzying heights. If he fell, he would be killed instantly. He took a last quick look down at the wolfdogs and began his climb.

At first it was easy. The branches were thick and it was simple to pull himself from one to the other. Blart allowed himself a smile, remembering the carefree days when he had climbed the trees around his grandfather's farm. And then he remembered his grandfather had sold him for a bag of gold and frowned.

But as he got higher, the branches became thinner. And then there was the wind, which was getting stronger. The tree felt like the *Golden Pig* – a great ship rolling and pitching upon the waves. Twice he nearly fell when a sudden gust shook the tree just as he was pulling himself precariously higher. He was tired and hungry.

It was then he heard voices.

'Didn't I say not to do that?'

'You said nothing of the sort.'

Voices he recognised.

'You are dried up and crackled.'

'You are mottled and diseased.'

Tree imps.

The voices of two tree imps to be precise. Possibly the only two tree imps left in the whole world. Sorel and Marjoram. Blart knew this because previously he and his fellow questors had introduced them after rescuing Marjoram, thus possibly saving the whole of the tree imp species from extinction. Blart could just make them out, bickering in the thin branches above him. From the sound of it, their non-extinction was not going smoothly.

'I wish I'd never met you.'

'I curse the day I laid eyes on you.'

Still, when you're trapped in a tree with vicious wolfdogs with healthy appetites waiting below, you're glad to see anyone.

'Hello, Sorel and Marjoram,' said Blart.

Sorel and Marjoram looked down at him in surprise. Tree imps are very small and green and have wrinkled faces. Their faces wrinkled even more at the sight of Blart.

'Of all the trees in all the world, you had to climb into this one,' observed Sorel. 'What are you doing here?'

'What are you doing here?' said Blart. 'The last time I saw you, you were in the great forest of Arcadia, many leagues from here.'

'We're on holiday,' snapped Marjoram angrily.

'Holiday?' repeated Blart, surprised.

'Yes,' said Sorel. 'Holiday. What's wrong with that? Just because we're nearly extinct do you think we're not entitled to have a holiday now and then?'

'Yes,' agreed Marjoram. 'It's tiring being the last surviving members of a nearly extinct species.'

'Why?' said Blart.

'You feel like you should be reproducing all the time,' explained Marjoram.

Worrying about tree-imp relationships wasn't top of Blart's list of problems.

'Will you help me?' he asked.

'No,' said Sorel. 'Ask me another.'

'And get out of our tree,' added Marjoram.

'I can't,' said Blart. And he explained why.

'Wolfdogs,' said Sorel when Blart had finished. 'They don't sound too frightening to me. Get out of our tree and go and fight them.'

'No,' said Blart. 'They'll eat me.'

'That's not our problem,' said Sorel.

'I'm staying here,' insisted Blart.

Sorel and Marjoram exchanged wrinkled looks.

'We'll never get any reproduction done with him here,' said Marjoram. 'Get rid of him.'

Sorel sighed.

'I suppose I'd better tell him about the creepers,' he said.

'You're going to help me after all,' said Blart. 'I knew you would. People always start off saying no, but in the end I get round them with my charm.'

Sorel and Marjoram exchanged extremely wrinkled looks and then Sorel reluctantly began to explain about creepers.

Unknown to people who don't spend their lives in the tops of trees (which is pretty much everyone when you come to think of it), there is a sophisticated network of creepers which can be used to travel from tree to tree. Each tree has a creeper which is hidden in its bark and accessed by simply pulling it out and swinging. The swinging creeper will deposit you on to a nearby tree at the exact point where you can pull out the next one and swing onwards. So once you find one creeper, you can move through an entire forest without once having to touch the ground.

'That means I can escape,' said Blart.

'That means you can leave us to the important business of trying to save our species,' corrected Sorel. 'Which you interrupted,' he added pointedly.

'It sounded like you were arguing,' said Blart.

'Foreplay,' explained Marjoram.

'What's –' began Blart.

Before he could finish his question, Sorel swiftly reached into a hole and hauled out a creeper, which he stuffed into Blart's hand.

'Get out of here. We never want to see you again.'

'Trees have got lots of holes,' said Blart. 'How will I know which one has got the creeper in?'

'Just stick your hand in the hole nearest to where you land,' said Sorel.

'What if there are two?' said Blart.

'Hope that you pick the right one,' said Sorel, 'otherwise an owl will have your fingers for breakfast.'

'But –'

'Goodbye,' said Sorel and Marjoram together, and the two tree imps disappeared into the tiny branches further up the tree where Blart couldn't follow.

Blart clutched the creeper. Did he trust the tree imps to help him?

Below him the wolfdogs howled longingly and scratched at the bark with their cruel claws.

Remembering the night when he had followed Tigrana and swung on a rope from the *Bloody Cutlass* over the treacherous seas to the safety of the *Golden Pig*, Blart closed his eyes, counted to three … opened them, congratulated himself on counting to three successfully, closed them again … and swung.

'Ahayahayaha,' cried Blart as he flew from one tree to the next.

The brief flight was exhilarating. The wind rushed through Blart's hair. But it was over too soon as the creeper deposited him on a flat branch wide enough to stand on and next to a hole.

Remembering Sorel's warning, Blart put his hand in tentatively.

Nothing bit his fingers. Instead he felt another creeper. *Those tree imps really must have wanted to get rid of me*, Blart reflected as he pulled it out. There was another howl from a wolfdog below.

Blart hoped they couldn't see him swinging through the trees. He grabbed a tight hold of the creeper and launched himself towards a nearby tree. No sooner had he landed on that tree than he pulled out another creeper and pushed himself off again. Through the forest he flew. Blart was doing something very unusual for him when there were no pigs in sight. He was having fun! He attempted more elaborate swings. He swung faster. He swung in arcs. He swung one-handed. He swung splat into the trunk of a nearby tree.

'Ow!' he said, feeling his nose to see whether it had been splayed across his face. It was a little sensitive to the touch, but at least it seemed to have survived the impact without a significant alteration in its shape. Blart told himself to swing more sensibly in the future. He reached into the nearby hole in the bark and pulled out the next creeper.

It was very short – too short to let him reach the next tree.

Blart stuck his hand in the hole again, hoping there was a spare creeper. There wasn't.

Hmm, thought Blart. As if in answer to his pondering, his eye was drawn by a glint of reflected light below him.

The river!

Blart remembered one thing he knew about wolves and

dogs, and so presumably about wolfdogs. They couldn't follow scent through water. If he could get across the river, then he might just stand a chance. He didn't exactly know what he'd do then, but he was sure he'd think of something.

Certain that the wolfdogs were still prowling around the tree they'd seen him climb, Blart climbed gingerly down towards the forest floor.

What he didn't know, however, was that the wolfdogs were working as a pack. One had settled down at the base of the tree while the others began to range through the forest, searching for any sight or smell of their prey.

Still, it was a large forest, and the chances of a wolfdog picking up on Blart almost as soon as he dropped quietly on to the forest floor were tiny ... Which is why Blart could consider himself very unlucky that the first sound he heard as his feet touched the ground was the bay of a wolfdog calling to the rest of the pack.

Blart ran through the trees and towards the glistening river. He emerged from the murk of the forest and gasped to find himself in bright sunlight. And then gasped again at what the sunlight revealed.

The river was there but it was a long way down.

There was a growl from behind. The first wolfdog appeared from the gloom and regarded him with hungry yellow eyes. Blart stepped out on to the rocky overhang and looked nervously down. The waters ran fiercely below him.

A second wolfdog appeared. Then a third. Then a fourth.

'Shoo!' said Blart desperately.

The wolfdogs did precisely the opposite. Knowing their prey was trapped, they padded stealthily towards him.

Blart comforted himself with the thought that it probably didn't matter if he could swim because the fall was likely to kill him anyway.

And then he jumped.

Moments later, he splashed.

Moments after that, he surfaced in the river, spluttering.

To add insult to injury, a log floating down the river clunked him heavily on the head. Dazed, Blart had only a second to fling out an arm to grab the log before he lapsed into unconsciousness and the river carried him away.

Chapter 29

Blart awoke face down in the mud, cuddling a wet log and with a toad on his head.

For most people this would be an unusual feeling, but not for Blart. Whenever he went on a quest he found himself dazed and half drowned at some point. However, the toad was a new touch.

Blart retched violently. Water spewed out of his mouth. The toad croaked and hopped into the river.

Far away Blart heard a howl. He jolted his head upright and turned. Silhouetted against the evening sky were four shimmering black forms. After all that, he hadn't even managed to cross the river; he'd just floated downstream and, unwilling to give up on their prey, the pack had bounded down the cliff and run alongside the river after him.

Blart had to find somewhere to hide. He turned round and there, to his amazement, was a building he recognised. It had high walls and patrolling guards. The jail!

Dropping the wet log and dragging himself to his feet,

Blart ran towards it and pounded upon the gate, gasping.

Nobody came. He glanced over his shoulder. The black forms were getting bigger. He pounded harder on the gate. This time he was rewarded. Caylus appeared on the other side.

'Let me in!' cried Blart.

'Come back to see your friends, have you?' said Caylus. 'I'm afraid visiting time's over for the day. But if you fill in a form I can give you first slot tomorrow.'

'I don't want to visit anyone,' said Blart. 'I want you to lock me back up in jail.'

Caylus looked puzzled.

'Nobody's ever asked to be locked back up,' he said.

'Hurry up!' urged Blart. The four wolfdogs were still padding along the side of the river. Any moment now they would pick up his scent.

'I'm afraid it's impossible,' said Caylus. 'You've been bailed, you see.'

'But I don't want to be bailed,' Blart whined.

'Forms have already been filled in,' said Caylus. 'You've made your smudge. Can't be changed now.'

Suddenly there was barking. The wolfdogs had found his scent.

'But I am a bad, bad person,' said Blart desperately. 'Everybody says so. I've done lots of bad things. I've thrown shoes at pirates. I've stood on an ill old man with leeches on his face. I don't want to save the world.'

'I don't think they're crimes,' said Caylus doubtfully.

'Of course they are,' insisted Blart. 'Especially not wanting to save the world. That makes me a menace to society.'

There was a howl from behind him.

'Those dogs look playful,' said Caylus.

'They're going to kill me,' cried Blart.

'Kill you?' laughed Caylus. 'Don't be silly. Just ignore them. If you ignore a dog, they think you are of higher status than them in the pack and respect you.'

'Please let me in.'

'Only criminals can come in.'

'That's not fair,' Blart protested.

'Would you like to make a complaint?' said Caylus, pulling out the complaint parchments that he had available at all times.

'Of course I wouldn't like to …' Blart stopped. He had an idea. He reached through the bars and snatched the parchment out of Caylus's hand.

The wolfdogs were pounding towards him. Soon they'd be upon him. Frantically he tore the complaint form into pieces.

'That's government property,' said Caylus disapprovingly.

Blart let the pieces fall to the ground.

'Look,' he shouted. 'I'm dropping litter. That's a crime in Triplicat, isn't it?'

Caylus nodded.

Blart dropped the last piece.

'Right,' he said. 'I'm turning myself in. For the crime of littering. I did it. I'm guilty. Arrest me.'

Blart threw an anxious glance over his shoulder. Now he could make out the ferocious teeth of the wolfdogs.

'It's most irregular,' said Caylus.

Blart shook the bars of the prison gate.

'Lock me up now!'

Reluctantly, Caylus put his key in the lock and opened the gate. Blart slipped inside straight away. The official shut the gate just as the four slavering wolfdogs threw themselves against it.

'They really are in a playful mood,' said Caylus, who was a dog lover.

Behind him the hounds howled piteously to the moon.

Chapter 30

'Where have you been?' demanded Beo.

'Nowhere,' said Blart truculently.

'Who came to visit you?'

'Nobody.'

The knight glared at Blart.

'We know where you've been and who visited you. Caylus told us. Deserting your comrades to rot in prison while you lie on luxurious beds.'

The questors stared at Blart.

'I only accepted bail so I could get the rest of you out,' he said. 'As soon as we were outside I told Zarzuela that she had to get four hundred more gold coins to bail you out. She didn't want to because … because … because she thought you might spoil our conversations about pigs. But I still said she had to get you out. And she said no. So I said I could never desert my comrades, and then she set her wolfdogs on me and I had to run through a forest and jump in a river and drop some litter to get back here.'

Blart looked at his fellow questors as though they should have been ashamed for doubting him. They weighed up what he had said. Finally Beo spoke.

'I believed you right up until that bit about dropping litter,' he said. And he stomped back towards the tunnel.

Blart couldn't believe it. A perfectly good lie ruined by a bit of truth. He had learnt a valuable lesson.

Herglotz went back to keeping watch and Olaf started singing to hide the noise of digging. Listening to the dreadful cacophony, Blart went to sit on his bunk wondering if he would have been better taking his chances with the wolfdogs.

Tigrana emerged from the tunnel, carrying handfuls of earth, which she hid under her bunk.

'The tunnel is coming on well, but we have to get rid of the dirt. Caylus may do a cell inspection at any moment.'

Blart looked under the bunk. There was already a sizeable mound of earth. A brilliant idea came to him straight away.

'Couldn't we hide it in the tunnel?'

Tigrana glared at him.

'I haf an idea,' said Herglotz. 'Vot if we conceal ze mud in ze turn-ups of our breeches and then, when we are taken out for exercise, we could shake it out secretly on ze ground.'

'We don't get any exercise,' pointed out Tigrana.

'I know,' said Blart. 'I'll eat it.'

Nobody could think of a better plan, so he began.

It was probably the first time on the quest that they had truly worked together as a team, and for a while it all went well.

'I'm getting a tummy ache,' complained Blart.

'Keep eating,' said Beo unsympathetically, dropping another armful of earth at Blart's feet.

'Earth hasn't got any flavour,' continued Blart, 'and if you bite on a stone by mistake, it really hurts your teeth.'

'*De do do do. De da da da*,' sang Olaf.

'And it's got things in it.'

'If a man says he will do a job, then he should do it,' said Beo. 'He should not whine and complain like a woman.'

Tigrana's head emerged from the tunnel. Beo, who had noticed that Tigrana was not in the habit of whining or complaining, looked unnaturally sheepish.

'I mean like most women.'

Blart kept munching – and a good thing too. Some time later Herglotz coughed three times. Tigrana and Beo rushed to climb out of the tunnel and replace the plank. Olaf sang even more loudly to mask the noise. But there was still a substantial portion of earth left.

'Get it down you,' hissed Beo as the key sounded in the door.

Blart crammed the last of the earth into his mouth and began to chomp.

'Daily cell inspection!' announced Caylus, opening the cell door and leading in four guards.

'*Numa numa nu*,' sang Olaf.

'Stop that,' said Caylus.

He produced a parchment and a quill. Pretending to

yawn, Blart forced the last handful of earth into his mouth. And chewed.

'Bunks. Five. Tick,' said Caylus as he began his inspection. 'Table. One. Tick.'

Blart had eaten so much earth that he was finding it very difficult to swallow this last mouthful.

'Chairs. Five. Tick. Prisoners …'

Caylus checked each of them individually. First he scrutinised Herglotz … then Olaf … then Beo … then Tigrana … then Blart … and then still Blart … and then Blart some more.

'Why do you have a worm dangling out of your mouth?'

The other questors held their breaths. Blart tried to think of a satisfactory explanation.

'I asked a question,' said Caylus. 'I expect an answer.'

Blart tried to look surprised.

'Ah,' he said, pulling the worm out of his mouth. 'I've been looking for him.'

'Why were you looking for him, then?' persisted Caylus.

'Er …' Blart hesitated. 'He's my pet.'

'Your pet?'

Blart nodded.

'I haf heard about zis phenomenon,' interjected Herglotz. 'I attended a symposium on social science. It voz in my younger days when I thought social science voz real science.' Herglotz laughed at his own naivety. 'It appears that ze incarcerated criminal feels alienated from society and seeks solace in a bond with a creature simpler than himself.'

'Slightly simpler,' Beo corrected him.

But Caylus was not moved by this explanation.

'Pets are against regulations, so I will have to confiscate him. Hand him over or I will have to order the guards to take him from you by force.'

The worm was handed over to Caylus.

'This completes the inspection,' announced the official. 'Tomorrow is cleaning day. We will move you to a different cell so this one can be thoroughly cleaned. Guards, follow me.'

And having ticked the final box on his parchment, Caylus led the men out of the cell and locked the door shut behind him

'Did you hear what he said?' said Tigrana. 'We are to be put in a different cell tomorrow. We must finish the tunnel and escape tonight!'

Realising the seriousness of the situation, the questors set about their various tunnelling tasks with an extra urgency.

All except Blart.

'What's the matter with you?' demanded Beo, catching sight of Blart's morose face.

'I'm missing my worm,' said Blart.

'He was only a worm,' said Beo.

'To you he was only a worm,' said Blart. 'To me he was a friend.'

Chapter 31

The questors tunnelled frantically, but progress was slow with only two of them actually removing earth. They had to take greater risks if they were to finish it before they were moved to another cell. First Blart, then Olaf, and finally Herglotz joined Beo and Tigrana in the tunnel. With nobody keeping watch, discovery was certain if Caylus and his guards were to return. And if discovered, how many more Triplicatian laws would they have broken and how much longer would they be fated to rot in jail? Such thoughts filled Tigrana especially with dread, for she couldn't bear not to be free.

'Sssshhh,' hissed Tigrana suddenly. 'Listen!'

They all listened. Above them was the sound of footsteps. They thumped overhead and then died away.

'We must have done it,' said Tigrana excitedly. 'We're outside the walls. I'm going to sneak a look.'

Very carefully, Tigrana pulled away the last pieces of earth. A shaft of moonlight shone into the tunnel. She raised her head and very quickly pulled it back in again.

'Guards!' she whispered.

As she spoke, two sets of footsteps thumped overhead. They were so near that the questors feared they must be discovered. But then the sound faded away again. Tigrana poked her head out once more. The next time she dropped into the tunnel she had more informaton.

'The prison walls are just over there,' she said, pointing. 'But there are two guards on patrol. If we try to run together, we will certainly be spotted. But if we move out one at a time, we have a chance to slip away into the cover of darkness before they turn around.'

'Thing is,' said Olaf, 'how do we know when to run?'

'I know,' said Herglotz. 'If we assume that ze guards are moving at a regular speed, which we call x, over a fixed distance, which we call y, then we can use zis information to predict when they will be where and calculate at precisely vot moment we haf to leap out of ze hole and run to give us ze best chance of success.'

This seemed a good idea to the other questors.

Except Blart.

'What's wrong with the other letters?'

'Vot?' Herglotz was puzzled.

'Why do we always have to call things x and y? What's wrong with j and q?'

'J and q?' said Herglotz dismissively. 'These are frivolous unscientific letters. X and y have value and worth, even if ve don't always know precisely vot that value is. Now be quiet, pliss. I haf to count.'

After listening to the footsteps of the guards and quickly poking his head out, Herglotz was able to reach a conclusion.

'I now know vot x and y are,' he told the questors. 'If I count to precisely fifty from now, it vill be time for ze first person to run. And then ze second person on another fifty. And so on.'

Herglotz began to count. Blart was impressed he could count up to such a big number without using his fingers. But then he reminded himself that Herglotz was a trained scientist.

Tigrana was to go first. Then Beo, Olaf and Blart. Herglotz would leave last, as he had to do the calculations.

'I'll signal my location when I'm out by calling like an owl,' said Tigrana. 'Run towards my hoots so you don't get lost.'

All the questors could do now was wait. The footsteps passed overhead and became fainter.

'Fifty,' said Herglotz.

Eyes gleaming with excitement, Tigrana pulled herself out of the hole and dashed for the safety of the darkness.

Herglotz started counting again.

'No shouts from the guards,' said Beo. 'She must have made it.'

The footsteps passed overhead again at the same regular pace. The guards hadn't noticed anything unusual.

The questors waited.

'Fifty!' whispered Herglotz.

Tigrana possessed a lithe agility that Beo did not. Beo possessed a large belly that Tigrana did not. Therefore the knight's exit from the hole needed the assistance of a hefty push. And the vibrations from his running for freedom shook the tunnel and sent earth falling down on the three remaining questors. Surely such a noise would alert the guards. But there was no cry of alarm, only the faint hooting of an owl.

Herglotz resumed counting.

Olaf went next. He was slower than Tigrana but faster than Beo.

It was Blart's turn.

The scientist began to count again. All this counting reminded Blart of the only difficult mathematical problem he had ever attempted.

'Once,' he whispered to Herglotz, 'I was looking after twenty-two pigs. And I had seven sties. And my grandfather told me to put an equal number of pigs in each sty. I tried all afternoon and I couldn't do it.'

Herglotz couldn't help thinking about it. Like all scientists, he couldn't resist a calculation. Fortunately, counting was easy, so he could keep doing it in the back of his brain while using the front to solve Blart's pig and sty problem.

But the more he thought about it, the more his brain puzzled over the question of twenty-two divided by seven.

Herglotz realised he had stumbled on an extraordinarily significant number.

'Zis is incredible,' he told Blart. 'I am dividing twenty-two by seven in my head and it appears to run to an infinite number of decimal places. Zis may be ze most significant number ever discovered. It is so important that it must haf a name.'

'Let's call it Pig,' said Blart.

'You cannot call a number Pig,' said Herglotz.

'You wouldn't have discovered it if it wasn't for me,' Blart reminded him.

Herglotz proposed a compromise.

'How about ve call it Pi?' he said. 'That's Pig for short.'

'I suppose,' agreed Blart.

'This is ze best moment of my life,' said the scientist.

'Your life must be even worse than mine,' said Blart.

'Fifty.'

Blart popped out of the tunnel. Unlike the other questors, he found himself emerging at precisely the wrong time. Herglotz had been so excited by the discovery of Pi that he had double-counted some numbers and his calculation had gone wrong. As a result, Blart found himself face to face with the guards. Actually, technically he wasn't face to face. As he was coming up from below ground and they were standing on it, it was more like face to foot. But whatever it was, it meant trouble.

'Aaaah,' cried the startled guards.

'Aaaah,' replied an equally startled Blart.

Whoever acted first would gain the advantage. Amazingly, this person turned out to be Blart. Before either of the guards could draw his sword he had hauled himself out of the tunnel.

'Stop!' shouted one guard.

'Prisoner escaping!' cried another, to alert the guards patrolling the walls.

The first guard slashed with his sword. Blart ducked beneath it. The second guard stabbed with his. Blart feinted to one side. He could hear the other guards rushing to help. Blart feinted one more time to throw them off balance and then ran, his heart pounding in his chest, fearing that at any moment he would be grabbed, until the darkness enveloped him and he crashed straight into Olaf.

'Ow!' said Olaf.

Blart turned and saw why he was still free.

Herglotz.

Hearing the shouts of the guards as they spied Blart, Herglotz had momentarily not known what to do – to stay hidden or to run. But he had not waited long. Maths told him that the two of them would stand a greater chance against the guards than one, and Herglotz was a servant to science. So he pulled himself out of the tunnel after Blart.

Unlike Blart, though, he lacked the crucial element of surprise. The guards were not as easily bamboozled by his attempts to avoid them, and others had arrived. The scientist was overwhelmed. In the confused effort to subdue him, a sword flashed in the moonlight.

'Remember Pi ze Number,' cried out Herglotz desperately. 'Remember Pi.'

And then he spoke no more. The guards pulled back. In the dark chaos Herglotz had been fatally wounded. He clutched his chest and then keeled over to one side.

Dead.

It happened so fast that none of the other questors had a chance to run back and help him. Herglotz the Scientist was no more.

'What did he want us to remember?' asked Tigrana.

'A pie,' said Olaf.

'A meat pie, I expect,' said Beo. 'He probably wanted one of us to eat a meat pie in his memory. Sure I'll eat one for him when we next reach a tavern.'

Blart decided it was all too complicated to explain the real reason. And so a great mathematical breakthrough was missed.

But more importantly, a comrade was lost.

The cold moon, now three-quarters full, shone down on Herglotz's body.

'We'll need some forms,' said a guard.

Chapter 32

'We must go now,' urged Tigrana, 'or we will be unable to go at all.'

The questors had no time to mourn. They had to get to the port and set sail on the *Golden Pig* before they could be recaptured.

'Hurry up!' she said.

'If I had a sword,' said Beo, looking angrily back at the jail.

None of them had weapons, though, as they had all been confiscated when they were imprisoned. With one last glance at the body of their fallen comrade, they fled into the night …

And immediately ran into another problem. None of them had ever been to the port before or had any idea where it was. But there, the questors had their first bit of luck.

Signposts.

Unlike all other lands, Triplicat had already developed a sophisticated system of signposts. Everywhere else in the world it was generally assumed that people knew where they were going and if they didn't, then they were probably lost and it served them right. Triplicat was different – which meant that each time the questors reached a crossroads, there was a sign with a helpful picture of a boat on it, pointing them in the right direction.

So after only an hour and a half the questors tasted the salt of the sea on their lips and beheld, in the first weak light of dawn, the looming grey shape of the *Golden Pig* – bigger and faster than any other vessel in the harbour. (The Triplicatians had never taken to seafaring because it was difficult to fill in forms while at sea – their quills kept slipping with the ebb and flow of the waves.)

They didn't have long. The inhabitants of ports rise early and every minute that passed made their discovery more likely.

Through the twisting cobbled streets they ran. They passed sleepy cats padding home from their nightly prowl, empty tables outside taverns and the occasional prone seaman who had drunk too much grog the evening before. Each quick step brought them closer to the *Golden Pig* and the promise of freedom. Now they were heading along the harbour's edge. All remained quiet. They finally reached the *Golden Pig*. She had been left unguarded. Her gangplank was down.

'Quick,' said Tigrana. 'Untie the ropes.'

Believing that any moment they would be spotted, the questors rushed to cast off the ropes that held the ship. But

212

the harbour remained silent, save for the creak of the ship's timbers in the early morning breeze. Moments later the *Golden Pig* was free. The questors hurried on board as, helped by tide and wind, the great ship began to drift away from the wharf.

'I never thought I'd be happy to be back at sea,' said Beo.

Blart collapsed on the deck, exhausted and thankful for the opportunity to rest.

'This is no time to rest,' Tigrana told them. 'We must raise the sails.'

'I'm just going to pop down and check the Triplicatians haven't impounded any of our things,' said Olaf.

'Yes, better make sure your long rope's safe,' Blart said sarcastically. 'What would we do without it?'

Olaf didn't respond and disappeared below deck. He was sensitive on the subject of his rope.

Tigrana watched him go in exasperation.

'We've got more important things to do. It's not easy sailing a ship with only four of us.'

But her exasperation was short-lived; Olaf was back on deck almost immediately – looking worried.

'Think you ought to know,' he announced, 'that we've got company.'

'Company?' said Beo.

Olaf nodded.

'Heard some snoring coming from the captain's cabin.'

'Think they can trespass on the *Golden Pig*, do they?' said

Beo. 'I'll rouse them with a prod of cold steel.'

'I'll come too,' said Tigrana. 'Let's grab some weapons from the armoury.'

But Beo was determined to keep this pesky damsel out of danger for once and held her back gently.

'Blart and I can deal with a sleeping enemy,' he said. 'You are needed to sail the ship.'

'Who said I was going?' said Blart.

'No leader lets a damsel go into danger when he could go there himself,' said Beo menacingly.

Knowing how Beo felt about damsels, Blart decided it was wisest not to argue.

'You go first,' he told Beo. 'I will lead from behind.'

They headed down below, equipping themselves with cutlasses on their way, and leaving a disappointed Tigrana to rig the ship.

If there had been snores coming from the captain's cabin, they had stopped by the time Beo and Blart reached the door.

'I believe Olaf was imagining things,' whispered Beo.

'Shall we go back up on deck, then?' said Blart, ready to turn round.

Just as he spoke there was a cough. Beo gripped his cutlass tight and flung open the cabin door.

'Let me see the snivelling thief that trespasses on the King of Illyria's ship,' bellowed the knight. 'I'll cleave him in two and feed his entrails to the seagulls.'

With his back to the two questors, a figure in black stood looking at himself in the captain's mirror.

'Prepare to meet your doom,' ordered Beo.

The figure in black turned round.

'Good morning, Beowulf. Still have your delightful turn of phrase, I see.'

Blart and Beo were speechless.

Standing in front of them was Uther the Merchant.

Chapter 33

It was Blart who found his voice first.

'You should be dead,' he said.

Uther frowned.

'I must say that is a little rude, Blart,' he observed. 'Especially from one of my old card-playing friends. No "Nice to see you, Uther." No "How have you been, Uther?"'

'But you should be dead,' repeated Blart.

'The boy is right,' agreed Beo. 'You should.'

'Sorry not to oblige,' said Uther. 'But I'm alive. You're probably thinking I shouldn't be because the last time you saw me on that isolated snow-covered mountaintop I was bleeding uncontrollably from a massive number of wounds.'

'You can't cheat death, merchant,' said Beo. 'I saw you fall with my own eyes. You stopped breathing.'

'Purely circumstancial,' cautioned Uther.

'Isn't it a safe bet to assume that someone's dead when they stop breathing?'

'Sometimes,' said Uther. 'Unless they have fallen into

216

an ice coma.'

'An ice coma?'

'Exactly,' said Uther. 'The doctor explained it to me. Apparently I should have died, but the freezing temperatures slowed down my body, so I was dying much more slowly than if I had been at sea level. A day later I was found by Yinsk, a wandering goat herder. He kindly carried me back down the mountain and took me to a doctor who staunched my wounds – and saved my life. I confess that I was a little off colour for a while. But a week of bed rest did wonders. And so as soon as I was recovered I paid the doctor –'

'What did you pay him with?' asked Blart suspiciously. 'You didn't have any gold.'

'I paid a visit to Yinsk to thank him for saving my life,' explained Uther calmly. 'And while I was there I taught him a card game. You remember the rules of Muggins, don't you, Blart?'

Blart remembered all too well.

'We played a friendly game at first,' said Uther. 'Yinsk was winning all the time. He proposed a little wager.'

'He did?' said Blart.

'Well, one of us did,' said Uther with a dismissive wave of the hand. 'And as soon as the wager was made, his luck some-how changed for the worse. I won all his savings – enough gold to pay off my bill from the doctor – and I'm also the proud owner of Yinsk's goats and his wife.'

'The man saves your life and you reduce him to penury

and turn his wife into a slave?' Beo shook his head at Uther's cruelty.

'I am not entirely without feeling,' said Uther. 'I rented his wife back to him at a generous discount. And, fully recovered, I set off to collect on my debts.'

'Debts?' said Blart.

'Ah,' said Uther, fishing in his black cowl and producing some papers. 'You're just like every debtor. Eager to borrow, slow to repay. Don't you remember all the IOUs that you, Beo, Capablanca and Princess Lois gave me for use of my lard?'

Reluctantly, Blart and Beo nodded. On their last quest they had been forced to risk starvation or buy and eat Uther's lard, for which he had charged extortionate prices.

'Through my network of business contacts I traced you to Triplicat and discovered that you were in jail. This was very disappointing as it is extremely difficult to get people to pay their debts when they are already in jail. However, I had a stroke of luck when I discovered that one of your possessions was still available and would adequately provide full and final settlement. I went to see the Triplicatian authorities and proposed that they give me –'

'The *Golden Pig*. So *you're* the one Caylus told us about. This is outrageous!' roared Beowulf. 'Even at your prices a few pieces of lard cannot be worth a great flagship.'

'Not at the time, no,' agreed Uther.

'What do you mean, "Not at the time"?' demanded Beo, pointing his cutlass threateningly at the merchant.

'It is one of the banes of my life as a businessman,' lamented Uther with a shrug of resignation. 'People who don't understand compound interest.'

'What?' said Beo and Blart.

'If only people would read the small print,' said Uther.

'I don't remember any small print,' said Beo.

Blart and Beo felt sure Uther was breaking some law, but neither of them was sufficiently aware of their statutory rights to know what it was.

'Luckily,' continued Uther, 'the authorities in Triplicat did understand compound interest and agreed with me that because of your refusal to service your debt –'

'We thought you were dead.'

'Because of your refusal to service your debt I could take the *Golden Pig*. I have the paperwork to prove my ownership here, so if you'll kindly leave my ship I have a voyage to the Treasure Islands of the South Seas to be getting on with. My crew are joining the ship this morning.'

Uther held out his ownership papers for the others to inspect.

Enraged, Beo slashed them in two with a sweep of his cutlass.

'You betrayed us on the last quest and would have handed us over to our enemies and a terrible death,' he said fiercely. 'The only debt I owe you is one of honour – to avenge your betrayal by killing you and then continuing on our quest.'

Uther looked puzzled.

'I've never understood these debts of honour,' he said. 'It seems impossible to trade them on the open market.'

'You will understand when there's a blade in your guts,' said the knight.

'I suppose I will have to fetch the authorities to throw you off my ship if you refuse to leave,' said Uther calmly.

Blart laughed.

'Look out of the porthole,' he suggested.

Uther did as Blart proposed and instantly realised the *Golden Pig* had drifted far from the Triplicatian Coast on the outgoing tide. He was trapped in his cabin, heading out on to the lawless high seas with two ex-comrades who both had an excellent reason to kill him.

'Did I hear someone say something about a new quest?' he said.

'Indeed,' said Beo. 'We must rescue Princess Lois before the moon is full once more or Illyria will be destroyed.'

'And then I die because I'm her husband,' Blart added. 'Even though nobody seems to care about that bit.'

'Why didn't you say so before?' said Uther. 'Naturally, I would have put all business concerns to one side until we had rescued Princess Lois. I always had a soft spot for her, if you remember. And the full moon is not long away now.'

Blart and Beo remembered that Uther would have sacrificed her just as willingly as he would have sacrificed them.

'Your end lies here, merchant,' said Beo. 'This time there

will be no ice coma for you. Prepare to meet your doom.'

Beo raised his cutlass.

'You can't kill me in cold blood,' protested Uther.

'True,' said Beo, remembering the chivalric code. 'I can't. Blart give him your cutlass and we will fight to the death.'

'What if he kills you?' said Blart. 'Then I won't have a cutlass and he'll kill me.'

'He won't kill me,' Beo assured Blart. 'Now hand him your cutlass or I'll be forced to fight you instead.'

Blart gave Uther his cutlass.

'Prepare to die,' said the knight.

Uther realised his mistake and dropped his cutlass immediately.

'You can't kill an unarmed man,' he said.

'Pick that cutlass up and fight like a man,' said Beo.

'No,' said Uther.

'Then you give me no choice,' said Beo, raising his own weapon. 'Farewell, merchant.'

The cabin door opened and Tigrana's head appeared.

'Is anybody going to come and help me with . . .' she began to say, and then she noticed Beo's attacking stance. 'What are you doing?' enquired Tigrana.

'They're killing me in cold blood,' said Uther. 'And all because of a slight business misunderstanding.'

Beo hesitated. The chivalric code was confusing him. He was obliged to seek vengeance on Uther for betraying his fellow questors, but he was also obliged to do his best to preserve the innocence of damsels. Killing a defenceless merchant in cold blood, even one as unscrupulous as Uther, could traumatise a sensitive maiden.

Reluctantly, Beo lowered his cutlass.

'I will kill you when there are no maidens about to be sullied by seeing you die,' he said.

Almost instantly Uther slid across the cabin to join Tigrana.

'Greetings,' he said with an oily smile. 'My name is Uther. I'm sure we're going to become very close friends.'

Chapter 34

And so the *Golden Pig* continued on its quest to save Princess Lois, and Blart wasted no time in reminding everyone that he was now captain. Tigrana took over general control of the ship and the navigation. She was assisted by Uther the Merchant, who had wisely decided the safest place for him was close to the innocent maiden. Olaf spent his time trying to remember all the deficiencies in his training that the quest had so far thrown up, while Beo brooded on the return of Uther.

Blart slipped off to the captain's cabin, which he had insisted Uther vacate. Sure that nobody was coming, he reached into his pocket, pulled out the Misty Mirror of Miracle and gave it a swift shake.

For once the mirror cooperated immediately. It revealed a face looking directly at him. The face was unmistakeable.

Captain Kozali.

'That wasn't what I wanted to see,' Blart told the mirror. 'I wanted to see the Illyrian armada sailing towards Styxia. Or

Capablanca coming to help. Or at least some pigs.'

Blart shook the mirror hard, hoping to force it to show him something he wanted to see. But the Misty Mirror of Miracle was an ancient artifact which bowed to the will of no man. It still showed Captain Kozali, but this time with Babel. They stood on the poop deck of the *Bloody Cutlass*. The ship was charred from the great fire that Tigrana had started, but somehow the pirates had saved it from destruction. Blart gulped as he imagined what would happen to him were he and Kozali ever to come face to face again. But he gulped even more at what the mirror showed him next. Behind the *Bloody Cutlass* was another pirate ship, proudly displaying its ragged Jolly Roger. And behind that ship another, and another, and another – a pirate fleet stretching across the entire Eastern Ocean.

And all intent on hunting down the *Golden Pig*.

Blart stuffed the mirror into his pocket, threw open the door of his cabin and rushed up to the wheel, which Tigrana was steering with an easy mastery while Olaf looked on.

'So you see,' said Uther, who was there too, 'it was all a complete misunderstanding.'

'We've got to change course,' gasped Blart.

'Change course?' said Tigrana. 'We're set fair for Styxia. A day or two of good wind will bring us to the coast.'

'Half a day will bring us into the hands of Captain Kozali,' said Blart.

'Kozali,' scoffed Olaf. 'We left his ship burning. He will

224

be no threat to anybody for a long time.'

'Nobody told him that,' said Blart. 'He's assembled a giant pirate armada and we're sailing straight towards it.'

'How do you know?' asked Tigrana. 'I was up in the crow's nest a moment ago and didn't see anything.'

'I saw it in the Misty Mirror of Miracle,' said Blart. 'Capablanca the Sorcerer gave it to me before we left Illyria. It shows you things.'

Tigrana looked doubtful.

'If we carry on, we'll just be sailing into a trap,' said Blart.

'But there is no other way to reach Styxia in time,' exclaimed Tigrana.

Uther coughed discreetly. Nobody noticed. It was windy.

Uther coughed a little less discreetly.

'I believe I may be of some assistance,' he said.

Blart regarded the merchant with suspicion. 'I don't want anything from you. You'll just betray us like you did before.'

Uther looked wounded.

'Can we not let bygones be bygones?' he asked. 'I'm willing to forget any differences we've had before and offer what help I can in this great quest.'

'Seems to me the fellow deserves a chance,' said Olaf.

'Please, please,' said Uther, a pained expression on his face. 'I have no wish to come between fellow questors. I simply wish to offer my assistance. As you know, I was about to set out on a voyage of my own and so I had acquired the very latest map. I can offer it to you at a very reasonable price – no more than a token. A businessman such as myself has a reputation to maintain.'

'Agreed,' said Olaf. 'Of course he does.'

'You're trained in business, then?' asked Blart. 'I didn't think there was anything you were trained in.'

'Not exactly,' admitted Olaf. 'But I'm studying.'

'Who with?' said Blart.

'Me,' said Uther smoothly. 'I have undertaken to introduce Count Olaf to the rudiments of business.'

'An entire course for just one estate,' said Olaf. 'I've got a real bargain.'

'Yes,' said Uther, shaking his head. 'I held out for three but he beat me down.'

Olaf smiled triumphantly at Blart.

'I doubt he'll give even ten gold pieces for this map,' said Uther.

'Ten,' said Olaf. 'I spit on your ten. I offer nine.'

'I have created a monster,' said Uther, sighing. 'What can I do in the face of such skilful bargaining? All right, I accept nine.' He reached into his pocket and pulled out an IOU and a quill. 'Sign here, would you,' he said smoothly.

Olaf signed with a flourish and, in return, Uther produced the folded-up map.

'A pleasure doing business with you, my good man,' said Olaf as he spread the map out.

Olaf, Blart and Tigrana scrutinised it.

'What do all these symbols mean?' said Olaf.

'You'll need the key to find out,' said Tigrana, who had studied nautical charts before. 'Sometimes it's on the back.'

Olaf turned over the parchment. There was nothing but mysterious outlines and strange symbols.

There was a small cough behind them.

'Did I not mention the key is sold separately?' said Uther casually.

Fortunately Olaf had forgotten none of his new skills. In only a moment he haggled Uther down to nine gold pieces (from ten) for the key. Studying it once more, the chart now made sense.

'Look,' said Tigrana, sweeping her hand across the map. 'There are new routes that I have never seen before – previously unexplored islands and sea channels between them.'

'Can you see a different way to Styxia?' asked Blart.

Tigrana studied the map carefully.

'I cannot,' she said.

'You mean the map was a waste of money,' said Olaf dolefully.

'A strict no-refund policy is in operation,' Uther informed nobody in particular.

'Wait!' said Tigrana. 'There! A tiny passage seems to be possible *here*.'

Blart looked at where she was pointing.

'There's some writing on it.'

Tigrana bent closer.

'*The Straits of No Return*,' she read.

'The Straits of No Return,' repeated Blart.

'There's something else written next to it in tiny letters,' said Tigrana.

'Always read the small print,' advised Uther.

Tigrana squinted and just about made out the words.

'*No ship to enter has ever returned*.'

'Perhaps we should find another way,' said Blart doubtfully.

But Tigrana was already turning the wheel of the *Golden Pig*. To her, the Straits of No Return sounded like fun.

Chapter 35

A day later the fun started.

Tigrana's kind of fun that is. Nobody else was quite sure about it. It began when they spied land, but land of a different kind than any of the questors had seen before. High in front of them rose a massive wall of rock, flat, hard and continuous. Tigrana checked the chart twice, then ordered some sails to be taken down to slow the ship. She steered a risky course close to the cliff face, while the others looked along its endless mass for any opening that could lead to the straits. Some of the questors began to doubt the map's accuracy. After all, it had been sold by Uther and, as Beo and Blart were well aware, he had never had a problem selling poor merchandise before.

As the day wore on, the sun rose in a clear blue sky, its rays beating down remorselessly. One by one the questors were driven into the shade. All except Tigrana, who could not admit defeat, and Olaf, who was determined to prove the map was a bargain.

'Wish I'd had more training in looking,' said Olaf, wiping his brow. 'Thing with looking is that you think you're good at it until you can't see something.'

'There!' Tigrana pointed.

At last, there was a gap in the rock. Olaf followed her finger.

'Don't wish to doubt your word,' he said, 'but it looks awfully narrow.'

'It's the only gap,' Tigrana insisted. 'It must be the entrance to the straits.'

'We'll never fit through that,' said Blart, returning from his sheltered spot beneath the sail to interfere.

'Of course we will.' Tigrana was determined. 'The *Golden Pig* has not let us down yet.'

And she set a course for the entrance to the straits. Immediately, there was a horrendous scraping noise from below.

'We'll be holed,' cried Olaf.

Tigrana twisted the wheel as hard as she could. There was an awful grinding sound and then there was silence.

'I think we're clear,' she said. 'Olaf, go below and see if we're shipping water.'

Blart looked ahead over the rail of the ship.

'What's that sticking up?' he said. 'And that? And that?'

'Curse the day I ever went to sea,' cried Beo. 'There are sharp rocks everywhere. We will be sunk before we even reach the straits.'

At the wheel, Tigrana flushed red with excitement.

'Just tell me where they are and I will steer us through them.'

'They're everywhere,' shouted Blart unhelpfully. 'Can't we go back?'

'If we turn her round she'll hit one for sure,' Tigrana replied.

'Can't see a leak,' said Olaf, emerging from below deck.

Blart stood at the front of the ship and stared intently at the clear green water for rocks. When he spotted one he shouted its location to Tigrana, who would steer to avoid it. But veering away from one rock brought the boat closer to another. And so the ship zigzagged towards what they hoped was the entrance to the straits.

It was strenuous work. Blart rubbed his eyes. All afternoon they had been straining to spot danger through the ripples and reflections on the water. His face was burning in the sun. The other questors had retired to the shade.

He blinked. There was a piece of grit in his eye. He tried to rub it away. It wouldn't go – in fact it seemed to get bigger.

There was a terrible tearing sound from below. The very last rock before the Straits of No Return.

Olaf ran below deck. He reappeared very quickly.

'I'd like to make it clear that I'm untrained,' he cried, 'but I think there's water pouring in through a hole in the side.'

'Blart,' shouted Beo. 'Why didn't you keep your eyes open?'

'Everybody always remembers the rock you didn't notice,' complained Blart.

But there was no time for recriminations.

'We need a bilge chain,' cried Tigrana. 'Uther, take the wheel and hold her steady. The rest of you get a bucket and form a line from the hole to the deck.'

So desperate was the situation that Beo took orders from a damsel without question and rushed after her.

'Spread out,' said Tigrana. 'I will fill the buckets and pass them along the chain. The person at the end of the chain throws the water back into the sea. That is our only chance of keeping the ship on an even keel.'

She sprinted down below to the breach. Olaf stood next to her at the bottom of the stairs, Beo at the top and Blart by the rail.

Tigrana scooped the first bucketful of water and passed it to Olaf, who then carried it up to Beo, who finally passed it across to Blart.

'Bucket needed at the hole,' cried Tigrana.

Blart obeyed the order immediately. He handed the bucket back to Beo, who passed it down to Olaf and on to Tigrana.

'I meant an empty bucket.'

Blart had forgotten to throw the water over the side.

'You didn't say empty,' protested Blart as the bucket was returned to him along with a cuff from Beo.

But after this initial hiccup the bilge chain began to work.

Buckets flew along the line. Water was dumped overboard faster than it could seep in. But would it be enough to give Tigrana the chance to steer the *Golden Pig* through the deadly walls of rock that guarded the entrance to the straits? She rushed back up on deck and grabbed the wheel from Uther. Now it was alive in her hands. Waves crashed angrily as the sea battered the rock wall. The gap seemed to shrink and the ship seemed to widen the closer they got. A deadly current took hold of the *Golden Pig*, pitching her forward towards the rocks. One wrong move and the ship would be lost.

But Tigrana refused to be quailed. It was almost as if she had become part of the ship. The current dragged her one way, immediately she turned the other. The waves drove against the *Golden Pig*, sending more water flooding through the gash in the ship's side. The bilge crew had to work faster. The ship rolled. The rock walls loomed overhead.

And then suddenly they were through.

The sea was green, clear and calm. There were no vicious rocks lurking underneath the water. The Straits of No Return widened to greet them.

Chapter 36

The following dawn found the *Golden Pig* floating serenely along the easy channel between the high rock walls. Through these calm waters Blart steered, while down below Tigrana and Beo completed the repairs to the hole in the side of the boat. On the foredeck Uther was continuing to give Olaf thorough training in how to become a successful merchant.

'It is common practice,' said Uther, 'when negotiating a price to offer below what the seller wants.'

Olaf nodded obediently.

'However,' said Uther, 'sometimes it is necessary to take the seller by surprise.'

Olaf nodded again. That made sense.

'Getting excellent training here,' he shouted to Blart.

'The best way to take your opponent by surprise is to do the opposite of what he expects,' continued Uther. 'For instance, by offering him more than he's asked for. Ambushed by this unusual tactic, he will have shaken your hand on a deal before he realises what's hit him.'

'Right-oh,' said Olaf. 'Take him by surprise by offering more.'

'This is advanced business,' said Uther sternly. 'Don't be too sure you'll be able to pull it off first time.'

'Don't wish to brag,' said Olaf, 'but I've got everything right first time before.'

'True,' admitted Uther.

The merchant pulled a handkerchief out from under his dark cloak.

'I want one gold piece for this handkerchief.'

'I'll pay two,' said Olaf.

Uther appeared bewildered.

'D-done,' he stuttered.

'Got you,' said Olaf.

Uther seemed to regain control of himself.

'You've taken me for a fool again,' he said, producing an IOU and a quill. 'Sign here, please.'

Olaf signed yet another IOU for Uther with a flourish.

'Can't wait to be doing more business with you,' said Olaf.

'Neither can I,' agreed Uther.

Minutes later, Olaf was becoming so accomplished a businessman that he had just paid Uther five times as much as he'd requested for a third handkerchief. Uther seemed to be finding it hard not to laugh out loud with pleasure at the advances of his student.

'Soon,' he told Olaf, putting away his most recent IOU and stifling a guffaw at the same time, 'you will have a monopoly on handkerchiefs. Securing a monopoly is a most sophisticated business strategy, and yet you have stumbled on it almost by accident. I believe you may be the most gifted student I have ever encountered. Buy just one more handkerchief and the monopoly is yours. If everyone on this ship caught a chill, you could make a fortune.'

Uther didn't seem to notice the burning sun, which made anyone catching a chill seem most unlikely.

'Follow me down to my cabin where my last handkerchief is stored,' said Uther, 'and we will conclude our negotiations there.'

Blart was left alone on deck. The *Golden Pig* continued to sail serenely through the Straits of No Return. Blart was beginning to feel the name was rather inappropriate. There hadn't been calmer water and easier sailing since they'd left the port in Illyria.

What was that?

There was a strange bubble to one side of the ship. Blart tried his best to look while keeping hold of the wheel. He couldn't see anything …

There it was again, this time on the other side of the ship. Had he caught a fleeting glimpse of a tentacle? Blart's imagination threw up visions of dreadful sea monsters lurking just beneath the surface, ready to drag the ship to its –

A terrible screech sounded from high above him. Blart's

head jolted upwards. Was that the shadow of some gigantic bird passing overhead, or was it –

Were the rock walls closer?

Now, you really are imagining things, Blart thought. *Rock walls don't move … They can't move …*

They were moving.

'We're being attacked by walls!' yelled Blart.

The other questors rushed up on deck.

'What nonsense are you shouting?' demanded Beo.

'Walls!' shouted Blart. 'They're attacking!'

'You imbecile,' shouted back Beo. 'Walls can't …'

And then he stopped.

There was a rumble which seemed to come from the very bowels of the earth.

Blart wasn't imagining anything. The rock walls were closing in.

'Raise the sails,' cried Tigrana, desperately rushing towards the mast.

But nobody followed her. The Straits of No Return stretched far ahead. The rock walls were closing in too fast. And nobody could fight rock.

'What are we going to do?' Blart moaned.

'*What are we going to do? What are we going to do? What are we going to do?*' The narrowing walls mocked his cry with echoes which bounced from side to side and slowly faded into nothingness.

There was nothing to do but wait.

The walls kept coming, shutting out more light the closer they got. Instinctively the questors backed away until they were all leaning against the mast.

'We are face to face with death,' announced Beo.

'*Death. Death. Death,*' echoed the walls.

'Nobody was talking to you,' said Blart to the walls.

'*To you. To you. To you.*'

'Be quiet.'

'*Quiet. Quiet. Quiet.*'

Even for Blart, this was stupidity at a truly advanced level. He was having an argument with an echo. The futility of his position didn't stop him for a second, though.

'Shut up!' he shouted angrily.

'*Shut up! Shut up! Shut up!*' bellowed back the walls.

'Blart,' hissed Beo.

'*Blart! Blart! Blart!*' hissed the walls.

'We are going to die,' whispered Beo. 'We should do so nobly. Has anyone any last words?'

The walls were now almost touching the sides of the *Golden Pig*.

'Not quite sure what to say,' mumbled Olaf.

'Why can't you take your money with you?' demanded Uther.

'These are not my last words,' claimed Tigrana.

'Comradeship and chivalry,' bellowed Beowulf.

Their echoes mingled and overlapped.

Only Blart was left to speak. The terrible walls reached

the sides of the ship. The awful creaking and splintering began.

'I like pigs!' shouted Blart.

'*Pigs! Pigs! Pigs! Pigs! Pigs! Pigs! Pigs! Pigs!*'

In the narrow channel the sound swelled until it almost deafened them. And then just as quickly it died away.

The walls stopped.

But like a vice they held the *Golden Pig* fast.

'What are we going to do?' asked Olaf.

It was not a situation in which a good plan automatically suggested itself. Below were the deep waters of the straits, to the sides barren rock. There was only one way to go.

'I'm going to climb out of here,' announced Beo. 'I may be able to find us a way to escape.'

'I'll come too,' said Tigrana immediately.

'I forbid it,' said Beo. 'You are a damsel. I do not know what I will find at the top. It is too perilous a deed and knights have got enough problems without damsels starting to do perilous deeds. There's only a limited number of perilous deeds to go round. The last thing we need is more competition.'

'But that's unfair,' said Tigrana. 'All I want is a level playing field.'

'You've got a wall of rock,' Beo snapped back. 'And anyway, Blart is the leader of this quest and he has commanded that he will accompany me on the climb.'

'When did I do that?' wondered Blart.

'Just now,' Beo assured him, tapping his sword in a menacing way. 'You insist.'

Tigrana huffed with anger but she had to accept Blart's authority.

Blart looked above him.

'Up there?'

It was sheer, dizzying, vertical rock.

'You have shown your prowess in climbing the rigging,' said Beo. 'Now you will show your prowess on rock.'

'That wasn't prowess,' said Blart. 'That was luck.'

'You are the leader of this quest,' said Beo. 'Now is the time to lead.'

'But Tigrana wants to go. I think now is the time to, er …' said Blart.

Delegate was the word he didn't know.

'You will lead this quest or I will throw you overboard.'

Blart had no choice. He was going to have to go.

'You will need food for such an arduous climb,' said Tigrana, who, despite her anger, still felt obliged to give her comrades the best chance of success.

Uther coughed.

'I happen to have some extra nourishing food. It has been designed specially for climbers.' He reached into his black cloak and pulled out a block of white fat.

'That's lard,' said Blart.

'Lard does not accurately describe it,' insisted Uther. 'It is known as Climber's Boost.'

'It looks like lard,' said Blart.

'Branding is a new technique in business,' Uther explained to Olaf. 'It can add value. Would you like to buy some?'

Whether it was lard or whether it was Climber's Boost didn't matter. It was food that, however bad it tasted, would reinvigorate tired limbs. Blart and Beo took some.

'I will prepare the bill for your return,' said Uther.

'You will need a rope to tie yourselves together,' said Tigrana. 'Then if one of you slips from the rock, the other one will be able to stop him falling to his death.'

Blart wasn't sure. He thought if Beo slipped, his great weight would simply pull Blart off after him. But Tigrana insisted that they be tied together.

'Climb safely, Beo,' said Tigrana. 'Make sure you return.'

'I'll do my best,' said Beo, and for a moment there seemed to be a tear in the great knight's eye. He brusquely rubbed it away.

'And you'd better come back, Blart,' said Uther. 'That lard – I mean Climber's Boost – wasn't free, you know.'

And so Blart and Beo went forth to climb the great wall of rock.

'Now,' said Uther to Olaf, pulling out another block of lard. 'Would you like to buy some Trapped Sailor's Tonic?'

Olaf was puzzled.

'That looks just the same as the Climber's Boost.'

Uther the Merchant allowed himself a smile.

'You're learning, my boy. You're learning.'

Blart and Beo stood ready to go, both looking up. The face was smooth except for one rocky protuberance that jutted out high above them.

'I will go first,' announced Beo.

He began to climb. Roped to him, Blart had no choice but to follow. Surprisingly, up close the sheer wall of rock turned out to have ample handholds. At every step, crevices easily accommodated a foot or a hand.

'This is easy,' cried Blart as they rose rapidly.

'Don't get cocky,' Beo growled from above him. For all his determination the knight was not comfortable climbing. He longed to be standing on an open field or sitting on a fiery charger with a lance in his hand.

But Blart had already convinced himself that he was a great climber. He had always been his own biggest admirer. He swung daringly between handholds. He leapt into toeholds. He had found something he could do better than the knight and he was determined to show it.

But the easy climbing did not last long. As they rose higher up the cliff, the gaps between available handholds grew wider. They were forced to plan the route much more carefully and progress slowed dramatically. Blart found that he had to stretch as far as he could to move from one handhold to the next and it was now Beo, with his greater reach, who had the advantage, though neither of them found it easy. The afternoon rapidly became evening and as the light faded it got colder. Growing more and more tired with each pull, Beo and Blart forced themselves to keep going.

Finally they reached the protuberance of rock they had seen from the bottom of the climb.

'Can we rest here?' said Blart. His muscles felt as though they had no strength left.

But the knight had already been waiting for him there a few minutes and shook his head.

'I can see the top. A half hour's climbing and we'll be there. The light will hold out that long.'

The news that the end was in sight seemed to put extra strength into Blart's legs. He followed Beo beyond the rocky outgrowth and then, looking up, he too could make out the summit. He felt a tug on the rope. Thrilled at the prospect of success, Beo was climbing faster than he had climbed all day. Blart was not going to allow the knight to accuse him of delay. Spotting a couple of nearby handholds he pulled himself up, then across to a foothold, then up to another handhold and then he heard the dreadful cry.

Beo had fallen off.

The knight dropped past him like a boulder.

Blart braced himself for the impact.

It came with a snap and a massive tug. Blart stood no chance of holding on. He was dragged straight off the rock face. Tied together, Blart and Beo were tumbling helplessly to their deaths.

Chapter 37

It would have been a pleasant sensation to drop through the air so freely if it wasn't for the certainty that their landing would be so abrupt and messy.

And doubtless it would have been ...

Were it not for the rocky protuberance.

Beo flew by it on one side. A moment later Blart flashed by on the other. The rope caught on the protuberance as though it were a giant hook. The sudden jolt that brought Blart to a swinging stop sent such a judder through his body that he felt as though all his bones had come loose.

When he was able to breathe again, Blart was pleasantly surprised to find that they were all apparently still attached. The pleasant feeling didn't last long, however. Before he could breathe twice he found himself being jerked up towards the rocky outgrowth. Evidently, at the other end of the rope, Beo was still descending, and his heavy weight was going to pull Bart up and over the huge hook of rock, at which point they would both plummet to their deaths. There was a horrible zipping noise as the rope slithered over the brutish stone, dragging Blart up with it, his body bashing viciously against the cliff face on the way.

There was nothing he could do. How cruel it was, thought Blart in the final moments of his ascent, for fate to dangle survival so temptingly before his eyes before whipping it away again. Faster and faster and higher and higher he rose. But any second now there would be that terrible fall over the other side. Blart closed his eyes …

And then suddenly and painfully slammed to a halt.

Tentatively he opened his eyes and looked about him. There wasn't much to see except rock. Blart found himself wedged in a narrow gap between the edge of the protuberance and the cliff face. Beo's great bulk could pull him no further. He was alive.

Alive but uncomfortable. The rope was stretched taut about him and the rocky fissure had him gripped firmly around the waist. Blart couldn't move. All he could do was hang tight and wait for Beo to climb back up the other side.

So he waited.

And waited.

The rope remained taut.

'Beo!' shouted Blart.

'*Beo! Beo! Beo! Beo! Beo! Beo!*' repeated the rocky walls.

Blart waited for a long time. Beo hadn't answered any of his calls. And from the continued tautness of the rope, he hadn't begun to climb back up either. Blart cursed the rocky protuberance, forgetting it had so recently saved his life, for now it blocked his view and prevented him looking down to where Beo hung. And attached as he was to Beo's great bulk, if he tried to manoeuvre himself out of the crack, he would be yanked straight up and over the other side of the rock. He had no choice but to wait. The last rays of daylight vanished. The moon rose, fuller again than the night before, and Blart was left to dwell on the hopelessness of his situation. Whatever happened regarding the rescue of Princess Lois, Blart's days were numbered. He suddenly felt very alone. He shouted Beo's name again and again but there was no reply.

Exhausted, Blart dozed through the night. Awful visions plagued his sleep – dreams in which the knight did not fly through the air unhurt as Blart had done but was smashed repeatedly against the rock face as he fell, and in which Beo's body now hung waiting for scavenging creatures to come and consume it. And then he had another dream where he wandered through a land of deserted sties as though some foul plague had come and taken all the pigs away.

He awoke with a jolt to a dirty grey dawn. A whole night had passed and the knight had neither shouted nor tugged on the rope. He must be dead. Truly this quest was exacting a high price. Beo the Knight, who with his great strength had stood side by side with Blart (when he wasn't threatening to cleave him in two), was no more. Even Blart, who was not very sensitive, spent a moment regretting the knight's loss.

I wish he could have died in battle, thought Blart.

There are those who might think that Blart should wish his

comrade hadn't died at all. But Blart's thoughts are his own and nobody can change them. And as hard as he was trying to think about his lost comrade, he had already become distracted by the rumblings in his stomach. He reached into his jerkin and pulled out a piece of Uther's lard and began to gnaw on it.

What was he to do now?

If he was ever going to be able to escape this barren rock, there was only one thing he could do.

Cut the rope.

Blart pulled out his dagger and held it over the cord that bound him to his fallen comrade. And then he paused. What if Beo was still alive?

Don't be stupid, Blart told himself. *He must be dead. You were sure of it a minute ago.* But somehow Blart wasn't quite so certain when he knew that with a few cuts he would sever the rope and send the knight's body plunging down into the abyss.

Get on with it, Blart told himself.

But he still couldn't bring himself to do it. Perhaps not being able to see the rope would make it easier. He closed his eyes. Gripping the knife tightly, he made a firm incision.

'Ow!'

The incision was in his finger. His blood dripped on to the rock. Wielding the dagger with his eyes shut was obviously not such a good idea. He was going to have to do it with his eyes wide open. He looked at the rope. If he did not cut it, he too was doomed. Better one questor lost than two. He had to do it. Hand shaking, he began to saw at the rope.

'What do you think you're doing?'

Blart looked up.

Beo the Knight's head poked over the rocky protuberance. While Blart had been agonising he had not noticed the changing tension on the rope as Beo climbed up the rock face.

'Beo!'

Blart laughed with relief. For once, he was happy to see Beo. However, from the angry look on the knight's face, the feeling was far from mutual.

'Were you cutting the rope?'

'Er …' Blart didn't think there was a good answer to this question. He had a knife in his hand and a rope which was half severed.

'You foul traitor,' growled Beo. 'Your comrade is knocked unconscious by a terrible fall and all you can think of is to cut him off and let him plunge to his death.'

'Er …' Blart was sure he'd been about to do the right thing. He was sure he could convince anyone of that. Except perhaps the person who he would have killed.

'It wasn't like that,' said Blart. 'You see –'

'I see!' shouted Beowulf in a rage. 'I see very clearly. Betraying your comrade to guarantee your own safety. I wonder how you'd like to be thrown to your death.'

One mighty fist grabbed Blart by the neck and plucked him out of the gap in which he'd been wedged. It held Blart over the precipice. Blart had only a moment to convince Beo that he hadn't been going to cut the rope. Unfortunately all the evidence pointed the other way. Then Blart spotted something that gave him an idea.

'I wasn't going to cut the rope,' he cried.

'Why did I see you with a knife in your hand, then?' demanded the knight.

The world turned in dizzying circles below.

'I was cutting some lard. But it slipped out of my hand. And the rope was under it. I cut it by mistake.'

'Liar!'

'It's the truth. I cut my finger at the same time. Look!' Blart waved his finger in the Beo's face. 'Why would I cut myself if I'd wanted to cut the rope? That proves it was an accident.'

Beo's grip relaxed. Blart was dragged back from the edge.

'Perhaps I was too hasty,' he said ruefully. 'But I am a fighting man who acts on what he sees. And you shouldn't have been chopping up your breakfast so near to the rope.'

Blart was so relieved that Beo had believed his lie that he readily agreed that he shouldn't.

'Now,' said Beo. 'We have wasted too much time. The others will be worried about us. We must make for the top of the cliff straight away.'

Blart stood up to continue the climb. The sooner he was off this rock face the better.

Beo held out his hand. 'Perhaps I'll take your dagger just until we reach the top,' he said. 'In case you get peckish again.'

Sucking on his bleeding finger, Blart handed his dagger over.

Chapter 38

'We've made it,' cried Beo as he hauled himself over the edge of the cliff and lay gasping on the ground.

Moments later Blart joined him. He didn't know what he'd been expecting but, whatever it was, he was disappointed. A featureless plateau stretched out in front of them. Well, featureless except for three giant boulders and a tree.

'Hmm,' said Beo, handing Blart back his knife. 'I know not where we are, and in this barren land there is nothing to give us a clue.'

'Apples!' Blart's sharp eyes had spied that the tree bore fruit. After a breakfast of lard, a ripe apple was not something he was going to resist.

'This is not the time to be giving in to your selfish urges,' cautioned Beo.

But Blart was already running towards the apple tree.

'Oi!' said Beo. 'Are you listening?'

Blart wasn't. He was already in the lower branches of the tree. Beo heard his own empty stomach rumbling.

'Well,' he said. 'If you must be getting yourself up there, then the least you can do is throw down a few juicy ones for me.'

Blart picked a couple of apples and dropped them into Beo's waiting hands. But the riper fruit seemed higher. Blart climbed towards it. Below, Beo leant against the trunk to enjoy his own snack.

'Mmmm.' Blart bit into the juiciest apple he had ever tasted. He looked across the plateau as he munched. And then nearly choked as he realised that it was not as barren or as empty as it had appeared a moment ago.

Stomping across it were twenty creatures. They were shorter than Blart but wider. And they were purple. At least their faces, arms and legs were purple. The rest of their bodies were hidden in studded brown armour. Some of them carried axes while others carried giant branches. They might have been shorter than Blart but they were undoubtedly much stronger.

'Beo!' hissed Blart.

'I'm enjoying my apple,' said the knight. 'I would prefer it were it inside a pie but I will not complain.'

'There's somebody coming,' said Blart.

'Excellent,' said Beo. 'Perhaps they will be able to help us.'

'They don't look like that kind of somebody,' said Blart.

Beo sighed. 'I can't even eat an apple in peace.' But fortunately the knight decided to look for himself.

The remainder of his apple dropped uneaten from his hand. He uttered one word.

'Trolls!'

'Trolls?' said Blart.

'Indeed,' said Beowulf. 'I killed one once.'

One of the advantages of having Beo on a quest was that he had usually killed at least one of any creature they encountered and so was often able to identify it.

'Will they help us?' asked Blart.

But Beo was already climbing into the lower branches of the tree.

'I think it is best if we keep ourselves hidden,' he said. 'Trolls are a simple race who are known for one thing.'

'What's that?'

'Killing anything that isn't a troll the moment they meet it.'

'Oh,' said Blart.

Beo pulled himself further up into the tree. His great bulk did not allow him to climb as far up as Blart but he was able to get high enough to ensure he was invisible to passing trolls.

Unfortunately, these trolls were definitely not passing. Instead, they stomped up to the three giant stones and stopped.

Peering through the leaves, Blart studied them. They were very ugly – their faces a mass of purple folds as though someone had just sat on them. But their arms were twice as thick as Beo's. These were creatures you didn't want to fight. Blart noticed one troll looking puzzled. It sniffed the air and then the ground.

'Can they smell us?' Blart whispered.

Beo didn't know. Another troll bent down and sniffed. It too seemed to smell something. However, the rest were looking over the precipice. One of them wore a gold helmet and appeared to be the leader. He grunted to the trolls who were snuffling about under the tree and obediently they stomped over to join him.

The chief troll pointed down into the gorge.

'Boat!'

Muttering among themselves, they split into three groups, one behind each of the giant boulders on the edge of the precipice. With another grunt each group chose a huge branch and wedged it under their boulder.

Horrified, Beo realised what was going to happen.

'They're going to force the boulders over the edge to destroy the *Golden Pig*,' he whispered to Blart.

'Why?'

'Don't you listen to anything I say? Trolls don't need a reason to kill things. They just do. Our comrades are doomed – they'll have no time to escape . . .' The knight tailed off.

Tigrana!

Beo remembered her face shining in the heat of battle. Maybe she wasn't a proper damsel, maybe she didn't know about needlework, but she was a maiden. And Beo the

Knight wasn't going to let any maiden be crushed as long as there was strength in his arm. He jumped from the tree, pulled his sword from his scabbard and charged.

The trolls all had their backs to him. None of them saw or heard him coming, especially not the one at the back whose head was cleaved from his body with one mighty swing. The others grunted in surprise and dropped their levers. Before any of them could reach for an axe, two more were dead – both stabbed expertly through the heart.

'Fight,' bellowed the troll leader.

The trolls advanced. Beo slashed. Another troll fell. Then another. Blart watched, breathless, from his vantage point, wondering if he should jump down and help. A fearsome blow from an axe, which Beo luckily managed to avoid, made up Blart's mind for him. If Beo wanted to throw his life away that was up to him, but anybody could see that even he was no match for the trolls now they were organised. They had formed a tight line which marched forward, hacking with their terrible axes. Beo could not defeat such overwhelming odds, however bravely he fought.

'Yield!' roared the head troll.

'Never,' said Beo.

'Die!' said the head troll.

Trolls were creatures of few words but, unfortunately for Beo, many axes. All of which were aimed at him. He was driven back. His sword was no longer used to attack but instead flashed high and low, desperately parrying. Further and further back he went until he backed into the tree and could go no further. Blart stretched to get a better view. Was the knight really going to die?

'Aaaarrgghh!'

A desperate last slash despatched one more troll, but it was only delaying the inevitable. A branch blocked Blart's view. He leant further and craned his neck. Beo knew his last moments had come.

'I die in the cause of chivalry,' he cried. 'To protect the lady Tigrana.'

What a noble picture! Beo faced death in the most honourable and dignified way possible. If he could have chosen a way of dying, this would have been it. So it was a shame Blart spoilt it by leaning over too far, falling out of the tree and landing with a crash on top of the knight, knocking him unconscious.

Not that spoiling Beo's noble death was uppermost in Blart's mind. He was more concerned that he was now lying at the mercy of fourteen armed trolls. Unlike Beo, Blart wasn't going to die a noble death with a defiant cry and a sword in his hand. He was going to die a pig boy's death with his eyes tight shut so that he didn't see the sweep of the axe that was destined to kill him.

Blart waited.

Nothing happened.

Blart waited some more.

Still nothing happened.

This was cruel torture. At least the trolls could kill him quickly.

Blart risked opening one eye.

The trolls were on their knees, faces buried in the ground in front of him. They were muttering. No, not exactly muttering. They were chanting.

Blart opened his other eye.

The head troll raised his head.

'We worship you, O God!'

'God?' said Blart. 'I'm Blart.'

'Praise to Blart the God,' chanted the trolls.

Chapter 39

The arrival of God was obviously a big day for the trolls. Velt, the chief troll, blew on a horn fashioned from a mammoth tusk, as Blart was carried aloft in a triumphant procession to the Valley of the Trolls.

Trolls are cave dwellers and, on hearing the horn, they rushed out of their homes built into the rocky sides of the valley. The horn had never been blown before, but all the trolls knew what it meant. The God of the Trolls had returned to his people. He had fulfilled the prophecy and fallen from the Great Tree of Trolledge and Destroyed an Enemy of the Trolls.

The trolls knew this but, unfortunately for Blart, he didn't, and none of the trolls had explained it to him because they thought, being God, he knew already. Instead, they had worshipped him for a bit longer, then picked him up (with eyes downcast at all times) and brought him back to the valley, so that the others could do some worshipping too. And worship they did. Immediately they caught sight of Blart they threw themselves face forward on to the ground. Many of the trolls were so enthusiastic in their desire to abase themselves that they cut their faces on the hard rock.

Blart wasn't sure what to do. He'd never been a god before and it was making him self-conscious. Should he wave? Should he smile? Or should he look angry?

But perhaps it didn't matter. After all, as soon as he appeared, the trolls looked at the ground, so he could probably pull faces at them and it wouldn't matter. Blart resisted the temptation. Being a god was all that was keeping him alive. And something told him gods didn't pull faces.

'What happened?' shouted a familiar voice from behind him. 'One minute I was fighting then it all went dark. Ow!'

Beo was still alive. For some mysterious reason the trolls had not killed him. Instead, they had tied him up and brought him along too. But unlike Blart, he had been dragged rather than carried, and so he was now bloody and bad-tempered.

'Where am I?' shouted the knight. 'Untie me! Let me fight like a man.'

The procession reached the end of the little valley. The trolls who had been carrying Blart laid him carefully down and then joined the other trolls in falling to the ground to worship him. Only Velt, the chief troll, remained standing, but even he had his head bowed reverentially.

'Please. May I speak to Blart the God of the Trolls?'

'Yes,' said Blart.

'All trolls worship Blart,' said Velt. 'Finest cave for Blart to sleep in. Tonight trolls have great feast in honour of Blart. Sacrifice Enemy of Trolls captured by Blart the God. Listen to commandments of Blart. Until then, free time. Blart rest in his cave or walk in land of trolls. Blart need anything, blow on horn. Trolls come.'

And Velt offered Blart the ceremonial horn.

'Er … thank you,' said Blart, taking the horn. 'Now you mention it, I am quite tired. Might nip into the cave for a lie down.'

And so Blart the God went into his cave for a lie down. Except he didn't lie down straight away. Instead, he stared at the piles of jewels that were strewn about the cave and the rich rugs that were ready for him to lie on. The trolls had obviously been waiting a long time for the coming of their god.

Blart sat down on one of the rugs and wondered what he should do. Things really were very serious: Tigrana, Olaf and Uther trapped on the *Golden Pig*, Beo in the hands of the trolls and due to be sacrificed, the quest hopelessly behind schedule. He was the leader. It was his responsibility to come up with a plan. It was his responsibility to … Impressed with the seriousness with which he was taking things, Blart promptly fell asleep.

And dreamt of pigs.

Lots of pigs happily eating apples and swill and snuffling in their sty. After a while, one pig noticed Blart watching and trotted over to greet him. Smiling, Blart patted the pig. And then … ugh! Where Blart had patted the pig there was a hole. The pig was punctured.

'Pssssstttt.'

The air inside the pig was rushing out.

'Pssstttt.'

Now the pig was deflating, getting smaller and smaller and …

Blart woke up.

'Pssstttt.'

He was in the troll's cave.

'Psssttt.'

Crouching at the back of the cave was Tigrana.

'I thought you were a pig full of air,' said Blart.

Tigrana looked confused. Nobody had ever thought she was that before.

'What are you doing here?' Blart wanted to know.

'I couldn't bear waiting around,' said Tigrana. 'So I climbed up the rock face as soon as it was daylight. I arrived just as you were being taken by the trolls. I followed at a safe distance and, when nobody was looking, I slipped into the cave.'

'They don't guard their gods very well,' said Blart.

'What?'

'Oh,' said Blart. 'Didn't I tell you? I'm a god.'

Tigrana's mouth opened but no words came out.

'Blart the God of the Trolls,' said Blart. 'They've been worshipping me.'

'Worshipping you?'

Blart nodded.

'It sounds more fun than it is. Once you've seen one troll

with his face in the mud, you've seen them all.'

'I wondered why they were doing that,' said Tigrana. 'But why don't they think Beo's a god?'

Blart explained what had happened earlier – somehow managing to give Tigrana the impression that he had nobly followed Beo to fight the trolls, rather than accidently fallen out of the tree. He finished his story with a shrug.

'I guess some of us have got it and some of us haven't.'

'They've pegged him out on the ground,' said Tigrana. 'I have to rescue him.'

'But Beo told me that trolls are very violent. They'll kill any non-troll they see.'

'I'll wait until nightfall,' said Tigrana.

'I think that might be too late,' said Blart. 'I think the trolls are going to sacrifice him to me.'

Tigrana was horrified.

'Sacrifice him?'

Blart nodded.

'I don't think they'd do it for just any god,' he explained. 'I guess I'm special.'

Tigrana ignored him.

'I'll think of something,' she said. 'You go out to see Beo and reassure him that he's going to be rescued.'

'But what if he isn't?' said Blart. 'Then we'll have got his hopes up for nothing.'

'He will be rescued,' insisted Tigrana. 'He fought the trolls to save us. I will not let him down.'

Blart sighed.

'You've saved my life lots of times,' he said, 'and I don't go on and on about it. I just say thank you and forget about it.'

'I don't remember you saying thank you.'

'Well, I don't actually say it,' admitted Blart.

'But you think it?' Tigrana suggested.

'I'm a god,' said Blart. 'I have more important things to think about.'

'If you're a god,' said Tigrana tetchily, 'then maybe you can tell us how we can get the rock walls to go back and release the *Golden Pig*, so that we can sail away once we've rescued Beo.'

'I've only been a god for a day,' said Blart. 'Don't expect miracles.'

And deciding that this was a good thing to say, Blart stepped out of his cave, leaving Tigrana to think of a way to rescue Beo.

'We worship you, O Blart, we worship you,' chanted the trolls outside, throwing themselves to the ground again as soon as they saw him.

'Nice day,' replied Blart, feeling that he should say something.

It was not difficult to spot Beo. The knight was staked out with his arms and legs spread as wide as possible. Blart walked towards him but was intercepted by Velt.

'Does God want anything?' he asked respectfully.

'I was going to see the Enemy of the Trolls,' said Blart.

'But God see him later when he is sacrificed,' said Velt.

'Better to see Enemy of Trolls dead than alive.'

'Yes,' agreed Blart. 'But I'd like to kick him a few times first.'

'Ah.' Velt nodded approvingly and backed away.

'Wait,' said Blart.

Obediently Velt stopped.

'You know there is a boat stuck in the Straits of No Return?'

'Yes, God. We go to smash it today but we find you instead and forget. Tomorrow, after feast, we go and smash it good. Then we trap another ship and smash it good. Then another.'

The repetitive cycle of mindless violence did not seem at all tedious to the troll.

'Excellent,' said Blart. 'But you'll have to make the rock walls go back to trap another boat.'

Velt nodded.

'And,' said Blart casually, 'how will you do that?'

Velt smiled.

'Blart God know already,' he said. 'Blart God know everything.'

'I do?' said Blart.

Velt nodded again.

Blart had run up against one of the thorniest problems of being a god. Your worshippers think you know every-thing. How was he going to find out the secret of how to release the walls of the Straits of No Return if Velt thought he knew already? Suddenly Blart had an idea.

'There is more than one way to open the straits,' he said. 'I wondered which one you were using.'

Velt looked surprised.

'More than one way? Trolls know only one way. We pull the tree.'

'The tree?'

'Blart God know. The tree he fall out of. Great Tree of Trolledge. Twenty trolls pull tree, big noise in ground, rocks go back.'

So that was why they thought he was a god. He'd fallen out of their holy tree. And the trolls thought the tree was holy because it was some kind of lever that could open and close the rock walls of the Straits of No Return. Blart was amazed. Velt was puzzled.

'But did not Blart God know that already?'

'Of course I did,' said Blart quickly. 'Now I must go and punish the Enemy of the Trolls. As I am God of the Trolls, I punish all their enemies.'

Blart walked quickly over towards Beo. Velt watched him thoughtfully – his head not bowed quite as low as before.

'What's happening?' Beo demanded angrily as Blart approached. 'One moment I'm fighting the trolls and then it all went dark and when I came round I was tied up.'

Blart kicked Beo.

'Ow!'

Blart kicked him again.

'What do you think you're doing?' growled the knight. 'If I

had a sword in my hand, then you'd not be as quick to kick me.'

Blart kicked again.

'I've got to,' he explained. 'You're an Enemy of the Trolls and I'm God of the Trolls. I can't let them think that we know each other.'

'What do you mean you're God?'

'I just am,' said Blart. 'And you're going to be sacrificed to me.'

'Sacrificed?'

Blart kicked him again.

'Couldn't you just pretend to kick me?'

Blart shook his head.

'The trolls have to think I'm kicking you for real.'

'You are kicking me for real.'

'It's the easiest way to convince them.'

'What do you mean I'm going to be sacrificed?' said Beo suspiciously. 'That had better not have been your idea.'

'That's what the trolls want,' insisted Blart. 'But don't worry. Tigrana said we're going to rescue you.'

'Tigrana?' Beo was surprised. 'She's on the *Golden Pig*.'

'Not any more. She said to tell you we're going to rescue you.'

Most people would be pleased to hear that they're going to be rescued rather than sacrificed to a god who is in fact a pig boy. But not Beo. He was angry.

'Now listen, Blart,' he said. 'You are not to let Tigrana rescue me. She is a damsel and I cannot have damsels risking their lives to save me. I would rather die than risk the hairs on an innocent maiden's head.'

'All right,' said Blart. 'But only if you help me.'

'How can I help you?' said Beo. 'I'm staked to the ground waiting to be sacrificed.'

'I need some help with my commandments,' said Blart.

'What?'

'The trolls are expecting some commandments and I can only think of two.'

'What are they?'

'They're good ones,' said Blart proudly. 'The first commandment is: Don't send Blart on More Quests. And the second commandment is: Be Nice to Pigs.'

'That's it?'

'That's all I can think of,' said Blart, 'but I've got a feeling they want more.'

'My commandment is: Get Out of My Sight and Make Sure Tigrana Doesn't Save Me,' said Beo, and he turned his head angrily away.

Blart kicked him twice more just to show he was an enemy and then walked back to his cave, being worshipped all the way by various prone trolls.

Back in the cave he found Tigrana pacing.

'Did you tell him?' she said.

Blart nodded.

'He said you can't rescue him,' said Blart.

'Why not?'

'Because you're a damsel.'

Tigrana paced harder.

'I'll rescue him if I want to,' she said. 'Just because he's got stupid old-fashioned ideas about damsels won't stop me.'

'He won't be very happy,' said Blart.

'It's even worse now he's told me not to,' said Tigrana. 'If I don't rescue him, he'll think I've obeyed him. And I'm not having that. But I can't think of a plan. Even if I managed to release him, the trolls are such an aggressive race that they'd just hack us to pieces straight away.'

'As you can't think of a plan,' said Blart, forgetting to sympathise, 'can you help with my commandments. I've only got –'

'Commandments?' snapped Tigrana. 'A fellow questor's life is in danger and …'

She stopped.

'You haven't finished,' said Blart helpfully.

'It might work,' Tigrana muttered quietly. 'It just might work.'

'What might work?' asked Blart.

'Of course it would mean that you saved him instead of me, but I can tell him it was my plan.'

'What do you mean I might save him?' said Blart. 'I've got commandments to think of.'

'Exactly,' said Tigrana. '*Exactly*.'

And she gave Blart a look that he didn't like one bit.

Chapter 40

'My fellow trolls,' shouted Velt. 'Today is great day!'
Every troll in the valley grunted its appreciation.
They were all assembled outside Blart's cave. A huge fire had
been built and lit. Beo had been trussed up and laid in front
of the entrance to the cave in preparation for his sacrifice.
He didn't look happy.

'Trolls wait long time. Today Blart the God has come.'

More happy grunts from the trolls.

'Soon there will be feast and sacrifice of troll enemy. But
first Blart God will give commandments. Praise Blart the God!'

Blart emerged from his cave. The trolls threw themselves
to the ground once more.

'We worship you, Blart the God. We worship you.'

Blart gulped as he looked at the large crowd of face-
down trolls. He had a very bad feeling about what he was
supposed to do next.

'Get on with it,' hissed Tigrana, concealed just inside
the cave.

'Trolls,' said Blart firmly.

'Yes, O Blart,' said the trolls.

'I have some commandments!'

The trolls listened.

'You must obey all these commandments, trolls.'

The trolls murmured in agreement.

'The first commandment: Do Not Send Blart on Any More Quests.'

The trolls grunted. They could do that.

'The second commandment: Be Nice to Pigs.'

This was a bit more difficult. Pigs were not trolls and so were usually attacked with axes like everything else. But it was only pigs, the trolls reasoned. If Blart the God said they had to be nice to them then they supposed they could be.

'The third commandment …' Blart gulped as he looked down at the crowd of ferocious trolls.

'Get on with it,' hissed Tigrana.

'Forgive Your Enemies!' said Blart.

The trolls were silent. And as all students of troll-lore know, a silent troll is an angry troll. But Blart was God. What were the trolls to do when God gave them such a strange commandment? Fortunately trolls were a primitive race. So they didn't do anything.

'Hurry!' hissed Tigrana.

'Look up and let me show you,' said Blart.

The trolls raised their ugly upset faces.

'Here is an enemy.' Blart indicated Beo trussed up in

front of him.

'Before I came you would kill him. Now, with new commandments, you will forgive him.'

Blart picked up the nearest axe and cut Beo's ties.

'Stand up!' he ordered.

Beo stood up, looking very confused.

'I forgive you, O Enemy of the Trolls,' said Blart. 'You are our enemy and you can go free.'

Beo stood there dumbfounded.

The trolls were still silent. This whole forgiveness idea wasn't convincing them.

'O Blart God,' said Velt. 'Who is that in your cave?'

Tigrana in her eagerness to see what was happening had stepped out of the shadows and been spotted.

'Who?' said Blart.

'In your cave, O Great One,' said Velt.

Blart didn't know what to say. Straight away he felt doubt spreading through the watching trolls. The one thing that a god was supposed to know was the answer to everything.

Blart couldn't think of a good lie, and he had to say something quickly. So he told the truth.

'That's Tigrana,' he said. 'Come here, Tigrana.'

Tigrana emerged from the cave.

The trolls were still silent. First there was the forgiveness and now there was a non-troll in Blart the God's cave. The trolls' faith was being sorely tested.

'Who is Tigrana?' asked Velt.

Desperately, Blart cast about for an explanation. As each second passed the silence grew more and more intense. Any moment now the trolls were going to stop believing in him. And that would be fatal.

'She's a spare,' said Blart suddenly.

'A spare, O God?'

'Yes. She's a spare enemy. I take her with me just in case there isn't another enemy around. So I've always got an enemy to forgive.'

'Oh,' said Velt suspiciously.

'That's all,' said Blart, adding quickly, 'so I and your enemies will be leaving you now. But I'll come back one day to see if you're obeying the commandments. And if you're not, I'll be very angry, so do as I say.'

Without waiting for a response, Blart the God hurriedly led his enemies from the mouth of the cave. The trolls parted like a sea to let them through. But they were silent and mistrustful. *Don't trip up*, Blart told himself as he walked.

Miraculously he didn't. Blart, Tigrana and Beowulf made it through the crowd of trolls and out of the Valley of the Trolls. Then behind them they heard a terrible roar.

The trolls had decided to become atheists.

The questors ran like they had never run before, except for all the other times on quests when they'd been running for their lives – which is quite a lot when you think back. Behind them came the thundering feet of the entire troll

271

nation, determined to expose the false god's mortality by tearing him limb from limb. Luckily for the questors, trolls are short, squat and muscle-bound, which is exactly the opposite shape to that required for long-distance running. Unluckily for the questors, trolls have an almost endless supply of stamina. The questors were the hare and the trolls were the tortoise, and we all know how that story turned out.

'This way,' said Tigrana, who'd memorised the route back to the straits.

Blart and Beo followed her. Across the plateau they ran. Behind them a huge cloud of dust rose. The trolls were coming. It was a long way to the cliff top. At first they managed to widen the gap between them and their pursuers, but eventually their legs ached and their pace slackened. The trolls began to close in on them.

'Leave me and go on,' gasped Beo. 'I will hold them up for as long as I can. You two can get away.'

'If that's what you want,' said Blart.

'Never,' said Tigrana. 'If you stop, I stop, and then you will have my death on your conscience, knight.'

And so Beo was forced to keep running. The last thing on the trolls' minds was forgiveness. They knew they were catching up and they gripped their axes tighter.

'Are we nearly there yet?' panted Blart.

They were. In the distance they saw the Tree of Trolledge and found one last surge of speed to get them there.

'What … do … we … do … now?' said Beo between huge gulps of air.

Blart told him about the tree. If they could push it over, the hidden forces would pull back the rock face and release the *Golden Pig*.

'But twenty trolls have great strength,' said Beo. 'Three of us cannot do it.' Closer and closer came the trolls, their purple faces burning with hatred and anger.

'I brought the Longest Rope in the World and hid it behind the tree,' said Tigrana. 'I borrowed it from Olaf. I've got an idea. We tie one end of the rope to the tree and then we tie one end to us. And then we jump over the cliff.'

Blart and Beo stared at her in disbelief.

Briefly.

After all, the trolls were still coming.

'You're mad,' said Blart. 'If we jump over that cliff, we'll be killed.'

'Have you got any better ideas?'

The murderous grunts of the trolls were growing louder.

'I haven't got time to tie my best knot,' said Tigrana. 'We'll have to make do with a Half Hitch Double Granny Bundle.'

'You mean I'm not even having a good knot round the tree when I jump to my death?' said Blart.

'Don't criticise her!' said Beo. 'Or I'll throw you over with no knot at all.'

The trolls were almost upon them. Tigrana's hands

whirled around the Tree of Trolledge as she tied the knot as fast as she could. Then, without pause, she rushed over to Beo and Blart standing by the edge of the cliff and threw the rope round them.

The trolls had their axes raised. They rushed for the questors.

'Done!' shouted Tigrana.

And they jumped.

The Longest Rope in the World unwound. And unwound and unwound. Down dropped the questors, past the rocky protuberance. Would the rope be long enough? Coil after coil snaked above them. They could see the straits and the *Golden Pig* coming closer and closer and … splash! The questors crashed into the water. *Snap!* The Longest Rope in the World snapped taut. High above them the Tree of Trolledge creaked and bent. The bowels of the earth rumbled and the rock face slowly parted. The *Golden Pig* was free.

Blart, Tigrana and Beo struggled and spluttered to the surface.

'I can't swim,' Blart reminded everyone.

'Greetings!' cried Olaf from the deck of the *Golden Pig*.

'Throw us a line and pull us in,' shouted Tigrana. 'We haven't got much time.'

And she was right. Far above the trolls had not given up. Under the orders of Velt they split into two groups. One group was ordered to pull the Tree of Trolledge back up to recapture the *Golden Pig*, the other to use the stout branches to lever the three huge boulders over the cliff edge.

Below, Tigrana, Blart and Beo clambered on board.

'Raise as much sail as you can,' shouted Tigrana. 'We must get moving.'

All the questors dashed to the rigging and desperately tried to raise some sails. The *Golden Pig* was not the majestic flagship that had set out from Illyria. She was battered and patched and warped. But she could still hold sail. The wind gusted through the straits. She was moving.

High above, the trolls levered the three great boulders over the edge. But the *Golden Pig* had sailed just far enough and they plunged into the straits behind her with a tremendous splash that created a great wave.

'The rock face is closing again,' shouted Olaf.

But the wave propelled the *Golden Pig* faster than any boat had ever travelled before. With the questors clinging as tightly as they could to mast, rail or barrel, the ship sped between the closing rock walls and out into the open ocean just as they smashed shut behind it.

'That was close,' said Blart.

'Look! The Great Illyrian Armada!' cried Tigrana. 'Land Ho!'

Uther's chart had proved correct. The Straits of No Return had brought them to their destination. And now, before them was a sight to chase away the recent close encounter with death. The port of Yort lay in the hands of the Illyrian fleet. No Styxian ship was to be seen. After so long sailing alone, each questor felt their heart swell with optimism. Now they had an army. Now they had a chance of success. But then Blart looked above the port to the grim, walled city of Yort itself. Something told him that things would not be so easy.

Chapter 41

The *Golden Pig* limped into the Styxian port, its mast damaged, its sails hanging limply, shipping water from the gash in its hull. Above the port, built high on a hill, towered the heavily fortified city of Yort, capital of Styxia and seat of power of Gregor the Grizzled. The city walls, thick and tall, were slashed with arrow slits and dominated by high turrets manned by well-armed sentries. The only way in was through the Great North Gate, which was itself a well-armed mini-fortress, bristling with armoured guards. It looked impregnable. Pegged out in front of the city was a village of improvised tents, looking very pregnable indeed.

'Do you think the quest's over?' said Blart.

'What do you mean over?' said Beo. 'If I have missed all the fighting and killing, then I will be sorely disappointed.'

'But if the Great Illyrian Armada has landed,' said Blart, 'then they must have defeated the Styxian fleet and won the war and rescued the Princess.'

'That would be most unfortunate for a merchant like

myself,' observed Uther. 'Quests are good for business. Wars are even better.'

Beo glared at Uther.

'I have not forgotten your treachery,' he said. 'The moment I find out this quest is over, there will be a reckoning twixt you and I, merchant.'

While the others had been musing on the state of the quest, Tigrana had been securing the *Golden Pig* in its moorings.

Waiting to meet them at the dock was a soldier. Just a single soldier. Blart felt it should have been more. After all, he was the commander of the armada.

He led his fellow questors ashore.

'Prince Blart, I presume?' said the soldier. 'My name is Captain Torres. I have been detailed to take you to Yspahan, Duke of Eixample, Temporary Commander of the Great Illyrian Armada. Follow me, please.'

Captain Torres led them through the improvised tented village. If the questors had thought they were bedraggled and battered, then the sight of the Illyrian troops made them feel clean and well dressed. The tents were filthy and tattered. The soldiers inside them, unshaven and dirty, looked morosely at the ground. In some tents injured men cried from untreated wounds, while in others they mumbled deliriously from fever. How far removed was this scene from the jaunty and hopeful armada that had set sail from Illyria.

Most of the questors were shocked and dismayed at what

they saw. But not Uther.

'This,' he explained to Olaf quietly, 'is the ideal situation for a merchant. Soldiers who appear to be on the verge of defeat lose all sense of the value of money. You can charge them anything.'

Despite his extensive business training, Olaf wasn't sure this was a good thing.

'See your point,' he said. 'But these men are on our side. Isn't it wrong to make money out of them?'

'None of this sentimentality,' said Uther. 'Money has no side but its own.'

Further ahead, Blart, Beo and Tigrana were still looking with horror at the state of the troops. Finally they reached the one tent that did not appear to be on the verge of collapse.

Captain Torres led them in.

'Prince Blart and retinue to see Duke Yspahan.'

Unlike everywhere else, this tent was clean and in perfect order. A tall thin man in an extravagant uniform adorned with medals was bending over a model. He looked up as they arrived.

'Prince Blart,' he held out his hand. 'Where have you been, man?'

'We were caught in a storm, then attacked by pirates, then put in prison …'

Duke Yspahan waved Blart's words away.

'No excuses, man. No excuses. This is war, you know.

First rule of being a general – turn up on time. Men expect it. Second rule – try to look the part. Suppose you can't help being short, but you could try to look less like a pig boy.'

'But I …'

Duke Yspahan shook his head.

'No excuses, man. No excuses. One thing I hate is a man who makes excuses. Suppose you'll want an update on the campaign?'

Blart nodded. 'It doesn't look like it's going too well.'

'Not going too well!' said Duke Yspahan. 'It's going splendidly.'

'But the mud, the men, the –'

'Mere trivialities,' said Yspahan, shaking his head. 'My plan is working superbly.'

'What plan?'

'Take you through it from the beginning,' said Yspahan, indicating the model. Blart realised that it was a scale model of where they were – the city of Yort dominating the surrounding area.

'Now,' said Yspahan, indicating the port. 'We arrived here. Expected resistance from the Styxian Navy but no sign. Dashed strange. Landed and made camp. Waited for you. No sign. Needed a new commander. Don't want to blow my own trumpet but I'm the best man for the job.'

'Why?' asked Blart.

'Because of his experience in battle,' said Beo in frustration. 'Can you not see all the medals on his chest? Duke

Yspahan must have spent many years fighting wars.'

Duke Yspahan eyed Beo doubtfully.

'Don't know what you're talking about. These medals belonged to my grandfather. Never fought a battle in my life.'

'So why were you picked to command?' asked Tigrana.

'What's this?' Duke Yspahan spluttered. 'Questions from a girl? Very bad show.'

'So why were you picked to command?' Blart asked.

'Discovered I had most noble lineage. The other suitors made me commander straight away.'

'So instead of picking a new leader based on merit, they picked one based on birth.' Tigrana was horrified.

'Amazing,' said Duke Yspahan. 'Girl understood something first time it was explained to her.'

Tigrana bristled.

'Anyway,' said Duke Yspahan. 'Sent message to Gregor the Grizzled stating we're ready to fight and will commence battle at dawn sharp. Next morning comes, but no enemy. Gregor the Grizzled sends a message saying he's not going to fight. Says he's going to sit in his city and watch us starve — wait until we're nearly dead then come out and massacre us. Says it will be more "fun". Well, I looked about, noticed nothing but burnt land for miles around. No food to forage for, no wood for shelters. Urgent action was required.'

'What did you do?' asked Beo.

'Built a model.'

'A model?' repeated Beo dubiously. 'Battles are won with

swords and blood, not models.'

Duke Yspahan shook his head.

'Old-fashioned,' he said. 'The commander with a model's always one step ahead of the commander without one. See this? High-quality model. Immediately employed it in a fool-proof plan.'

'Did you use a battering ram to charge the great gate?' suggested Beo, who had laid siege to a number of cities in the past.

'That's just what they would have been expecting,' said Yspahan. 'An attack at their weakest point. Where's the element of surprise in that?'

'When you're laying siege to a city you don't normally have an element of surprise,' said Beo. 'Because they can see you.'

'Defeatist attitude,' huffed Yspahan. 'They expect an attack on the gate, so attack the walls instead.'

'The walls?' said Beo. 'But that's much more dangerous.'

'Now you're getting the idea, man,' said Yspahan. 'They wouldn't expect it.'

'If I was fighting someone, they wouldn't expect me to stab myself,' said Beo. 'But that doesn't make it a good idea.'

'What happened?' Tigrana wanted to know.

Yspahan patiently tapped his foot and showed no signs of having heard Tigrana.

'She asked you a question,' Beo pointed out.

'She is a girl,' said Yspahan. 'Might as well talk tactics with a monkey. Should be at home sewing.'

Beo opened his mouth to argue. And then closed it again. What Yspahan had said sounded uncomfortably like something he might have thought himself not very long ago.

'What happened?' repeated Blart.

'Ah,' said Yspahan. 'Excellent question. Attacked the walls on three sides simultaneously. Plan worked perfectly. The Styxians expected an attack on the gate and were taken completely by surprise. Army climbed walls, overpowered Styxians and were victorious.'

The questors were all confused.

'So why are you out here in tents,' Blart wanted to know, 'when you've defeated the Styxians?'

Now it was Yspahan's turn to look confused. Then suddenly there was a flash of understanding.

'Oh,' he said. 'See what you mean. Plan worked perfectly. On the model.'

'The model,' said Beo in frustration. 'But what happened in the real attack?'

'Hardly relevant,' said Yspahan. 'Slightly different result.'

'How different?' said Blart.

'Wasn't there myself,' said Yspahan. 'Had to guard the model. But it seems that it took some time for the soldiers to scale the walls – they were much faster on the model. The Styxians saw them and fired arrows at them and poured boiling oil on their heads. Most unfortunate.'

'And what happened then?' said Beo.

'Quite a lot of deaths,' acknowledged Yspahan. 'All the

suitors died apart from me. And most of the men. Still, what's war without death, I say.'

'And the Styxians? Any casualties?'

'Had a report that one of them burnt a thumb,' said Yspahan. 'So far unconfirmed.'

'You mean that most of the army is dead,' said Blart. 'And all we've done is burn the thumb of one Styxian?'

'*Possibly* burn,' corrected Yspahan.

'And what were you doing here?' demanded Beo. 'A commander should lead his men on the field of battle, not skulk about in tents, playing with models.'

'Commanders like me are too valuable to risk,' said Yspahan.

'Pah!' said Beo.

Duke Yspahan was not used to being spoken to like this and his temper snapped.

'I was going to leave you the model,' he said. 'But I see that it will not be appreciated. That concludes my report. I now return overall command of the army to Prince Blart of Illyria. Myself and my model are leaving.'

The duke picked up his model and stamped out of the tent, leaving Blart in command of a ragged and demoralised army.

None of the questors said anything for a moment. After all the risks they had taken to get there, they would have hoped to have found a better situation. Well, most of them would. Tigrana's eyes were shining at the prospect of a desperate quest.

'This is what I came for.'

Chapter 42

'They are hungry, thirsty, sick, angry, demoralised and on the point of rising up and cutting their commander's throat.'

Being the commander in question, Blart received Captain Torres' report about the state of his troops without enthusiasm.

'Do they have any fight left in them?' demanded Beo.

'Do they know I'm their commander?' asked Blart.

Torres explained that it was possible that the soldiers had one final battle in them.

'A battle we cannot fight,' lamented Beo. 'For those cowardly Styxians sit in their city and watch us starve. And yet we must. It is only two days until the next full moon.'

'If we are to fight again, it must be soon,' said Torres gravely. 'Disease is rife in the camp. There is little food. Those men who are not ill are restive. Mutiny and murder is talked of around campfires. I fear that military discipline may break down any day now with terrible consequences.'

Blart understood the consequences would be particularly terrifying for him.

'Perhaps you would take me to visit any ill soldiers,' said Uther. 'It is just possible I may be able to help them. I happen to have a few bottles of medicine with me.'

'You'd better not be trying to make a profit from the men,' threatened Beo.

'Perish the thought,' said Uther. 'But I will take Olaf with me to confirm I don't charge them a penny. My services will be entirely free.'

Uther and Olaf followed Captain Torres out of the commander's tent.

'This quest is rubbish,' said Blart. 'Everybody wants to kill me now. The Guild of Assassins. The Styxians. And now my own army. It's not fair.'

Blart seemed to have a point. But the knight was not convinced.

'This is the time to lead,' he said. 'Now we must reach for glory. There comes a time in the affairs —'

'I don't want to lead,' Blart interrupted. 'I want to resign.'

'You are the leader of an army. To talk of resignation is tantamount to speaking of surrender.'

'I would surrender,' said Blart. 'Except that I'd have to surrender to Gregor and he'd kill me. Just tell me who to resign to and I will.'

Angrily, Beo pointed out that the only person empowered to accept Blart's resignation was the King of Illyria and before it could be communicated to him, Blart's men would have mutinied and killed him. Blart was therefore stuck with being the leader.

Tigrana was pacing about the tent.

'If we could only open the gates to the city,' she said.

'Yort is the most well-defended city in the world,' said Beo. 'Even if we were to attack the gate –'

'Not open from the outside,' said Tigrana. 'From the inside.'

'How will we do that?' snapped Beo, almost losing his temper with a damsel for the first time in his life. 'Ask the Styxians to open the gate tomorrow and let us all in?'

'There must be a way,' said Tigrana. 'If we could get just a few of us inside, then, under cover of darkness, they could open the gate for the rest of the army.'

They lapsed into a moody silence as each of them tried to figure out how to do this.

Presently, Uther and Olaf returned. Olaf confirmed that the merchant had taken no money for the medicine he had given to the diseased soldiers. He didn't, however, mention the service charge that Uther had been most reluctantly forced to levy for bringing the medicine to the patient's bed-side. The merchant had explained to him that this was a separate matter of no interest to the others, and no one seemed to notice that Uther's pockets were bulging with money, so preoccupied were they with coming up with a plan.

Uther and Olaf joined in the pacing up and down the

tent. There was much beard stroking. For those who didn't have beards there was chin stroking. For those like Olaf who didn't have much of a chin there was nose scratching. Occasionally the silence would be broken when one questor or another cried, 'Aha!' or 'What if?' or 'How about?' The remaining questors would turn to look at whoever had exclaimed, only to see his or her brow furrow as a fundamental flaw in their plan suddenly became clear. Then they would shake their head and go back to thinking.

An hour passed. Blart had never thought for so long before. Fearing that if he overtaxed his brain he might break it, he decided to allow himself a little rest, and imagined a few pigs in a sty, snuffling about as pigs do. What he wouldn't give to look at a pig right now. If only someone would open the tent flap and say that a present had arrived for Blart, and then he would go outside and to his delight he would see a pig waiting for him. That would really –

'Aha! What if? How about?' said Blart suddenly.

The other questors turned to look at him.

'I've got it,' said Blart proudly. 'The perfect plan to get into the city.'

'Tell us, then,' said Beo.

Blart had hoped for a bit of praise first, but it appeared that the other questors wanted to hear the plan first.

'Yes,' said Tigrana. 'Let us hear it.'

'Right,' said Blart. 'First, we tell the Styxians that we are giving up and going home. Then we make the troops sail away. But we leave a present for the Styxians outside the city.'

Blart paused dramatically.

'Your plan is to give our enemies a present?' said Beo.

'A really big present,' said Blart.

'That makes it better, I suppose,' said Beo. 'As they're our mortal enemies, a token gift wouldn't be enough.'

'No,' said Blart. 'For inside the present we hide a small group of soldiers. The Styxians will come out and take the present into their city. While they're asleep, the soldiers will sneak out and open the gates to let the rest of the troops in.'

'Small point,' said Olaf. 'But didn't the other troops retreat earlier in the plan?'

Blart decided to ignore Olaf's small point. 'You haven't heard the best bit yet,' he said.

Beo, however, felt that Olaf's small point needed addressing, and came up with a solution.

'The Styxians will be fooled into thinking our men are cowardly deserters, but in the night the army can sail back, creep up to the gate and, when the soldiers on the other side open it, attack the sleeping city and free Princess Lois!'

There was silence while the other questors considered this plan.

'But why would we leave them a gift?' Tigrana broke in.

'As a trained negotiator in surrender,' Olaf piped up, 'I believe I can offer some advice on that. It would be a jolly nice gesture to leave some kind of gift to say thanks for having us and to signal our goodwill – a sort of peace offering, you might say.'

'Peace?' said Beo doubtfully.

'It didn't appeal to the trolls,' said Tigrana.

'Just one small thing, Blart,' said Uther. 'I was interested as to what this gift of yours might be that would so tempt the Styxians.'

Blart allowed himself a smile of satisfaction. This was his masterstroke. This was what he'd been waiting to tell them; what made the plan so certain to work.

'A wooden pig.'

Chapter 43

'A wooden pig!'

    'A wooden pig!'

'A wooden pig!'

'It's a great idea, isn't it?' said Blart, convinced that his fellow questors were repeating his words out of admiration. 'I just thought of the present I'd like most in the world.'

'It's terrible.'

'It's stupid.'

'It's idiotic.'

Blart was amazed. How could they not see that his plan was a work of genius?

'Should we reappoint Duke Yspahan?' suggested Olaf. 'At least he had a model.'

'Couldn't we at least make something more noble? Like a horse,' said Beo.

It wasn't fair. Blart had come up with a superb plan and all they could do was pick holes in it. So it wasn't flawless, but it did have a giant pig in it, and that, thought Blart, made it the best plan around.

'Has anybody got a better idea?' asked Blart.

The other questors were silenced. If the quest was not to fail, they had to act. And if none of them had a better plan, then they were going to have to act with the only one they'd got.

A wooden pig.

'It seems everyone is agreed,' said Uther. 'But I think I may be able to raise one last difficulty.'

'What is it?' asked Tigrana.

'Gregor has burnt everything for miles around,' said Uther. 'If we are going to build a giant wooden pig then we are going to need a considerable amount of wood.'

'I've thought of that too,' said Blart.

'Oh,' said Uther, shocked. 'And what is your solution?'

'We will chop up our ship,' said Blart. 'The *Golden Pig* will become the Great Wooden Pig.'

'Very clever,' said Olaf.

'Clever?' said Uther. 'Do I have to remind everybody that I am the rightful owner of the *Golden Pig*? I am not going to stand by and watch it chopped to pieces.'

'I'll chop you to pieces first,' offered Beo. 'Then you won't need to watch.'

'You can have the wooden pig when we're finished with it,' said Blart.

'A ship is more valuable than an over-sized figurine,' said Uther. 'I demand compensation.'

Uther stood firm. The other questors knew that he would negotiate until the bitter end and, if not satisfied, he might betray their plan in some way to secure his own fortune. Beo was forced to offer a deal.

'Your compensation will be your life,' said the knight. 'If you give us the ship and agree to serve in the quest, then I will agree to put our previous dispute to one side and when the quest is over I will not celebrate by killing you, even if there are no maidens around.'

Uther considered Beo's offer. The knight pulled his mighty sword from its scabbard while he did so. It concentrated the merchant's mind.

'You have a deal,' he said. 'The ship is yours.'

The *Golden Pig*, the great ship that had seen the questors through so many adventures, was to be chopped to pieces. It was almost as if they were losing a fellow comrade.

There was a lot to do and they worked all through the next day. The plan was passed down to the soldiers by their officers and Beo the Knight was suddenly to be found everywhere in the camp, chivvying the men into action. Some were reminded of their duties with a sharp word, while others were encouraged with a friendly cuff. But somehow the spirit of the knight spread through what remained of the army, and its men found new heart.

And so the *Golden Pig* was chopped to pieces and from its wreckage there grew a new pig. Tigrana watched sadly as the mast was pulled down, the great wheel she and Blart had fought with was torn out, and the creaking hull was ripped to pieces. Alongside her, Blart had no regrets. He was much more concerned about the new pig. As commander, Blart had put himself in charge of this part of the project, convinced that it was the most important. He was perhaps unnecessarily critical of the carpenters, constantly insisting that the snout needed to be flatter or the tail curlier.

'Is this sort of detail really necessary?' Tigrana asked.

'Of course,' said Blart. 'I wouldn't take it if it didn't look like a proper pig, so why would the Styxians?'

Tigrana didn't have an answer.

And gradually, the Great Wooden Pig was assembled. Giant trotters first. Then huge hams. Then a vast belly. And finally a massive head. It was the biggest pig the world had ever seen. Blart stood admiring it, the hint of a tear glistening in his eye.

'If only it were real,' he said, 'I would give it an enormous apple to munch.'

Meanwhile, under the supervision of Beo, Uther and Olaf, the makeshift tents were ripped down and the injured and the sick were carried on board the various ships of the Illyrian armada. After them came the able-bodied, including a very grumpy Duke Yspahan, clutching his model tightly to his chest. With surprising speed the army packed up, and by mid-afternoon they were almost ready to depart. Only a few soldiers now remained on land. Under the command of

Captain Torres they were to push the wooden pig up to the gates of Yort.

From Yort there had been no sign of any response to the besieging force's departure, even though a messenger carrying a huge white flag had been dispatched to inform the Styxians of the Illyrian armada's intentions. The messenger had passed the message through the gate and was returning when he was cruelly hit in the back by an arrow – a terrible act by the Styxians, which left Beo fuming about their contempt for the basic rules of war.

Only one thing remained: to decide upon those who would be hidden in the wooden pig. The questors stood underneath it, conferring.

'It should be as small a group as possible,' said Beo. 'And nobody in it should have a cold.'

'A cold?' said Olaf.

'Indeed,' said Beo. 'An unfortunate cough at the wrong time could reveal the existence of the secret force to the Styxians.'

'I will go,' said Tigrana immediately.

'Never!' said Beo. 'The stomach of a wooden pig is no place for a damsel. I forbid it.'

'I appeal to the commander of the quest for permission,' said Tigrana, looking at Blart, fire in her eyes.

Blart disagreed with Beo. He felt the stomach of a wooden pig was a perfectly good place for a damsel. *Where else*, Blart wondered, *would any sensible damsel want to be?*

'She can go if she wants to,' he said.

Beo was furious.

'Then I must go too,' he said. 'For if I know a damsel is to be sent into peril, I must accompany her.'

'You're quite big for a secret mission, aren't you?' remarked Uther. 'And you do make a lot of noise. I would have thought that the best people to put in the pig would be those who can move silently and without attracting attention.'

'Like you, merchant,' said Beo. 'Never have I known a man who can appear and disappear so silently.'

Too late Uther realised his mistake. By pointing out Beo's unsuitability, he had drawn attention to his own qualifications.

'You will join me in the belly of the pig,' said the knight.

'But –' protested Uther.

'No buts,' said Beo grimly. 'I have sworn that our feud will be forgotten at the end of the quest. But the quest is not yet over and therefore I can still demand vengeance.'

Uther had no reply, nor any option but to agree to join.

'I will come too,' said Olaf. 'As one of the few remaining suitors I must honour my oath.'

'Four's enough,' said Blart. 'I wish you all success.'

'What?' said Tigrana. 'You're not coming?'

'I'm the commander,' explained Blart. 'I'd like to come but I'm too important.'

'Nonsense,' cried Beo. 'A commander should be in the place of most danger, leading his men by example.'

'That's not what Duke Yspahan thinks,' said Blart.

'What does he know?' scoffed Beo. 'Every great commander must lead his men in mind and in body.'

'You're right,' agreed Blart suddenly. 'I will go. I am the leader. I must a … a … aaaaCHOOO!'

Blart sneezed.

'What?'

'AaaaCHOOO!'

Beo and Tigrana stared at Blart contemptuously.

'I think I'm getting a cold,' sniffed Blart. 'What a shame! That's the one thing that definitely stops me going inside the wooden pig and risking my life.'

As he spoke, Captain Torres approached. He had been supervising the final embarkation of the army. He looked worried.

'Prince Blart,' he said. 'I am sorry to report that the mood of the men towards you is turning ugly again. I could not guarantee your safety on any of the ships, as your presence there would indicate a lack of faith in your own plan, and be seen as an act of cowardice. The men already refer to you as "Yellow Blart" on account of your late arrival at the siege. It is likely that as soon as we are out of the port the men will throw you overboard.'

Immediately Blart turned to Beo.

'No, you're right. I will lead you into the belly of the

Great Wooden Pig.'

   'Thought you had a cold,' said Beo.

   'Seems to have cleared up,' said Blart.

Chapter 44

From his peephole just below the curly tail of the Great Wooden Pig, Blart watched the Illyrian armada set sail. The Great Wooden Pig, with the five questors inside, stood in front of the gates of Yort. What would be its fate?

'What can you see, Blart?' whispered Beo.

'The plan seems to be working,' answered Blart. 'The fleet is out of the harbour now, into the open sea. When we can't see it any more, then the Styxians will come and – oh.'

'What is it?'

'Oh no.'

'What?' hissed the other questors, none of whom had access to the peephole.

'Oh no!'

'Stop saying that and tell us what's going on.'

Blart uttered one word which sent a chill through the other questors.

'Kozali!'

For as soon as the Illyrian armada was out to sea and

vulnerable, from around the headland had come the pirate fleet.

'He must have been waiting for us!' said Blart.

The fast ships of the pirates, their sails billowing boldly, sped towards the Illyrian armada. Blart watched in horror as the most bloody and one-sided sea battle in history unfolded in front of him. The pirate fleet was fresh, ready and packed with reinforcements. The Illyrian armada was exhausted, ill and depleted. Ship after ship was boarded, the sailors and soldiers overwhelmed and put to the sword, the ships stripped of any booty and then set on fire. From his vantage point, Blart reported the destruction. Within an hour, the entire Illyrian armada was gone.

'Every ship?' repeated Beo in disbelief. 'The entire armada?'

It dawned on each questor simultaneously what this meant for them. Even if they succeeded in their mission, there would be no army to return to charge into Yort. They were all alone outside a hostile city, inside a wooden pig.

'We've got to get out of here,' said Blart, who was always quick thinking when it came to his own safety.

'The boy is right,' said Uther, who was almost as fast.

'Kick open the door,' said Blart. 'If we jump down we can run before —'

There was a clang outside as the gates of Styxia swung open. It was too late. They heard the sound of marching feet coming towards the pig. And then harsh voices.

'Did you see what happened?'

'You mean the Illyrian armada?'

'Every ship destroyed.'

'All their men put to the sword.'

'We defeated them without even losing a man.'

'My thumb still hurts.'

'Forget your thumb. Styxia has triumphed,' said one particularly gruff voice.

'King Gregor is a genius.'

'Styxia will rule for ever!'

There was a cheer and then the marching feet stopped underneath them.

'It really is a pig,' said one puzzled Styxian voice.

'Why would they leave a pig for a gift?'

'The Illyrians are a strange people. They eat fruit.'

'And they give each other things.'

'And they don't settle arguments by fighting to the death.'

'They are strange.'

'But still,' persisted one Styxian soldier, 'a pig is no kind of gift for the end of a war. If they'd given us a horse, I could understand it.'

Beo, who had suggested replacing the pig with a horse, shot Blart a significant look. But it was dark in the belly of the pig and Blart didn't see it.

'You are not required to understand things,' said the Styxian with a harsher tone than the others. 'You are required to obey the orders of King Gregor and you are to obey them without question. Bring the pig into the city.'

'Yes, Abakash,' said the other soldiers, and the questors could hear the fear in their voices. There was the sound of movement again as the soldiers positioned themselves around the base of the pig.

'Heave!'

The Great Wooden Pig began to move. With his eye stuck to the peephole beneath the pig's tail, Blart could make out a little of where they were being taken. They were pushed up the ramp that led into the forbidding walled city of Yort. They passed through the vast gates, which clanged shut behind them, and then by the fortified gatehouse itself. Blart spied the lever which controlled the great gate – one of the reasons the peephole had been built into the wooden pig. This part of the plan had worked superbly, unlike the bit about the army charging in.

Now they were in the great city itself. All about them there was the sound of cheering as Abakash the General led the symbol of Styxian victory through the streets. To the listening questors the cheers sounded barbaric and cruel. The Styxians were a people whose only pleasure came from destroying their enemies, and even their celebrations sounded like murderous war cries. Through the cacophony they were pushed, the derisive cheers becoming ever louder until they reached a climax as the wooden pig came to halt in the main square of Yort.

'Everybody in Styxia seems to be a soldier,' said Blart.

'That's because they are,' said Uther. 'Styxia has no respect for anything but military might. Even money is regarded as unimportant. Horrible, isn't it?'

The cheering was abating.

'Why've they gone quiet?' whispered Tigrana.

Chapter 45

Blart saw why. High above them, standing on the battlements, stood the grim, grey figure of Gregor the Grizzled.

'Subjects,' he said in a strangled hiss.

It was an awful voice. It spoke of years of rage and violence that had ripped the power out of it and replaced it with a barb of deadly menace. This was not simply the voice of a fearsomely potent king, but a cunning and devious tyrant.

'Subjects, the Illyrians and their allies are defeated – so terrified that not only do they retreat but they leave us a gift. A gift to beg us for peace. But their pathetic offering will not save them from the wrath of Styxia.'

Harsh cheers shattered the silence. Gregor the Grizzled waited for them to subside.

'Know that we shall celebrate our victory with a night of feasting. And we celebrate doubly because the hated pig boy, Blart, has been killed.'

More cheers rang round the square. Blart was touched.

He had no idea he had the capacity to cause such jubilation simply by being dead. It was nice to know someone cared.

'Then tomorrow at dawn,' continued Gregor, 'my son Anatoly will marry Princess Lois, fulfilling the prophecy and safeguarding Styxia for ever.'

And he beckoned the engaged couple forward on to the balcony. More cheering broke out. A smiling Prince Anatoly, gripping an angry Princess Lois, waved to the throng below in the square. The crowd didn't seem to notice the fury in the face of the red-headed Princess. Or if they did, they didn't care.

'But that is only the beginning,' Gregor told his people. 'The moment the wedding is over we will burn the wooden pig to show what is to come – the destruction of all the lands of Illyria and beyond. We will burn and slaughter and Styxia will rule the world!'

Inside the pig the noise of the cheering was deafening. The questors covered their ears in an attempt to keep it out, as wave after wave reverberated around them. They were five against a multitude. If they were discovered, they would be torn to pieces. If they were not, they would be burnt alive.

And then the feasting began. And then the drinking. And then the fighting.

In Styxia there was no music. There was no dancing or storytelling. There were few of the entertainments that in other lands bring people happiness. In Styxia a person ate, then drank and then fought. All through the night the main square echoed to the sounds of violence as Styxians beat each other senseless in celebration.

'What are we going to do?' said Blart. The one advantage of the violence below was that there was no chance of anyone hearing them. He could see the moon from the spyhole. It would be full on the morrow and all would be lost.

'Thought you were in charge, old boy,' said Olaf.

'I have sworn to defend Princess Lois,' said Beo. 'And I will die in the attempt to keep my vow. And as her husband, Blart, I expect you to do the same. And should you not attempt to, then I will use my sword to remind you of your duties.'

There was a loud crash underneath the pig as the drinking and the fighting continued.

'You'd think they'd get tired of fighting,' remarked Olaf, 'and want to sleep.'

'If they fall asleep,' said Tigrana, 'we can slip out of the pig, find some drunken Styxians and steal their uniforms.'

'Styxians never get tired of fighting,' said Uther. 'They will fight and drink until dawn.'

'Perhaps we could still sneak out.'

'What foolishness you talk,' Uther snapped at Tigrana. 'We are hidden inside a large wooden pig in the middle of the main square. We would be spotted straight away.'

Uther's sharp tone angered Beo.

'Don't talk to her like that, merchant, or your next conversation will be with the point of my sword.'

'This is your chivalry again, is it, knight?' sneered Uther. 'When will you learn that nobody but you believes in it any more? The future lies in trade, not in old-fashioned ideas about damsels and maidens.'

'You dare to speak ill of damsels and maidens?'

Even in the confined space of the pig's belly Beo was about to reach for his sword, when the one damsel present intervened.

'Stop!' Tigrana said. 'Are we to become like the Styxians – fighting among ourselves? We must work together. If we can do nothing but die, then, when morning comes, that is what we will do.'

Beo's grip on his sword slackened. Uther said nothing further. Blart was put out.

'I would have said that,' said Blart, trying to regain some authority, 'had I thought of it.'

But nobody even acknowledged that he had spoken. For now nobody said anything for fear of restarting a quarrel. All they could do was listen to the foul oaths and cruel blows below as the Styxian celebrations continued.

Blart turned away and pulled out the Misty Mirror of Miracle. He had to hold it close to the peephole to see anything. The first thing he saw was his own fearful face. He shook the Misty Mirror as hard as he could to make it show something else.

And for once the mirror obliged. But it did not show him something he wanted to see. He recognised Capablanca's bedchamber, but the bed was empty. For a moment Blart allowed himself to hope. Could it be that the wizard was recovered? But then he saw the tears in the eyes of Lowenthal the Court Physician, who was carefully placing his leeches back in their bowl and shaking his head with remorse. The new treatment must have failed. Capablanca the Sorcerer was dead. Blart felt a tear prick in his own eye as he shook the mirror once more to remove the terrible sight of Capablanca's empty bed.

The mirror misted over again. So too, despite his best efforts, did Blart's eyes. When he could see again, the next image the mirror had chosen to show him was just vanishing. Blart had seen it for less than a second. It was ... Blart wasn't sure. He shook the mirror, but now it would only show him his own face again. What was the image Blart had missed? He had an awful feeling it was very important.

'Listen!' whispered Tigrana. 'The noise is stopping.'

It was true. Finally the Styxians were exhausted by their night of celebration and the square was quiet.

'What do you see?' asked Olaf.

Blart looked. There were sleeping bodies in the square. There were also the first streaks of light in the sky.

'Dawn is going to break soon,' he said.

'It's now or never,' said Beo.

'What are we going to do when we're out of the pig?' said Olaf.

'We'll think of something,' said Beo as he pulled open the

secret hatch in the underbelly of the pig. They dropped silently to the ground, each waiting for the cry that would mean their discovery. But it did not come. Many of the Styxians had staggered home to sleep off their night of riotous celebration, while those who had celebrated too hard lay sleeping where they had fallen.

'Quick!' said Uther. 'Find a Styxian and strip him of his uniform. Then we will be able to slip through them unnoticed.'

In a city in which every citizen would happily kill them, even Beo the Knight was not going to argue with a little bit of trickery. Like all the other questors, he looked for a drunken Styxian whose uniform he could steal.

Blart tiptoed over to a snoring soldier about his size, sporting a badly bruised eye. He lifted his arms. The soldier muttered in his sleep. Holding his breath, Blart took hold of the soldier's jerkin and pulled. The soldier moaned as if in the middle of a bad dream. Blart kept pulling. The soldier's eyes opened. Blart froze. They closed again. He was still asleep. With one last pull the jerkin came off and a moment later Blart was dressed in the uniform of a Styxian soldier.

Nearby, Tigrana was also pulling on a Styxian uniform. Beo and Uther were still looking for suitable candidates, whereas Olaf was tugging fiercely at the jerkin of another prone figure. Sadly for the questors, Olaf had not had any training in stealing clothes, especially when those clothes were still being worn. He gave a final yank to pull the uniform free, but unfortunately his tug was so violent it woke the sleeping Styxian.

'What? Thief! Murderer! Impostor!' shouted the soldier.

Chapter 46

Olaf was caught in the act. As were Beo and Uther. Every soldier in the square was waking up.

'Imposters!'

'Kill them!'

All round the square, bleary-eyed Styxians were standing up, grabbing their swords and then charging towards Olaf, Uther and Beo, who had no hope of defending themselves.

Nevertheless, Beo reached for his sword. But before he could raise it, the Styxian at the front of the mob cried, 'I have an order from King Gregor. Take them alive. Anyone who disobeys his order will be tortured and killed.'

Quite how an order could have been passed down this quickly was a mystery, but such was the fear of King Gregor that the mention of his name stopped the Styxians from attacking with deadly force. Nobody wanted to risk torture and death by doing the wrong thing. The questors were over-powered and in the confusion the soldier who had given the order slipped away.

'Who's stolen my uniform?'

'And mine!'

Two Styxians stood up in their shifts.

'There's more of them.'

'They're in disguise.'

Panic and anger swept through the square. Blart was terrified. His fellow questors were captured and the Styxians
were searching for him. High above on the battlements he
saw the grey figure of Gregor the Grizzled scanning the
crowd. He felt as though at any moment the tyrant's eyes
would hone in on him. Something would give him away. As
quickly as he could, he edged his way out of the square.
Almost everybody else was crowding in, attracted by the
hubbub and the prospect of a public marriage, so Blart's
progress was slow. But he was nearly out when an arm
clapped down heavily on his shoulder.

'Stop!' said a voice in a harsh Styxian accent.

This was it. He was caught. He turned round.

It was Tigrana.

'You sounded like a Styxian.'

'I've spent months pretending to be a boy,' answered
Tigrana. 'You think I can't put on accents?'

'They've captured the others,' said Blart. 'They would
have killed them if a Styxian soldier had not told them that
the King wanted them alive.'

'Wonder who that could have been?' said Tigrana, with a

knowing smile. 'But now we must act to rescue them.'

'Two of us cannot defeat the Styxians,' said Blart. 'Shouldn't we get out of the city and find help?'

'There is no help to be found,' said Tigrana. 'What are we going to do? Ask Captain Kozali if we can join his pirates?'

Pirates! The fleeting picture that Blart had seen in the Misty Mirror of Miracle flashed in front of his eyes. Maybe there was still some hope.

'Follow me!' said Blart.

And he said it with such authority that Tigrana followed him. Through the streets of the walled city they dashed, doubling back whenever they spied a group of soldiers searching for impostors. Word had spread throughout the city faster than fire, and street after street was being patrolled by the search parties. Unlike Tigrana, Blart was sure that he could not fake a Styxian accent. But, for once, luck was with them. The search was chaotic as groups of soldiers kept stopping to interrogate each other. The two questors were able to stay ahead of them as they headed out of the centre down a series of quiet back streets, and eventually they found their way back to the gatehouse.

'What are we doing here?' Tigrana wanted to know.

'Sticking to my plan,' said Blart. 'We're going to open the gates.'

Tigrana looked at him in disbelief.

'What for?' she said. 'The pirates destroyed the Illyrian

armada. There is nobody to come through them.'

'We'll see,' said Blart.

'People said you were a coward, Blart,' said Tigrana. 'If this is simply you trying to escape, then I will hand you over to the Styxians myself.'

'Quick,' said Blart, tugging her by the sleeve. 'There are soldiers coming.'

They dashed across the last street and through the door to the gatehouse.

A guard sitting at a desk looked up at them.

'Orders from the King,' said Tigrana. 'Search the gatehouse for imposters.'

Her accent was perfect. He nodded them through. As fast as they could, they ran up the steps. From across the street they heard loud voices.

Their luck had run out. The real search party was approaching the gatehouse. The Styxians would soon know where they were. They reached the top of the stairs. Another blow. There was a guardroom through which they would have to go if they wanted to reach the great lever that Blart had spotted the night before, and inside it were five Styxian soldiers. However convincing Tigrana's accent was, there was no way that she could persuade them to raise the gate without a good reason. Voices sounded from below. Time was running out.

Tigrana whipped out a dagger and held it to Blart's chest. 'Die!' she whispered.

'What?'

'Hold it under your arm as though you've been stabbed, stagger backwards into the guardroom and die!'

'Why?'

'Do it. Or we're both dead for real.'

There were footsteps on the stairs.

Blart stuck the dagger under his arm and prepared to die.

'Remember to moan,' Tigrana hissed.

'Aaaahhhhhooouuurrgghhh!' shouted Blart and he staggered back into the guardroom and collapsed on the floor.

The guards, seeing what looked to be a Styxian comrade dying, crowded round his body to see what had happened. The moment of distraction was all Tigrana needed. She leapt into the room, a dagger in each hand. The two Styxians nearest the door were dead before they knew it, despatched with deadly stabs through their necks. Tigrana pulled her daggers free and threw them in one fluid movement. The two Styxians furthest away had no chance to move before the daggers arrowed into their hearts. Only one remained. He faced up to Tigrana, grimacing and drawing out his sword, but his expression quickly turned to disbelief when the corpse he had just been examining came back to life, pulled the dagger from its chest and killed him.

'The lever!' cried Blart.

Tigrana and Blart pulled. The great gate opened. And from outside there was a mighty roar.

'What's that?' said Tigrana.

'Pirates!' said Blart.

That was what Blart had glimpsed in the Misty Mirror of Miracle. The pirates, having destroyed the Illyrian armada, had landed in Styxia and were advancing on the city of Yort. Blart thought it might be a good idea to let them in.

From below they heard the shout of Captain Kozali.

'I vowed vengeance on Blart the Pig Boy, and I will have vengeance. Torres told me he was here. Bring me his body.'

'Oh,' said Blart, wondering if it was such a good idea after all. 'I just let in even more people who want to kill me.'

But fortunately for Blart, the pirates and the Styxians were entirely unaware of their common agenda. Even more fortunately, they tended invariably to kill their enemies and ask questions later, which made for some very unsatisfactory answers. It also made for war. The pirates swarming into the city threw themselves into battle with the Styxians, who responded with vigour. But Blart and Tigrana had no time to congratulate themselves. The Styxian search party had reached the top of the steps and were advancing.

'Blart!' said Tigrana, indicating another set of steps which spiralled upwards. 'We have to go higher.'

'Stop!'

Up the steps they sprinted. The Styxians were close now. One slip, one trip would bring Blart and Tigrana into their grasp. The steps were narrow, but neither questor made a false move as they climbed higher and higher and suddenly emerged with a gasp into the bright dawn on the battlements.

'Which way?' shouted Tigrana.

Blart had no idea. He had run out of plan.

'This way,' he said, pointing one way and running the other in his confusion.

Tigrana sprinted after him along the battlements.

'Stop in the name of King Gregor!'

The search party, twenty strong and well-armed, charged along behind them. Blart and Tigrana had nowhere to go, but still they kept running. Something might save them if they just kept running. And then they saw a terrible sight: King Gregor, Anatoly the Handsome, Princess Lois and a troop of the imperial guard, directly ahead.

They hadn't been spotted yet, for King Gregor was looking down with cold fury on the main square, where pirates and Styxians fought hand to hand. Bodies piled up. The streets ran with blood.

'How did this happen?' Gregor demanded. 'Who opened the gate?'

Blart and Tigrana got closer. Dressed as Styxian soldiers they attracted little notice. Everyone was concentrating on the battle below. Behind King Gregor they saw Beo, Olaf and Uther.

The cries of the wounded echoed round the square. The closest members of the imperial guard turned to challenge Blart and Tigrana as they pounded towards them.

'I'll tell them we're part of the search party,' said Tigrana. 'You just nod.'

'Halt,' said a guard. 'Who goes there?'

Tigrana opened her mouth to speak, but another voice rang out clear and certain.

'That's Blart the Pig Boy.'

Chapter 47

In all the excitement Blart had forgotten one very important thing – Anatoly the Handsome had seen him before.

Gregor the Grizzled's attention was no longer on the battle below. His dead grey eyes were focused on Blart.

'So,' he said. 'We meet at last, Blart the Pig Boy. Kill him.'

Ten members of the imperial guard advanced, each grim-faced and brandishing a huge sword. Blart and Tigrana backed away, but they were moving towards the Styxian search party. They had come this far and, finally, they had nowhere left to go.

'I think this time we might really be in trouble,' said Tigrana.

The imperial guard prepared to charge.

And then a blue firebolt smashed into them.

There was only one person Blart knew who could fire blue firebolts.

'Capablanca!'

Flying down towards them on Pig the Horse, firebolts

thundering from his wand, was the greatest sorcerer in the world.

There was chaos on the battlements. The search party panicked. The imperial guard panicked. Firebolt after firebolt rained down on them. They were blown to smithereens or blasted from the battlements into the soldiers and pirates below. Or most of them were. A group of guards from Gregor's elite protection force had ushered the King, Anatoly and their prisoners through a pair of doors leading back into the royal apartments. Two guards remained and were now too close to Blart and Tigrana for Capablanca to risk firing another bolt from his wand.

Trained from birth to obey the orders of Gregor in any circumstance, the guards had been told to kill and that was precisely what they intended to do. They advanced on Blart and Tigrana, their great swords raised.

'Butt their bellies!' shouted Tigrana.

Simultaneously, Blart and Tigrana threw themselves head first into the stomachs of the guards. Surprised by this curious form of attack, they were knocked off balance, their arms flailing.

'Now push,' shouted Tigrana.

And with terrible cries the guards toppled over the edge of the battlements and crashed down into the melee below, crushing a pirate and two Styxians. Through the streets and main square of Yort the battle raged on.

Pig the Horse landed on the battlements. Capablanca

jumped off the mighty steed, looking fit and well and much younger than Blart remembered him.

'Greetings, Blart!'

'I thought you were dead,' said Blart.

Capablanca was momentarily taken aback.

'Why?'

'I looked in the Misty Mirror of Miracle. Lowenthal, your doctor, was standing by your bed, crying.'

'One of his leeches sucked too much of my blood and exploded,' explained Capablanca. 'He's very sentimental about his leeches.'

'Oh,' said Blart. 'Well, if you're not dead, why didn't you get here sooner?'

'Perhaps you'd introduce me to your new friend?' said Capablanca, ignoring Blart's remark.

'This is Tigrana,' said Blart. 'She keeps saving my life.'

'And now we must save the others,' said Tigrana, acknowledging Capablanca with a brief nod. 'Gregor took them from the battlements when you attacked.'

'A young person who is happy to battle with evil,' said Capablanca approvingly. 'She should be an example to you, Blart.'

'It's all right for her,' said Blart. 'She hasn't got everybody in the whole world wanting to kill her like I have.'

'This is no time for self-pity,' said Capablanca. 'Our comrades are in peril. Follow me!'

'I thought I was the leader,' protested Blart. 'You can't

321

just turn up right at the end of the quest after I've done all the brave things and start ordering me around.'

'I'll give you a carrot for a nose if you don't do as I say,' threatened Capablanca. And he led the way towards the door to the royal apartments, followed closely by Tigrana and Pig the Horse.

Blart looked down at the battle. More and more pirates and Styxians lay dead or injured, but the violence showed no signs of abating. How long it would rage on was impossible to tell.

Then, surprisingly, Blart had the strange feeling that someone was looking at him from right in the middle of the battle. Looking up with hatred and only one eye.

Captain Kozali.

'Blart the Pig Boy,' he yelled. 'You will hang from my yardarm yet.'

'Wait for me!' said Blart, hurrying after the others. He decided that the best place to be at this moment was at the side of the most powerful wizard in the world.

The doors to the royal apartments had been locked and bolted from the inside, but they proved no barrier to Capablanca. Blue firebolts shot from his powerful wand and smashed the doors open.

'You didn't used to be able to do that,' said Blart, stepping through a shattered door after the wizard.

'That rest in Illyria has made me a new wizard,' said Capablanca and with a few effortless flicks of his wand he sent deadly blue fireballs whooshing into four guards who charged towards them. 'I explained to you before that magic powers get used up. And I've been so busy fighting evil over the years that I've never properly had time to recover. But after these weeks of rest my powers are now ten times greater than they've ever been.'

Capablanca nonchantly flicked his wand again. Another blue fireball shot out and smashed the door to the next chamber to pieces.

'We'll find Gregor, rescue our comrades and have this quest resolved in minutes,' announced the wizard.

'I don't think that door was actually locked,' pointed out Tigrana.

This time eight imperial guards were waiting for them inside. But it made no difference. Capablanca's fireballs were just as deadly.

'It's almost too easy,' said the wizard breezily. 'I feel two hundred years younger.'

Blart had never missed the old Capablanca, the wizard who used to lecture and criticise – until now. The new one, who was all swagger and smugness, was more than he could bear.

'Don't start saying that this quest hasn't been hard, because it has,' said Blart.

Another door exploded.

'That one wasn't even shut,' Tigrana observed.

The remainder of the imperial guards poured through

the door. Surely this was too many even for the wizard. Ten … fifteen … twenty thundered across the room. Capablanca raised his arms and spoke words from an ancient tongue. A line of blue flame shot up from the floor. When it burned down the guards had vanished.

Blart and Tigrana looked at Capablanca in amazement.

'The Impossible Spell of Consuming Conflagration,' said Capablanca. 'I think you'll find it hasn't been performed for seven centuries.'

But Blart noticed that, despite Capablanca's smile, the furrows in his brow were more pronounced. All this magic was taking its toll. But perhaps it didn't matter. Only King Gregor and Anatoly the Handsome now stood between the questors and their goal.

Tigrana pushed open the throne-room door to be met by a terrible sight. There, standing in front of his throne, was King Gregor the Grizzled. Gripped like a shield in front of him, he held Princess Lois — at her neck, a knife. There was no hint of mercy in his dead grey eyes.

'Stop!' he ordered.

Chapter 48

Blart, Capablanca and Tigrana froze. Beo, Olaf and Uther were tied up in the far corner. Anatoly the Handsome stood guard over them.

'Drop your wand!' commanded Gregor. 'Or the Princess loses her head.'

Reluctantly Capablanca dropped his wand to the floor.

'Hello, Princess Lois,' said the wizard.

'Where've you all been?' demanded the Princess, her freckles burning with anger. 'It's not that far from Illyria. I've been waiting and waiting to be rescued. I've had to put up with soppy face Anatoly over there telling me how beautiful I am for ages.'

'We got a bit lost,' said Blart.

'Lost?' said Princess Lois. 'Trust you to get lost. It's not that big an ocean.'

'You two are married?' said Tigrana incredulously, taken aback by Princess Lois's greeting.

'It was complicated,' said Capablanca. 'We needed to save the world.'

orld again,' said Princess Lois. 'Is that why I'm

...o appear to feature in a lot of prophecies,' admit-
... ...ablanca.

'Prophecies,' sighed Blart. 'I hate prophecies.'

'Silence!' said Gregor. 'If the Princess dies then Illyria will be destroyed. And if I don't get what I want then I'm going to kill her.'

'Kill me instead!' shouted Beo. 'I would rather die than allow a damsel to suffer.'

'No, kill me instead,' shouted Tigrana. 'I will die in his place.'

For a moment Gregor was confused by all these people competing to die. Then a look of cunning crossed his face. He tightened his grip on the Princess's neck.

'I will exchange the Princess as a hostage,' he offered. 'But not for either of you – I will swap her for Blart.'

Everybody in the room looked at Blart.

'I didn't actually say I'd swap,' he said.

'You're a disgrace, lad,' bellowed Beo from the corner. 'You have a chance to free your wife from the grip of a merciless tyrant and you hesitate for a second. If I wasn't tied up, I'd kill you.'

'Thank you, Beowulf,' said Capablanca. 'Your interventions are helpful as always. Blart will, of course, change places with Princess Lois.'

'Will I?' said Blart.

Capablanca nodded.

'But he wants to kill me.'

'It's probably just a figure of speech,' Capablanca assured him. 'There's really nothing to worry about.'

In the distance they could hear the cries of battle. Whoever was winning was getting closer.

'Don't make me wait any longer,' said Gregor, tightening his grip on the dagger, 'or the Princess dies.'

Everybody in the throne room looked at Blart.

'It always ends up like this,' he said bitterly. 'Everybody says we're all comrades together but when it gets to the end I'm the one who seems to get killed. Why is it never someone else's turn?'

Nobody said anything. They all just kept staring at him. With an ill grace, Blart accepted his heroic destiny once more and nodded.

'Let the Princess go first,' said Capablanca.

'Do you think I'm a fool, wizard?' said Gregor. 'The moment she is free you'll kill me. When I have Blart at my mercy, then she'll go. Throw away your weapons, boy, and get over here now.'

The wizard was forced to accept Gregor's terms. So Blart dropped his dagger and walked across the huge throne room, his every step echoing against the granite walls. From somewhere beyond the chamber the sounds of battle grew louder.

'Come here, boy,' said Gregor with an evil smile.

Blart saw that Gregor's other hand also held a dagger. He stopped.

'Come here!'

Somehow Blart forced his shaking legs forward. When he was close enough, Gregor shot out a hand. Blart gasped. The King was surprisingly strong for his years. He held Princess Lois in one arm and Blart in the other, daggers at their necks.

'Now release the Princess!' said Capablanca.

'Release the Princess?' repeated Gregor. 'I don't think so.'

'You're outnumbered,' said Capablanca. 'You can't get away.'

'Get away?' said Gregor. 'That's the last thing on my mind.'

'What are you going to do?' said Blart.

'A good question,' said Gregor. 'I'm going to kill you and then use my power as King to marry Anatoly to the Princess, who'll say "I do" or have her head chopped off – and the prophecy will do the rest.'

'You're mad,' said Capablanca. But the other questors could hear doubt in his voice. If Gregor succeeded in doing what he proposed, then the prophecy would be fulfilled, Styxia saved and Illyria destroyed. And as Capablanca was always pointing out, you couldn't argue with a prophecy.

'Get over here, Prince Anatoly,' said King Gregor. 'You're about to be married.'

'This is the happiest day –' began Anatoly.

'Just get over here,' ordered King Gregor. 'Now, Princess Lois, prepare to become a widow and then get married again all in the same minute.'

Blart felt the knife biting into his neck. He closed his eyes and tried to picture his beloved pigs. If he was going to die, he would at least part this world with happy thoughts in his mind . . .

'Stop!'

Olaf stood up, the rope that had tied his hands falling to the floor.

'This does not concern you,' said Gregor.

'Have to disagree with you there,' said Olaf. 'I'm the last surviving suitor who vowed to defend Blart's marriage to Princess Lois, and even though they don't seem to like each other much I intend to defend it. Anatoly, I challenge you to a duel.'

'Stop it!' shouted Gregor.

But Olaf was determined to stand by his oath. He picked up the dagger that Blart had dropped on the floor and advanced towards Anatoly. Anatoly reached for his sword.

'I should warn you,' said Olaf. 'That we're on land. Indoors. One on one. This time, I've had training.'

And with that Olaf attacked. But Anatoly was a Styxian. He too had received extensive training. He parried Olaf's blow and attempted one of his own. Olaf ducked and thrust again. Expertly Anatoly avoided the thrust and with Olaf off-balance stabbed him straight through the heart.

The watching questors cried in horror. Olaf sank to his knees, his hands clutched desperately to his chest.

'I can't die,' he said. 'I haven't had any …'

He fell forward dead. It appeared no training was necessary.

'Now perhaps we can get on with the wedding!' said Gregor. 'After we've dealt with the matter of the funeral. Goodbye, Blart!'

The knife bit further. Blart felt blood running down his neck. He twisted back and forth but he couldn't escape the deadly grip.

'Stamp on his feet,' cried Tigrana.

In perfect harmony, as only a married couple could, Princess Lois and Blart stamped down hard. Gregor howled in pain and dropped his daggers.

Princess Lois scooped one up and charged at Anatoly the Handsome.

'This is for every soppy compliment you've ever given me,' she shouted.

Moments later Anatoly the Handsome lay dying on the floor of the throne room. He looked up at Princess Lois with the eyes of a puppy.

'Dearest!' he said.

'Shut up,' said Princess Lois.

Olaf had been avenged. Anatoly was dead.

Chapter 49

'Look out! The King's escaping!' shouted Tigrana.

King Gregor had used the distraction of his son's death to slip out by a hidden door in the back wall of the throne room.

'Don't let him get away!' said Capablanca, bending down and grabbing his wand.

With Tigrana and Princess Lois, he ran after Gregor. Blart, overwhelmed by his near-death experience, didn't follow them immediately.

'Cut my bonds, lad,' said Beo urgently. 'My sword arm aches for action.'

Blart did as he was told. Beo grabbed a sword and charged through the door.

The sound of Beo's footsteps clattered away in one direction, while the din of battle grew louder in the other. There was a small cough.

'I would be grateful if you'd untie me too,' said Uther.

Blart, still dazed, cut Uther's bonds and dropped his

dagger to the floor.

'I suppose we should go after Gregor the Grizzled,' he moaned. 'If we don't, they'll all go on at me and say I'm a coward. They never remember that I'm the one who nearly always gets killed.'

Rubbing his wrists, Uther glanced about him. 'We are alone at last. I have something to tell you.'

'What is it?' said Blart.

'It's about pigs,' said Uther.

'Pigs?' said Blart, coming closer.

Suddenly Uther whipped out a dagger from his dark cloak.

'When I say it's about pigs,' said Uther, 'I really mean it's about killing you.'

'What do you mean, killing me? You're on my side,' said Blart.

'As I explained to Olaf,' said Uther, 'money doesn't really have a side.'

'Money?' said Blart. 'What's money got to do with it?'

'Oh,' said Uther. 'Didn't I mention I was a member of the Guild of Assassins?'

'No,' said Blart.

'Now I want you to understand,' said Uther, advancing, 'that there is nothing personal here. It is simply business.'

Blart backed into a corner.

'If only the bounty on your head wasn't so huge, then even I might overlook it,' explained Uther. 'But what kind of businessman would I be to forego such an easy profit?'

'But,' said Blart desperately, 'Gregor the Grizzled took out the contract. If he's dead –'

'He was still alive the last time I saw him,' said Uther, 'which is why I must kill you quickly. So if you wouldn't mind just standing still.'

Uther raised his dagger. Blart was defenceless and doomed to die. Again.

There was a tremendous crash as Gregor the Grizzled burst through the door, Beowulf's sword embedded in his chest.

He staggered into his throne, sending it toppling over, and then collapsed dead on top of the body of his son, Prince Anatoly.

Uther allowed himself a tut of annoyance.

'Curses!' he said. 'Would it have hurt him to wait one more minute?'

And as Beo, Capablanca, Princess Lois and Tigrana dashed into the room, his dagger disappeared.

'As I said, Blart,' he whispered, 'it was nothing personal.'

Beo stood over the body of Gregor the Grizzled.

'There's nothing like killing an enemy to make the day feel better,' he observed.

'But the loss of a comrade is grievous,' said Tigrana, kneeling by the body of Olaf.

'Indeed,' said Capablanca. 'But he died for a noble cause.'

There was a moment of silence. For Olaf. For Herglotz.

Blart interrupted it.

'Did you know that Uther is –'

'A person who has promised to buy Blart a pig farm,' said Uther. 'As a token of his ability to keep his mouth closed.'

'I didn't know Blart could keep his mouth closed,' said Princess Lois.

'He might be able to if it's a big pig farm,' said Blart. 'A very big one.'

Uther agreed it would be a very big pig farm.

Outside, the noise of the battle was very close indeed. It sounded like the fighting had now reached the royal apartments.

'Perhaps,' said Capablanca, 'we should delay talk of pig farms until we have removed ourselves from Yort. Princess Lois is saved. Illyria will not be destroyed and, as we can hear outside, Styxia soon will be. It shows the prophecy was right.'

And then Blart remembered something bad. Something very bad indeed.

'It's all right for the rest of you,' he said. 'The prophecy said that I'd die anyway. I've done all the brave deeds on this quest and I'm still going to die. It's not fair.'

The questors were silent. It was true. As the husband of Princess Lois, Blart was destined to die.

'What did the prophecy say?' asked Princess Lois, who was the only person not to have heard it.

'It said that on his return your husband must die,' said Blart. 'I'm your husband, so I must die.'

'Is that all?' said Princess Lois.

Blart felt this was a bit much. He'd come all this way to rescue Princess Lois. The least he deserved was a bit of sympathy.

'Isn't it enough?' he said.

'We can solve that problem easily,' she said.

'Can we?' asked Blart.

'Yes,' said Princess Lois. 'Would you like a divorce?'

'What?' said Blart.

'Think, stupid boy,' said Princess Lois. 'Then you'd return but you wouldn't be my husband any more, so the prophecy wouldn't apply to you.'

'That would work,' said Capablanca in amazement.

'Divorce!' shouted Beo in outrage. 'I will not hear of it. The whole quest was designed to save your marriage and the moment it's over you want to end it?'

'We were never well suited,' said Blart.

'Well suited?' spluttered Beo. 'Marriage isn't about being well suited. And divorce is unchivalrous.'

'But the marriage is going to end either way,' said Tigrana. 'Either they get divorced or Blart dies and Princess Lois is a widow.'

'And then I'd be a damsel in distress,' said the Princess. 'And you wouldn't want that.'

'For a very reasonable price,' said Uther, pulling a parchment from his cowl, 'I have divorce papers pre-signed by a monk available for purchase. Simply make your mark and the marriage is over.'

Blart gave Uther a fierce stare.

'In the circumstances,' said Uther, 'I'll give you them for free.'

Princess Lois signed with a quill he offered her. Blart made his smudge. Uther wiped away a tear.

'I always cry at divorces.'

There was a shout from the next room. The battle was almost upon them.

'I think it's time to go,' said Capablanca. 'This door leads to the battlements where Pig the Horse is waiting for us.'

Moments later Captain Kozali and Babel the Butcher of Barca crashed into the throne room to find only the dead bodies of Olaf, Gregor and Anatoly. Moving as fast as he could, Kozali reached the window. He looked out, his wild eye rolling berserkly.

'Where is he?' he shouted vainly. 'Where is the boy who destroyed my ship? Where is Blart?'

Babel pointed upwards.

There, far above them, silhouetted black against the sun, flying high on the back of Pig the Horse, were Capablanca the Wizard, Beowulf the Knight, Uther the Merchant, Tigrana the Cabin Girl, Lois the Princess and Blart the Pig Boy.

The moon would be full that night. But by then they would be safely back in Illyria. The quest was a success. Unquestionably.

THE END